FEYO

TRAVIS MICHAEL

ACKNOWLEDGMENTS

If you've made it this far, thank you so much! This story has taken on many forms in my head over the years. I'm happy to finally have it on paper. I hope that something within these pages has helped you in some way.

We all deal with our own struggles. It's important to know that even though that struggle may feel impossible to overcome, the power to continue exists in all of us. Have faith in yourself and give yourself a chance to carry on. Power through the dark so that you can better enjoy the light. I have lived the lows that this story represents. I am proof that even when you think you can't carry on, you can.

Special thanks to my amazing wife Haley, who had to listen to this book and all of its variations no less than twenty times. Thank you so much for lending me your ear throughout this journey. You can play your sims in peace now that I won't be reading in your ear (for now.) I love that you and the girls have given me the space to create something like this.

To Summer Michael and Casey Edmonds who stuck it out for this entire process… Thanks so much! Without you two, there is just no way I would have been able to sift through those edits. I am very grateful you both chose to play such an integral part of this book.

To MaKayla Dillard and Craig Taylor, thank both of you for giving me writing advice along the way! Now is the time for you to put your stories on paper too!

To Mr. Bruce Morgan, my high school forensics teacher

who told me I should be writing stories instead of joining the Army. I misunderstood an assignment and wrote an entire ten page short story for something that was supposed to be a few paragraphs and he really enjoyed it and encouraged me to try and write more. Had I listened, I likely wouldn't have required so many rounds of editing for this book. I hate that he did not get stick around long enough to get a copy of this one. Rest in Peace.

To the ones I have lost along the way, specifically from the weight of life becoming too heavy to hold, it is in your loving memory that I wrote this book. No matter how big or small your presence, it means something.

* * *

For my wife, who never stops finding ways to make this life worth living. This book and my presence in this world would not have been possible without your continued support. Thank you.

For those who have ever found themselves facing the welcoming hands of death, and chose life... There is beauty and purpose in you. Look into yourself and find it.

* * *

CHAPTER 1

$\mathcal{I}$ pull out the top drawer of my bedside table and sift through all of the junk I had thrown in there last time I "cleaned up." I can't find a single one of my good pens. I guess the one I found in the kitchen will have to work. Seems fitting to have to use something of lower quality in this moment. Story of my fucking life… I sit down at my desk and begin to write.

To whom it may concern

— No, that's not me. I would never say that. I hear my phone ringing on my dresser, probably some more bullshit. That has to be the fifth time in the last few minutes. Whatever, I'll let it go to voicemail. If it's a real emergency I'm sure they'll call the station anyway.

I begin to write again.

To the Culver Forensic Team members that have to get me out of here: I apologize. I didn't have a cleaner way of pulling this off. I know I'm not doing you any favors but I felt like the least I could do was to make sure to put the air conditioner on low. Maybe I won't stink too bad by the time you get here. This isn't anyone's fault but my own. I just don't have it in me anymore. This life isn't going anywhere and I don't know what to do to make it better. These days seem to run together into one big shitty movie that isn't worth watching. Just cremate me and spread my ashes wherever you'd like, as long as it isn't here in Culver. I need someone honorable to take my dog. She deserves nothing but the best. If this demand is not met, it is my dying wish for the city to burn my home to the ground so that no one can profit from it.

Chief Marks, I have left the deed of this home and the title to my car in the kitchen. You can have them both, again only if Daisy has a home. Sell them so you can put some money towards getting the camper you wanted.

Mom, I hope this takes me to you. We never could agree on God, but maybe if he's real you can convince him to at least let me see you before they throw me in hell. Can't be any worse than it is here.

Daisy, this isn't your fault. I am so sorry I had to lock you out of here, I wanted you to see me in one piece for the last time. Leaving you is the hardest part. You are the best girl in the whole world and I love you with all my heart. I am so sorry. I hope you understand. -DM

. . .

I PUT the pen down and finish the last of my whiskey, the burn lingering in my throat like the dying embers of a campfire. I grab my service pistol and make sure it's loaded. I push it to my temple and close my eyes. Placing my finger on the trigger, I hold my breath. The cold barrel pressing into the same spot it has many times before. This time I can smell the lubricant from the last time I cleaned it. Seems at least a little ironic that the most work this pistol will do after this is sit on a shelf in evidence alongside every other dusty box holding the floors down at the station. A life born of nothing soon to return again to that nothing. *Will I feel anything? Will this hurt Daisy's ears? I wish she could understand all of this... Will she think I abandoned her?* My hands begin to sweat. I set the pistol down and wipe my hand on my shorts. I would hate to slip up and just injure myself. *How embarrassing...* I hear Daisy whining from the other side of the door, scratching wildly at it in between her fits. My phone begins to ring again. *God damnit, what could be so important right now?* I look at the pistol again, contemplating everything and nothing all at once. I decide to walk to the dresser to pick the phone up.

"Damon! I need you on Bradbury Road right now! There is a fucking body hanging from the ceiling of the church!"

The caller ID reads: "Raymond Stokes." The town drunk. Had I been sober enough, I probably wouldn't have answered. *Why would he be calling me and not just 911 anyways? Am I hearing him right?*

"Mr. Stokes, can you repeat that? I'm sorry. I didn't hear you," I say, hoping my brain didn't twist his words.

"There's a body hanging from the ceiling, man! Get down here! I called everyone else but no one will answer!"

"Mr. Stokes, I will be there shortly. Hang up and dial 9-1-1 and stay on the phone with them until everyone shows up."

I hang up and call Deputy Chief Marks. Before I can get a word in, he cuts me off, "Already on the way, meet you there. It's the older church closer to the end of Bradbury." He hangs up. I now see where he has called me five times already. I didn't realize I was that focused on my...*note*. Chief Marks has a way of saying a lot without actually saying it. It's kind of his super power. Most people think he's an asshole, but I prefer that over the type of person who will spend thirty minutes explaining their cup of coffee in the morning. I'm not much of a talker myself. I rub my temple, still feeling the pressure from the pistol from a few moments ago. I take one last look at the words I had written down before trading my shorts and t shirt for my uniform.

* * *

As I BACK OUT of my driveway, I notice Daisy poking her head between the curtains of the living room window. She is the best dog I've ever had. The vet said she is a Lab-mix but to me she looks pure bred. Either way, she's good company. She doesn't know any tricks or anything but she knows the rules of the house and what not to chew on. *I wonder where she thinks I'm going when I take off in the middle of the night like this?* I guess it's better than seeing them carry me out in a body bag. Speaking of, this church situation seems too interesting to pass up, so I guess that'll have to wait.

I've really been needing something to go right for a while, so maybe this can get my mind off of things and focused in the right place for at least a few days. *Of all the times for something like this to happen...* I focus hard on the lines of the road as I make my way to the church on Bradbury Road.

11:45 P.M.

. . .

As I arrive at the church, I see Chief Marks talking to Raymond, who is sitting on the back of his old Lincoln. He looks pretty shaken up, but to be fair, I'm not sure if I have ever seen him in a normal state of mind. There are already quite a few officers here, all parked right in the grass at the front of the church. I'm not sure why they've made a point to roll up on scene all crooked, as if the dead body might try to make a run for it. There are way too many cops here for a suicide, especially this time of year. Usually during the summer, Union County gets around five or six suicides, and about ten to twelve per year. This one would make three for the year, and the first one that I have been called to. They typically happen on night shift and don't require too much cause for emergency. This one must be particularly bad. The number of suicides has increased by at least 2 every year since I've been working here. I'm not sure if it's because of money, or just because there isn't anything to do here and people get a little crazy. I can't really cast judgement since I was almost a part of that number just a little bit ago.

I grab a piece of gum out of my center console to mask the smell of whiskey on my breath and step out of my car. It's a horrible mixture as far as taste goes but the last thing I need right now is for anyone to notice I rolled up to a crime scene like this. I have to side step around one of the patrol cars to get to the front doors of the church. The doors burst open and Sergeant Hamilton storms past me. He always seems to be in some type of mood, but so is everyone else on night shift. This time he looks more confused than angry, though. I approach an officer standing near the doorway.

"Pastor Tim is going to be pissed off about you guys tearing up his grass," I say, looking back at the cars haphazardly strewn across the grass leading up to the doors of the church.

"I don't think he'll be too worried about it. He was pretty upset when we called him," he says, putting his thumbs into his vest.

"So, where's the body?" I ask. I had almost forgotten why I was here.

"Right in the middle. Can't miss it," he says. "Follow me."

* * *

I HAVE NEVER BEEN to this church before, or any of the others in Union County. It isn't for lack of options though. My partner, Detective Davidson always says, "If you can't see a church or a boutique, you ain't in the city of Culver anymore." We always joke that it should be the town's motto. Magnolia, a neighboring town in Union County isn't as saturated, but you can still bet on seeing one or the other on accident every now and then. The officer and I snake through the lobby and down a short set of stairs before we reach the walkway that leads to the main hall. As soon as we walk through the double doors, my heart begins to race. Raymond Stokes wasn't exaggerating when he called me.

Hanging from what appears to be a steel cable about fifteen feet above the pews, right in the center aisle, hangs a white male. He is completely naked, and hanging parallel to the floor. His stomach is facing down towards the ground with a black fabric bag over his head. Eight years of law enforcement really takes away the "shock factor" involved with walking into situations like this, but this one is intense. I have never seen anyone hanging this way. Something is just so off putting about the whole thing. I stare up at him and run my tongue across my teeth, contemplating how someone might even accomplish such a task.

"Doesn't make any damn sense does it?" asks Chief Marks as he jogs down the aisle. I swear he's bigger every time I see him. His wife of twenty-five years passed away around this time last year and his way of coping has been to order takeout every night.

"Yea, I'm not sure how he could've done that to himself. Extra points for creativity, I guess," I say. A little morbid humor is necessary in this line of work. Some people look at it as disrespectful, but we look at it as a way to view bad things in a better light so that we don't end up hanging from a ceiling somewhere too.

"You think this is a suicide? Open your eyes detective," says Chief, motioning sarcastically up to the man.

I guess I didn't really think about any alternative to suicide as a possibility until now. We don't have many murders here. I can think of only four in my entire career. When I was still a regular officer, I was first on scene when Marty Hadley was killed by his wife for sleeping with some younger woman at the paper plant in Magnolia. She used a hammer to knock him out while he was sleeping then cut his throat with a little pocket knife. Gruesome stuff. That was the first time I had ever really seen anything like that.

"I mean, why wouldn't it be?" I ask, walking a little closer. "This seems like too much work for a murder... and for what? Maybe it was just his way of feeling important after the fact. Knowing it would make a lot of people scratch their heads? Who knows."

"If you think hanging him up was too much work, wait until you get a closer look," says a voice from one of the first pews. I look to see who it is, as I don't recognize the voice. A slender man in his late fifties stands up and walks our way.

"James Scott, Coroner," he says, stretching his arm toward me for a handshake. I had forgotten that last November, pretty much all of the old dogs in local government retired.

This made way for a lot of new names and faces I have yet to learn. I should probably pay more attention to things like that, but I have never been one to care about elected officials. I just stay to myself and hope everything works the way it's supposed to.

"Nice to meet you. I'm Detective Damon McKay," I say, releasing what had to be a five minute handshake.

"Go look at his back, then tell me what you think," he says, pointing to a large ladder that lay folded in front of the altar.

He seems a little too excited about it, but I'm interested to see how someone would end up like this. I stand the ladder up as close as I can to the body without touching it, and start to climb. As soon as I get close, I get a strange feeling. I hadn't noticed it when I walked in, but the man is grey all the way through. Normally, when someone dies, the blood will pool towards the bottom and create a dark purplish color. Maybe this isn't a suicide... Reaching the top, it appears that his back is also grey as well. I understand what James meant now, as my eyes fall on what holds the man in place.

The steel cable stops about an inch away from the body and is wrapped around a long metal rod. The rod runs parallel to the man's back, starting at the middle of his neck and ending at his backside. From the rod, three black bars poke down into his skin. They go directly into his neck and spine, but as I look closer it appears that they are offset by a quarter of an inch to the right.

I look down to James, who is now standing almost directly below me. "Are these hooks?" I ask.

"I believe so," he says. "Take a look to the left of the point of entry."

To the left of his spine and I can see where his skin is protruding up, likely due to the sharp part of the hook not making it all the way back through.

"I'm just thinking out loud here," I say, almost losing my balance on the ladder. I really should've eaten something before coming to sober myself up a little. "No discoloration. This man was already dead when this happened. I'd say someone stole a corpse and strung it up like this."

"Ahh, my thoughts exactly. You might grow up to be a detective one day," he says, smiling at Chief Marks. "The forensics team has already taken their pictures, so let's see what's under the bag."

I know whatever is under the bag isn't going to be pretty, but I'm curious as to who it could be. *If they were okay with displaying the rest, what was so bad about the head that it needed to be covered?* I slide my gloves on and start to roll the bag up from the bottom. I don't want to just yank it off, in case something is inside. Halfway up his head, there is a hole that couldn't be any bigger around than a quarter. I pull out my flashlight and click it on. The light shines through, unobstructed, illuminating the ground below.

What the hell happened here? Did someone stab a dead body with a pole or something and hang it up as some fucked up joke? What type of person would go through this much trouble? I have to figure out who this guy is. He must have pissed off someone so badly that his death wasn't enough and they decided to add their own personal touch.

"Gunshot wound?" asks Chief as he stares up to me.

"No. Same size all the way through. Someone really must've hated this guy," I say.

I finish rolling the bag off of his head and look inside. It's empty, just like that hole through his skull. I step back down the ladder and place the bag on a pew. Chief grabs a clear evidence bag, and places it inside. I shine my light up at the man's face, hoping that from this perspective I may recognize him. He looks very familiar. I think back to a bad dream I had a few nights ago, where a man similar to this one had tried to break into my house. Maybe that's why he looks familiar, but then again he looks pretty generic. Middle to late fifties, beer belly and a scruffy white beard. Pretty on brand for every other man of his age around here. Death makes people look different, though. I'll have to wait for positive identification and go from there.

I take my gloves off and head towards the back of the church. I need to get whatever information Raymond Stokes has while it's still fresh on his mind. With as few brain cells that man has left, we might be losing information by the second. That man is one hard fall away from a total reset, I'm sure of it. As I reach the back of the pews, I hear a loud crackling noise behind me. I turn around just in time to see the body slamming into the middle aisle way with a loud *THUD*. Broken bits of wood flutter through the air, as Chief Marks sprints my way.

"God damn, y'all alright?" he asks, brushing wood from his uniform. I haven't seen him move that fast since Bobby Springfield's kid shot at him with a paintball gun in 2013.

Looking up at the ceiling, it is obvious that whoever anchored the man with those cables either underestimated his weight, or didn't know those boards weren't meant to hold weight that way. In hindsight, we probably should've looked at that a little closer before being under it. *A cleanup crew will have fun with this one.* The remaining splinters and decades of dust descend upon the church, leaving a film over everything. I feel as if the film has landed on my mind as well, slowing my thoughts as I try and make sense of the last few hours. I turn and head towards the door.

CHAPTER 2

12:15 A.M.

"So tell me what happened here, Mr. Stokes. How did you end up here? Why are you at a church this late?" I flip open my notepad, and lean against the back of his car beside him. "…Mr. Stokes?"

He rocks his weight back and forth for a moment, never taking his eyes off the ground, "You… you ain't gonna believe me anyways."

"What makes you say that?" I ask, wafting his cigarette smoke away from my face.

"Well, I just had a feelin'. Somethin' just told me I should go to the church."

"Like a dream?" I ask, closing my notepad. I don't expect this to be a very productive conversation. I can smell the alcohol on his breath, and that's saying a lot.

He looks up at me, "No. No, like a *feelin'.* Like when you

know somethin' bad is about to happen. Ain't it called into… uh, into-bishin or somethin' like that?"

"I know what you mean, Mr. Stokes. So where were you when you got this feeling?"

"I was sitting on my porch having a few beers, windin' down," he says, scratching his nose.

"So you decided you would drive drunk to a church?" I ask.

He rolls his eyes and shakes his head, "Look, you know I ain't no saint. Never claimed to be. If y'all wanna charge me or somethin' that's some bullshit. It ought to cancel out since I… you know."

"I'm not worried about that right now, I'm just asking," I say. I feel like it would be wrong to even pursue that given the fact that I did the exact same thing, and the nature of the circumstance.

"Aight then, good. Anyways," he leans back against the car, "I just kinda went into autopilot or somethin' and when I got here I just walked in."

"Walked in?" I ask. "So the door was unlocked? Any signs of forced entry or anything?"

"Naw, nothin' like that. Pastor Tim always keeps the doors open and the lights on in case anyone needs a place to stay, or if they feel inclined to come in and praise God. You know he's a good man like that."

Pastor Tim is definitely a good man. He is the kind of man who knows everyone no matter what. It might be through a friend of a friend of an uncle of an aunt, but he'll address you by a nickname you forgot you had. He is very personable and kind. Always there to lend a hand to those in need, whether they deserve it or not.

"That's good," I say. "Did you see anyone around when you walked in?"

"Nope. Not a soul. Hell I screamed so loud when I seen

him hangin up there, I bet if anyone were around they took off," he says, putting his hand on the back of his neck.

"Do you know who would do something like this? Is there anyone that you know of that has been acting suspicious or even just a little different lately?" I ask.

"Hell naw, man! That's some horror movie stuff right there. And I know some tough bastards that would prolly kill someone, but no one that would do *THAT*."

"Thank you for your time, Mr. Stokes," I say, placing my hand on his shoulder. "Is there anyone that can give you a ride home?"

"Yea my ol' lady is already on the way. She's gonna whoop my ass for doin' this. I just hope y'all get who did this quick. The town is gonna turn upside down when they find out."

He is right. One of the worst parts of living in an area this size is that everyone becomes a keyboard detective at the first sign of a crime. The rumors and allegations always bounce back and forth across social media and at community events. Before you know it, something that was as minor as a traffic stop turns into a full scale investigation by our local "expert investigatory reporter" Parker Cowan with WCDX news. *Makes me sick.*

An old green Ford pickup truck whips into the first parking spot. It's Pastor Tim.

"Can you fine young gentlemen remove your cars from my grass please?" he asks. I smirk as the officers by the door scramble to move their cars back to the parking lot.

"I told them you'd be mad, but they didn't listen," I say, reaching the front door of the church just as he does.

"Damon? I'll be doggone. It's been too long!"

Pastor Tim stands about six foot three and was born for this career. He could tell you the sky was falling and you'd run for cover. I couldn't imagine him doing anything else besides preaching. I remember him coming to congratulate me the day I got promoted to detective, even though I had only spoken to him a few times in passing.

"Yes sir, I apologize for it being under these circumstances," I say.

"It's quite alright son, everything happens for a reason. I can't go in there can I?" he asks, trying to look through the dim entryway.

"No sir, not until they get it cleaned up anyways. They did some damage to your ceiling too, you might have to cancel this Sundays service," I say.

"Oh, absolutely not! We have this whole dang parking lot we can use if the need arises. I'll take the word to the people if I have to. God ain't ever took a day off, and I ain't planning to either," he says, pointing up into the night sky. "You have any idea who did this yet?"

I cross my arms and scan the roof of the front area of the church, "No idea as of yet. Do you happen to have any cameras that could've seen anything?"

"Noooo no no. Only camera in the whole church is a set up on the back wall to record my service for my website. I made a page so when people are sick they don't have to miss out," he says, patting me on the back for some reason.

"That's really nice of you," I say, turning my body to make sure he can hear me, but not reach me. "Anything out of the ordinary happen lately at any of your services? Any unsavory characters or outbursts?"

"Not at all son, just the same fifty to sixty people as always. People have their ups and downs but I can't imagine any one of my members being in a place so low that they would have killed someone. I would've seen it in them, I'm good at that," he says, again finding a way to put his hand on my shoulder, "There's only one thing to lead a man to do something like that..."

"What's that?" I ask.

"The Devil. You know the Lord is strong in this county. It's Satan and I *know* it. I can *feel* it."

I guess everyone is *feeling* something tonight. My *feeling* is that this has nothing to do with the Devil, and everything to do with some sick person trying to make a scene. They got what they wanted, I guess.

"This place is going to be off limits for at least a day. Someone will let you know when it's safe to go back inside. Here is my card. Call me if you need anything or hear something new," I say, handing him one of the few remaining business cards I had made when I got promoted. To think I was proud of these at one time.

"Thank you son, and may the Lord guide you all to the poor soul that is responsible, so that he can face judgement for this unforgivable sin," he says, walking back to his truck. Before he gets in, he glances back at the church and shakes his head. I can only imagine what the news is going to say about this. I pull out my flashlight and do a quick perimeter check to see if the brilliant patrol officers that arrived on scene may have missed anything. The hiring pool around here doesn't afford us the opportunity of preference and we have to bend the minimum requirements more than we'd like, to make sure both shifts are covered.

If I was going to bring a large man in here, how would I do it? Both side access doors are far too small to have made sense, and even if they did, they're both still locked. The back door is up a small set of stairs, so that one is off the table as well. Front door it is then. Bold of whoever to just drag that man in there like that, but I'm guessing this had to take more than one person to do anyways.

"Damon, wrap it up!" says Chief, walking out with the coroner. "Don't expect you'll find much else, especially now that the body bounced off the damn floor. Go back home and get some rest. Since you came in this late, just try to be in by lunch."

"Yes sir," I say, clicking my flashlight off and putting it back in my pocket. Walking back to my car I take another look at the church. What an odd night. Maybe I'll still have time for a few more drinks when I get home. Watching the man's body slam into the ground like that was just enough to sober me back up.

2:30 A.M.

WHEN I WAS YOUNGER, my mother always told me I should leave Culver. She said that I would understand when I got older, but if I ever wanted to be something, I would need to do it elsewhere. She always wanted the best for me. If she only knew now that I never took her advice and fell into the trap of this place, she'd be disappointed to say the least. She was so different from all the other women her age here, in a way that I didn't respect until now. She wasn't involved in any of the small town politics and made sure I had what I needed to get by, no matter what. Likely due to us moving here from an area with a totally different culture.

I remember thinking she was mean and I didn't understand what she was talking about half the time, just like any other little kid growing up. It turns out she was the most independent and intelligent woman I have ever met. She had me at eighteen years old and raised me all by herself. In today's world everyone seems to have some type of support and isn't present in raising their young. She didn't have a single bit of help. I still look up to her for that. My piece of shit father never put anything towards raising me, and I think I'm better for it. Well, mostly.

Putting her picture down, I realize my phone is vibrating. It's a text from Chief:

> Got a suspect for last night's murder. Gonna
> let Davidson interrogate since you just got
> off. Just letting you know.

That's weird. Someone must have confessed. It usually takes weeks for any real suspects to be identified in situations like this. I look over to Daisy, as she sits on the couch like she owns the place.

"Who do you think did it?"

She raises her head up as if she is going to answer, then sits it back down on the edge of the cushion and sighs.

"Me neither."

I need some friends before I go crazy. If someone knew how much I talk to my dog they'd probably have me in a mental institution. The problem with being in your mid thirties and single in Culver is that every woman is already married, has four kids or is over fifty. This isn't a bachelors town but I'm not that worried about it, I guess. My house and car are paid for, and Daisy probably wouldn't let another woman stay the night here anyway.

Looking to my distorted reflection in what is left of my bourbon for guidance, I ponder on what this lonely life would be like had my mother not been taken so early.

You would think I wouldn't drink so much knowing that the demise of the sweet, selfless Suzanne McKay had been at the hands of a drunk driver.

I need some sleep.

CHAPTER 3

9:45 A.M.

"You oughta just get you a damn cot in here," I hear from over my shoulder as I walk through the side door of the station. It is supposed to be for "emergencies only" per Chief's orders, but around here the only emergency is when anyone needs a smoke break. We usually keep it propped open with an old boot.

"You're one to talk, you haven't clocked out in five years!" I say with the same sarcasm. I knew it was Earl Davidson the moment that "oughta" hit my ears. Davidson is a seasoned detective, and you can see those fifteen years he has spent running the streets of Culver on the bottom of his boots he has resting on his desk. He always jokes that when he retires we will have to use his boots to prop the doors open for good luck.

"Any luck on your suspect?" I ask.

"Well...honestly I'm happy you came in early. I can't get

him to say a damn thing. Maybe you'll have better luck. You know you're the smart one anyways," Davidson says, pulling his feet off of his desk and sitting upright.

"He wouldn't speak? So how did you guys decide he was a suspect? Did Mr. Stokes remember something else after I talked to him?" I ask.

"Well that's the thing, man. Chief said when they started to leave this guy uh… Preston was just standing at the end of the parking lot of the church sobbing with his head in his hands. They thought maybe he saw the body or something but when they asked him what he was doing there he just kept saying he was sorry."

Davidson seems to look more confused as he speaks, as if he is hearing the information again for the first time. "Then, I shit you not he put himself in the back of a patrol car and shut the door. Then when they got him here he wouldn't say anything about it other than it was his fault, and not to let him go. I was hoping you would have better luck than I did."

"Interesting… lets go talk to him," I say, grabbing my notepad off of the corner of my desk.

I wonder why someone would go through so much work to hang that body up, just to immediately turn themselves in? If he wanted to go to jail, there are much easier ways to get there besides desecrating a corpse and traumatizing a few police officers. I guess I'll ask him myself, but something tells me that this isn't our guy.

10:30 A.M.

"I am Detective Damon McKay, and this is Detective Earl

Davidson. I am informing you that this conversation will be recorded. State your name for us, please."

"Preston Walsh," he says, calmly placing his hands on the table.

"It is my understanding that you have waived your right to having an attorney present, is that correct?" I ask.

"Yes."

The man on the other side of the table does not seem like the type to hurt anyone, much less hang a grown man from the ceiling of a church. He is young with a clean shaven face. His hair is short and messy, but in a way that is likely intentional. He's dressed nicely, and sits with great posture. It feels more like he is here for a job interview than to confess to a crime. I'm pretty confident this is a waste of our time.

"Are you ready to tell us why you were at the church last night?" I ask.

"I-I-I...well... I really can't say," he says in a frustrated tone.

"What do you mean?"

"I just don't really know to be honest and you guys are going to think I'm fucking crazy," he says, slumping forward and looking away.

"Well, how about you just walk us through your night and we'll go from there?" I ask.

"I guess I'll try... I was walking my dog around nine-thirty and I just kind of zoned out for a minute."

"Walking your dog? Do you always do that so late?" I ask.

"Yea, I could set my watch to my dogs nightly restroom breaks. Every night at 9:30 exactly, Scout picks a new spot in the yard. I've been doing it for six years now."

"Then what?"

"Well, like I said I had just zoned out for a minute. Then I just had like a weird feeling and like a... uh... vision or something..." He stares at the wall, then rubs his hair.

"Can you describe this vision?" I ask.

I notice Preston get visibly uncomfortable for a second. I share a quick glance with Davidson, as he must have noticed it too.

"It was like I was flying for a second, but just through the woods and towards the church at the end of Bradbury Road. Then I kind of… went through the door and on the inside it was dark and it felt…bad in there," he says.

"What do you mean bad? What did you see?"

"That's the part that will make you think I'm crazy… I didn't *SEE* anything really. It was just a feeling. A really bad feeling, like something horrible was present. Then I came back to reality when Scout started licking my hand," he says, staring down again.

I'm fairly certain this is just another person who's on drugs. If we had a dollar for every crackhead we've had in this room, we would've already retired.

"So, then what did you do?" I ask.

"I put Scout back up and I tried to sleep but I couldn't shake the thought of that bad feeling and I figured I had to check it out. So I drove to that gas station up the road and was going to get out and walk up there when I saw all the police. I went to drive back home but all of a sudden I felt like I *HAD* to go and see. Like the church was pulling me into it. And as soon as I got to the parking lot and could actually see what was going on, I just had an overwhelming feeling of guilt and sadness. I just couldn't stop crying. I don't know why, and didn't know what to do," he says.

I honestly don't know what to even write down for this. This man got into a police car and spent the night in jail all because of a drug induced premonition. I wonder what drug it was though, because I mean his feeling wasn't too far off. It would make my job easier if I could take something and just *FEEL* my way through the investigation.

"Mr. Walsh, do you know what happened in that church last night?" I ask.

"Not really I don't guess, but I feel like it HAS to be my fault somehow. When I was in that parking lot I felt like I had been there before...and that I did something terrible. I have been sleepwalking lately and I-I think maybe I hurt someone in there and my vision was some form of recollection. That happens sometimes after I sleepwalk, I'll remember some small details a few days later. I figured if I forced myself to stay here it would come to me but it just... hasn't yet," he says.

This isn't making any sense. I've heard of sleepwalkers hurting other people or themselves without knowing, but never something as complex as this. I think maybe this guy should be evaluated by a professional, but that isn't something we really have the funds for right now. Maybe he just needs some time.

"That's all for now Mr. Walsh, thank you. This is Detective Damon McKay ending the interrogation."

Davidson and I walk into the small hallway that connects the two interrogation rooms to the holding area.

"I think we should let him go," Davidson says in a concerned tone.

"What makes you say that?"

"It can't possibly be him. He said his dog went out at nine-thirty. Booking says he lives near Springhill and that's a thirty minute drive. He also works at the distribution center in the industrial park, and his employer said he was at work from seven a.m. to seven p.m. yesterday. Pastor Tim holds youth group Thursdays at five so the body couldn't have been there then. Meaning he had around an hour to take that body, get it in there, then UP there somehow and not be seen by anyone. There's just no way. Plus he had no idea what really happened. A man wouldn't go through all that mess and not brag about it if he was the one who did it."

"You're right," I say. "But I still want to hold him for the full seventy-two hours in case he remembers something else. He could always be lying about the dog situation, it isn't like the dog can verify his alibi. I wonder what kind of drugs he's on."

He laughs, "They drug tested him when he came in, and he had THC in his system but no other drugs or alcohol. Our rinky dink test wouldn't pick up anything crazy enough to cause visions like *that*, though."

"Lets go down to Doc Thompsons office and see if he has any information for us," I say, tossing my notepad down on my desk and heading for the coffee pot.

Davidson is right about Preston not being worth keeping. *But what about his so called "vision"? How would he have known something bad would be going on there? Why would he react that way if he didn't at least know something?* Then again I think he just had some really good, or really bad drugs. My head begins to throb as I pour myself a cup of coffee. Maybe this will help.

CHAPTER 4

"*T*hat steering wheel ain't gonna fly away, son," Davidson says from the passenger seat.

I didn't even realize I had been holding onto it so tight. I relax my grip, then grab my coffee from the cupholder and take a long drink.

"Sorry man, I'm just tired as hell," I say.

I wasn't lying, but I wasn't telling the whole truth either. I am tired on most days, but after watching that man fall from that church ceiling last night over and over in my head, I am a different kind of tired. Something was so odd about the scene. Surely all of this was for some reason. No one goes through all that, just to display their victim as a trophy. It has to be deeper. At least I hope so for the sake of all the work we're likely about to do to get to the bottom of it.

The church HAD to mean something. Hanging him up like that HAD to mean something. Why there? Why him? Why here of all places?

"Don't you feel like this is a waste of time?" I ask, without taking my eyes off of the road.

"Why would you think that?"

"I don't know man, I just feel like the guy was already dead so what can he really tell us?" I ask. "I think the ball is more in forensics court on this one. Hopefully, whoever did this left something behind and that's what will get the ball rolling."

"I think it will be worth our time. Whether he was dead or not, maybe Doc will find something that we aren't seeing. He has his way with—Mother FUCKERS!"

Before I could ask, I notice what has Davidson so excited. I see the "WCDX NEWS" logo across the side of an old Ford Windstar van. It is in the first parking spot in front of Doc Thompson's office, camera crew and overdressed reporter at the ready.

"Those slimy bastards are the scum of the Earth. I wish we could drive through the side of that ugly ass van," says Davidson, echoing the entire police department's opinion.

WCDX news is notorious for being the first to report anything and everything, no matter how exaggerated or untrue the story may be. That claim to fame has awarded them the sponsorship of every local lawyer, politician and restaurant. That's how they afford to drive everywhere all the time, and have a commercial on every channel, even their own. I don't even know what shade of green I'd call their van, but it's somewhere in between a Granny Smith apple and baby shit.

I take a deep breath and grab the door handle. "Let's get this over with."

"Hellllooooo Culver, Parker Cowan here with WCDX news on the scene with the developing story from last night's sacrificial murder at the church! Sir, can you fill us in on the details of what happened?? Sir? Sir!!"

The reporter is cut short as we all but sprint into the double doors at the front of the building. Chiefs policy is to only speak to Parker Cowan if there is no other option, and it's always fun to see the disappointment in his face when we scurry away. A staff member locks the doors behind us.

"Doc is waiting for you in the exam room, let me know when you're ready to leave and I'll let you out the side door so maybe those vultures will leave you alone."

"Won't be necessary ma'am, we might get lucky and bounce one of those doors off Parker Cowan's crooked ass nose on the way out," says Davidson, causing the young woman to laugh as she walks back into her office.

Walking down this hallway is never a good feeling. I'm only ever here when something bad happens, and my stomach turns in preparation of what I know I'm about to see. Dead bodies don't bother me, but seeing them in here makes me uneasy. Maybe it's just the cold and lifeless examination room with its tools, tables and lack of any distinct smells. Something about looking at a body this way is so dehumanizing, and it makes me feel like I'm looking at an educational diagram, not what used to be a person.

"Sorry gentlemen, my red carpet is at the cleaners or I would've given you a more grandiose entrance," says Doc Thompson with his monotone voice that seems to come from everywhere all at once. "Please grab yourself some gloves and come with me to table two. This is a weird one, no doubt."

Yea, no shit.

Mike "Doc" Thompson is the most intelligent man I've ever met. "Over educated and under compensated" as he would tell you. He was top of his class at Johns Hopkins University and even taught forensic pathology for a few years at Penn State before his father fell ill, landing him here in the city of Culver. His brilliance was immediately praised and before he could escape the web of this place, he took up residency as the expert for any and all abnormalities in the world of death. Twenty-five years and counting.

He is a stocky, well-built man that could very easily pass for a retired football player, but speaks in a kind way that makes you feel comfortable, even in a cold room just a few feet away from a dead body.

"Well Doc, who is it?" Davidson asks.

"Unfortunately, I don't know. Keep in mind it's only been a day and this entire county moves like cold honey. I assume you two cowboys have already called and asked around and don't know either," Doc says, staring at the covered body.

"Unfortunately not. No missing person report has been filed matching the description of this guy within a fifty mile radius. We'll expand our search, but for now we thought we'd see what you have for us," I say.

Without saying a word, Doc rolls the sheet all the way off the man, placing it at his feet. He walks to the head and clicks on a bright, articulating light.

"I'd like to be able to answer the questions I'm sure you both have, but for now all I have are bits of information that will likely create further confusion," he says, sounding oddly upbeat given the circumstance.

He continues, "I'll start by saying that this is no dead man that was exhumed. My cut into his chest was the first one, and he has no embalming fluid in his system. Not a trace of decomposition that would correspond with a person who has been deceased for any amount of time at all. I also found no signs of bruising or damage to any organs or soft tissues. Outside of his obvious indulgence of calories and his high mileage liver, this man should've been happy and breathing."

"Well, what about the hole in his head?" asks Davidson, almost implying that Doc Thompson had somehow missed it.

"Even more peculiar, as there are no marks indicating that this was done while he was still alive. Not bruising, not any distinct markings on the bone, and not even a singular crack in the surrounding area of the skull. It's like he was dried out, and cross sectioned like an ice sample in the Antarctic. It's still too early to admit defeat here, but I'm sorry to say I have no idea how this man ended up this way as of yet. The only thing I found that may be of assistance is this," he says pointing to a faded tattoo on the man's right shoulder that reads "Gina" in a red heart.

This isn't good. Doc always has the answer. I expected to show up here and leave with enough information to move forward with either releasing Preston Walsh, or moving to prosecute. Now I'm even more confused and feel like we won't be solving this any time soon. *What the fuck is going on here?*

"Will you call us if you find something?" asks Davidson, breaking my dizzying chain of thought.

"Of course I will. I won't sleep until I have something definitive on cause of death, and I will work my way from there," Doc says, pulling out a small notebook and scribbling into it.

Walking towards the double doors, I can feel the tension building in the air. It isn't because of Parker Cowan and the baby shit van waiting for us outside, it is because I know Davidson and I both have no idea what to think about this. I have even less of a clue on what to tell Chief Marks when we get back. I'm not used to leaving here empty handed. It's like we know less with each passing moment.

2:00 P.M.

"SURELY HE'LL FIND SOMETHING. That man should be working for NASA instead of dissecting the dead out here. Give him time," says Chief, finishing a glass of tea. He rolls his chair to his computer and types slowly on the keyboard for a minute.

"Y'all think it may have something to do with a ritual? Like the news said?" he asks.

"Possibly," I say. "I would've thought there would be more than just the body there if that was the case, though. The only element that makes it feel that way, at least to me, is that it was in a church. Remove the church setting and it's still weird, but less…cult-ish. Are there even any groups like that around here?"

He turns his computer screen to face us, "That's what I was lookin' for but I really don't even know what to search. It's not like cults have billboards or advertisements."

"No, that would make them a church then, wouldn't it?" I ask sarcastically.

"Hey now," Davidson says, shaking his head.

* * *

We spend the next few hours scavenging the internet for local groups that might be worth looking into, but don't find anything convincing. There is a possibility that this is some new group trying to make their presence known. If that's the case they aren't helping us out any since there wasn't any real evidence at the scene. I've lived here since I was twelve and I can only think of one time anything like that ever happened. There was some old lady who went around killing cats. Everyone at school thought she was a witch and swears she turned a few kids into toads. I think she just hated cats and loved methamphetamine.

Chief Marks informed us that he had some officers go to our suspect Preston's house to execute a search warrant in the hopes of finding anything of interest. The only thing they found that would raise an eyebrow was his extensive vintage porn collection. Other than that he seems like any other guy, which gets us absolutely nowhere.

* * *

"I HATE that my off days line up with this just getting started," I say.

"Yea it really sucks to get a Saturday off, must be horrible. I can't stand weekends," says Davidson rolling his eyes.

I gather my things and head to my car. It's very rare that off days line up like this, and I'm looking forward to it. In a weird way I wish that I wasn't off, though. Something interesting like this popping up has me a little motivated. I haven't had to solve a real problem for a long time. I wish I could be this motivated to solve my own problems, but I'll take what I can get. I pull out of the parking lot and head towards the package store near the station.

CHAPTER 5

I place my glass back on the nightstand and look at the clock.

2:34 A.M.

I NEED to go to sleep so I can actually salvage some of my days off, but I just can't get this murder out of my head. Most of the crimes around here are pretty cut and dry. Most of my job is filtering out the "he said-she said" and then taking action, but this one is just so far from normal and it's effecting everyone. Even Chief Marks seemed perplexed in a way that I've never seen once we told him the news from Doc. The only decision he seemed to be able to confidently make was to release Preston Walsh immediately. It's not like I disagree with him or anything. I just wish he would've kept him for a while.

What If he decides to "sleepwalk" again and we have another murder? What if he knows exactly what he did, but is just playing some fucked up game with us? I guess I'm not going to solve it with this bourbon tonight anyways. I'll just make sure Daisy has some water and sleep it off.

"Ready to lay down?" I ask into the dark of the hallway, expecting her to come running in from the living room.

"Daisy?"

That's weird. Maybe she fell asleep on the couch or something. Grabbing her empty water bowl, I head towards the kitchen. As I round the end of the hallway, I hear a low growl coming from the living room.

"Daisy? You okay in there girl?"

More growling, this time a little louder.

What the hell could she be growling at?

I reach for the light switch blindly, finding it after the third try and it illuminates the room. Daisy is standing with her tail tucked behind her, in the middle of the living room. Her head is low to the ground, nose pointing directly at the front door. Her hair is standing up, teeth showing and no sign of breaking her gaze.

Before I can call her off I hear the slightest tapping coming from the door.

Tap-Tap-Tap

Daisy raises the volume of her growl and takes a step towards the sound, ready to engage with whoever may be on the other side.

Tap-Tap-Tap

. . .

THIS TIME, the tap also increases in volume prompting me to interject.

"Who is it?" I ask towards the door.

TAP-TAP-TAP

OKAY, *fuck this.* I walk to the door, now annoyed at who might be playing some stupid prank this late.

"Daisy, SIT!" She complies and I reach for the door. I turn the knob and swing the door open as hard as I can.

"CAN I HELP-" I stop mid sentence, as my porch light illuminates a woman in a short black dress, standing as still as a statue at the end of my porch steps. I clear my throat and try again.

"Uh…Ma'am can I help you?" I ask.

"Ma'am?"

Okay, this is fucking creepy. The woman is very short, and very pale. She has a blank expression, with her lips pressed tightly together. Her eyes seem totally blank, almost completely black and are staring right through me.

"Ma'am?"

My voice cracks, and I clear my throat again.

"MA'AM! I NEED YOU TO FUCK OFF OKAY IT IS TOO LATE FOR THIS!"

Instead of responding, her eyes seem to cut into me and her lips start to curl into a small smile.

I try to speak again, but this time, nothing comes out.

Her smile gets bigger.

I hear Daisy start barking behind me.

"Please get the fuck out of here," I try to say, only mouthing it as no sound is coming out of me.

What the fuck is happening… Am I really this drunk? Why

can't I speak? Daisy's bark stops suddenly, and I look back quickly to see if she's okay. It looks like she's still barking, I just can't hear it. Her fur is moving wildly, and slobber is coming from her mouth as she puts all of her energy into trying to scare this woman away.

I turn back to face the woman and she is now no more than six inches from my face, smiling from ear to ear. She is still motionless. I try to throw my hands up to push her away but I can't move. My arms are stuck at my side and my legs are planted still underneath me. Its as if her gaze has turned my bones to concrete. *What is this, some new age fucking medusa or something? Surely I'm not THAT drunk...*

With her this close, I can see her more clearly now. My stomach turns. Her paper white skin, a stark contrast to her dress, is... unnatural. Her eyes seem so... *lifeless.* Her teeth are so white that I can see the reflection of my porch light as it starts to dim. The light of the moon behind her begins to fade and a wave of panic hits my body.

I try with all of my strength to move to run, but I can't. It is still totally silent... The light is slowly fading around me and I can't look away from her. My heart is about to beat out of my chest. All I can feel is the cold sweat rolling down my forehead.

How is she doing this? Is she about to kill me? Is she the one who killed the man at the church? Why didn't I grab my pistol before I opened the door?

"I won't hurt you, but I will be seeing you soon."

Her words hit my ears as if they were coming out of a loudspeaker inside of my head, but her smile never changes and her teeth remain pressed together.

Before I can even try to respond, all of the remaining light goes away at once.

* * *

I FEEL A POUNDING in my head, and all the sound and lights come crashing back to me. As I focus, I no longer see the woman, but instead…the white of my ceiling. I jump up with all of my strength, accidentally throwing my phone across my bedroom. My heart is pounding. My body is covered in sweat.

Where is she? What did she do? I grab my pistol sitting beside my bed and run into the hallway.

"WHERE ARE YOU, YOU CREEPY BITCH?"

As I reach the end of the hall, I bring the sights of the pistol to the center of the living room. I sprint across to the door, twisting the knob and swinging it inward against the wall. I align the center dot of the sights with the center of the sidewalk leading up to the porch.

Nothing. I look around and see that the moon has my entire yard lit up, and nothing is there but the wind. Closing my eyes, I listen intently, hoping to hear the crunch of a footstep or maybe heavy breathing that could point me towards the woman that was just on my porch. In the distance I hear a lone owl calling into the night. It seems to be mocking me… *Who? Who? Who are you looking for you idiot? No one is out here!* I lower my pistol to my side and turn back to my living room to see Daisy sitting up on the couch, with her head slightly tilted, looking at me like I am playing some game.

I glance at the clock on the wall behind her.

2:34 A.M.

WHAT THE HELL? Daisy lays back down on the couch and rolls to her side, inviting me to come rub her belly. Her tail starts wagging, hitting the remote on the armrest.

TAP-TAP-TAP

I LAUGH to myself as I sit next to her. I rest my arm on her back and feel the sleepiness seeping back into my bones. I yawn. *What a dream.*

CHAPTER 6

12:30 P.M.

I place my glass from last night in the sink, and reach into the cabinet for some ibuprofen to knock my headache down. Usually I'll drink some pickle juice before bed to get ahead of these things, but with the weird dream from last night, I must've forgotten. Hopefully tonight I'll get some better rest so that my off days aren't wasted. I was only supposed to get one off day this week, but Chief decided with recent events it was best for everyone to have some time to rest up and get focused. I think he has a feeling this will get worse before it gets better and he wants us all as ready as possible. According to a text from Davidson, some of the newer guys are going to make the rounds and ask questions in the neighborhoods around the church. Chief is to follow up with Raymond Stokes as well as check on Preston Walsh to see if his mind has cleared any. Maybe something will turn up.

I spend the rest of the afternoon cleaning up and doing laundry, which has become my dreaded off day ritual. Working long hours doesn't allow for much other than a hot meal from a drive-through on the way home and a few glasses of something strong to get me to sleep. It seems like that isn't even enough on most nights anymore, though. I think my brain knows it doesn't want to be alone with itself and would rather me be at work focused on something. I think I might go out somewhere tonight instead of adding more dishes to the sink.

"Nah," I mutter out loud, thinking of how used to these walls I've gotten. The last time I went out it ended with a bartender convincing me to call my ex-girlfriend a whore on social media, so I might just stay here and make sure Daisy has company. On the same note, the last few nights I've been alone with my thoughts haven't gone too well either. Maybe I'll go out and just turn my phone off once I get tipsy.

"What should I do?" I ask to Daisy.

She trots into the kitchen beside me and sits, wagging her tail across the floor, ejecting hair across the freshly cleaned tile.

"You're right! Bar food sounds great!" I say, as if she had weighed the pros and cons out in her response. It's early enough that if I get ready and go soon, I will have time to hang out and sober up before coming home to get some decent rest. I head to my room to look for something more than these pajamas to wear out. I move a pile of dirty clothes and find my note from the other night on the floor.

I pick it up and read back through it. "Drunk words are sober thoughts" is what I remember one of my friends telling me back in school. I never know how I feel about that statement, especially now. I grab the pen laying on the floor near it and scribble the words "just kidding" at the bottom. I smile and crumple it up, tossing it in the trash. This case has definitely pulled me out of where I was when I had written it. It's given me the motivation to push forward, at least for now. I'd hate to miss out on finding out who killed the man in the church. If everything goes the way it's supposed to, I'll be the one to figure it out.

7:00 P.M.

I PULL up to "Big Lew's Tavern", a small bar outside of Magnolia. Magnolia is only thirty minutes away from Culver, but just far enough that I won't be seeing any familiar faces. Walking in, I make sure to lock my car twice, looking back to verify the lights are flashing. This isn't the safest area, and I've gotten into the habit of leaving my doors unlocked accidentally when I get to drive my personal vehicle. I really like this place. They have the best burgers you can get on this side of the Mississippi River. It's been a while but I hope they're still as good as I remember.

I walk into to the bar and notice that I'm one of only six or seven people in the whole place. Perfect. I read the room quickly before choosing a spot at the end of the bar in the corner. That way I can see everyone at once without having to turn around. I take note of only two women in here, hopefully they will leave me alone with the burger I'm about to order. It's kind of hard to flirt while eating like a slob.

"What can I get you?" asks the bartender, who is facing away cleaning a glass.

"Double whiskey coke…and do you guys still have a food menu?" I ask hopefully.

"Of course, I'll grab you one." As he turns around, I realize it is the same bartender I had from last time. *Maybe he won't remember me...*

I place my order, selecting "The Lew" from the menu, just like the last time I was here. The bartender scribbles onto a small notepad, then looks up at me.

"Been what, eight or nine months, huh?" he asks as he types my order into a screen that I hadn't noticed until now.

"I wondered if you would remember me," I say.

"How could I forget? I see the same one hundred or so people in here every week and you definitely aren't the typical customer. No worries though, no peer pressure this time!" He smiles as he walks to the back.

I think this is what I needed. The atmosphere here is equally relaxing and stimulating, as the music perfectly drowns out the chatter of the people at the pool tables in the far left corner. A few more people have poured in, but even at its busiest, "Big Lew's" never has more than thirty or so sad souls in it at a time. It has a ton of neon lights that adorn the walls and the lingering clouds of cigarette smoke make it seem as if you've been transported into a sad country music video. Just the type of place you'd go to try and escape your troubles, or find some new "trouble" to get involved in.

The waiter walks from the back to bring me the burger, and my stomach growls. Glad that was quick, as that first drink went down faster than I thought. Maybe I should pace myself. Then again, I didn't come here to waste money so I guess I need to make my time worth it.

* * *

"So why do they call this one "The Lew"?" I ask the bartender after he delivers my second drink.

"You won't believe this but uh..." he says with a smirk, "Big Lew's Tavern...BLT...you know for...Bacon Lettuce

Tomato? The Lew just makes it seem like it's a trade secret. Sounds a little cooler than ordering a BLT like you're at some regular burger joint. Come on, man… this is Big Lew's!" He points sarcastically at the large worn sign on the back wall of the tavern that used to hang on the outside of the building. It had to be replaced a few years ago after some storms came through and knocked it down.

I laugh and take a long sip, before asking him another question, "Who is Lew anyways?"

He shifts his weight to his other side and his smile fades just for a second. He places both of his hands on the bar in front of me and lets out a small sigh.

"Well, I really don't know much about him other than he opened this place after his wife died around twenty years ago. He put his heart and soul into keeping this place running and always made sure he spent at least a few hours here every night. I only got to see him for about a year when I first started bartending here."

"Oh, so did he pass away?" I ask, hoping it wasn't too intrusive.

"No sir!," he says. "He's still around, just not around here. About five years ago he sold the place to the current owners, some friends he'd made over the years. Nice couple in their forties who really have kept Lew's vision alive. He let them keep the name and all of the recipes. All he asked is that they reach out if they need any help."

Thinking back, I never even imagined that "Big Lew" was a real person.

"So what made him want to sell?" I ask.

He looks down briefly, and in a genuinely heartfelt tone says, "He was getting up there in years, and had started showing signs of uh…decline… He wanted to make use of the years he still has left so he cashed out and got him a nice place off the beaten path, tucked into the woods near the valley. Last I heard he was happy with his decision. Want another?"

I didn't realize I had already finished another drink. This guy is easy to talk to, but I guess he wouldn't have been a bartender if he wasn't.

"Yes sir," I say, pushing my empty glass and plate towards him. I think about what "Big Lew's" life must be like. *How cool would it be to be able to cash out and move to somewhere away from everyone? Then again, what's the point of waiting until you're that old before enjoying life? I guess that's normal, but maybe that's why I'm so unhappy. I still have twenty something years before I can retire, and even then it wouldn't be a nice enough retirement to have anything too special. So what's the point anyways? Am I just unhappy because of how boring my job is? If I changed jobs would this feeling go away, or would I be right back to writing suicide notes in my bedroom in a few months?*

I make my way to the back right corner of the tavern to get my first restroom visit of the night over with. As I wash up I hear a man walk in behind me. He doesn't go to a stall, he just stands a few feet behind me. I briefly glance up to the mirror and notice he's staring at me.

"Don't worry son, I won't hurt ya," he says in a thick southern accent.

I zone out, rethinking my dream from last night…*"I won't hurt you" echoing in my ears, the sight of her clenched teeth and big smile…"I will be seeing you soon."*

"You good, buddy?" the man asks. "I was just jokin' with ya, I got some dang ketchup in my beard and was gonna dip in that sink."

I quickly wash my hands while apologizing, and hurry back to the bar. Hopefully this next drink will get that creepy bitch out of my head. When I get back to my spot, there is a group of college-aged guys sitting at a round table behind me. I can overhear bits and pieces of their conversation, but it seems mostly about girls and sports, so I carry on sipping my drink. I think maybe I should socialize with the guys by the pool table instead of sitting here like some sad bastard, even though that isn't far from the truth.

As I get up to walk over to the corner, I overhear one of the guys say, "Yea man, it's getting weird around here. I just think we need to take a vacation or something." I sit back into my chair, hoping no one will notice. "Yea dude, first there was that murder over in Culver, then all the Foster's animals losing their shit and now I heard someone killed a few of the mayor's cows. Probably some satanic fuck trying to call Papa Lucifer home or something!" The table all laughs together, then stands up and heads towards the pool tables in the back. *Damn, there goes that idea.*

"Any idea what those kids were talking about?" I ask the bartender.

He perks up and walks closer to my side of the bar, "You're a cop, right? You didn't hear about any of that?"

"A detective, yea, but I didn't know anything about weird animal stuff," I say.

"Ahh, well I'll fill you in. The Foster family owns a big farm out there near the end of Sunridge Valley. The other day, every damn one of their horses and cattle went through the fence and high tailed it about ten miles into downtown and just stood around. And when I say through the fence, I mean it. They tore down about half a mile of three tier wooden fence. It really was a sight to see all those animals just hanging out in town blocking the road like that," he says, now leaned on to my side of the bar only a foot or so away from me.

I take a long drink, finishing off my glass and sliding it towards him, "Something must've spooked them, huh? What about the mayor's cows?"

He grabs my glass, "Ohhh that's the weird one alright, his

farm backs up to the Foster farm, and someone put a hole in two of his cows." I raise my eyebrow, but before I could ask what he meant, he interrupts. "What I mean is they somehow shot them in the head or something but they didn't bleed out or anything. A farm hand walked out and found them early in the morning. They called a vet out but he said he had never seen anything like it. The reason they didn't bleed out is because there was no blood in either one of them. Ol' mayor came in here and cleared out my Jim Beam that day."

Kind of like that poor motherfucker that we found in Pastor Tim's church. There might be some kind of connection there... maybe the guy practiced this sick shit on some cows before he decided to escalate.

"Damn, that's weird. What did they do with the cows?" I ask. If they are still around, maybe I can have Doc Thompson take a look and compare the holes in the cows to the hole in our mystery man.

"They buried them at the edge of the property so the coyotes and vultures wouldn't get them," he says. "You guys have anything else weird besides that church thing?"

"No, but I have a feeling that we will soon though," I say as I accept another drink. I'm definitely buzzed now, but I don't know if I should keep drinking or not since apparently Culver isn't the only place with mysterious events going down.

No Damon, you didn't come here to work. Relax.

* * *

OVER THE NEXT HOUR, I make sure to keep the conversations with the bartender and any unfortunate soul who accidentally sits next to me strictly casual without asking anymore questions. From sports and music, to relationships and life advice, I talk my way around the bar. My fourth and fifth drink have me in a perfect state of extroversion that I know will come crashing down if I proceed. I put an order in for two more burgers and a basket of fries, then retire to my corner of the bar to wait.

"How do you have room for all of this?" asks the bartender as he brings the bag my way.

"Well, one of the burgers is for my dog. Can't go out on the town and not bring her something back," I say, mouth already watering at the smell.

"Very kind of you. I appreciate the business tonight. Can I expect to see you back here soon?" he asks as he brings me my tab.

"Depends on work, honestly," I say through the chewing of the fry I snuck out of the bag, "But when I come back I'll make sure I fill you in. My name is Damon McKay, by the way, what's yours?" I ask, reaching out my hand to him.

"Jacob Greene, and thanks again. I'll see you soon."

Ugh. If another person says that I'm going to lose it. The only thing I want to see soon is my dog and my bed. I walk to my car and start to eat my food, in hopes that it will level out the alcohol in my system. Just as good now as it was a few hours ago. I make sure to save Daisy a few fries before rolling the bag up and tossing it into the passenger seat. As I start my car, I notice a woman standing right outside the entrance of the tavern. I didn't see her earlier when I was leaving. There seemed to be a disproportionate amount of men in there for a Saturday.

She has a cigarette in one hand, and a cell phone in the other. She seems to be typing vigorously. How long has she been there? Did she watch me eat that whole burger in forty-five seconds like some barbarian? Oh well. I watch her put her cigarette out, before briefly glancing my way and walking inside. Should I go back in? She seems much more attractive than any of the women I'd spoken to tonight...but that isn't saying much. She is just a blob I saw from across the street. For all I know that was a man and I just looked like a creep staring out of my car like that. *But what if it was a woman, and she's worth talking to?*

I should put myself out there again, though. Fuck it, I'll go see what she's about. I reach for my keys to turn my car off but in my rearview mirror I notice a group of people walk around the end of the block and head towards the bar. Ahh, I guess I'll take my chances next time. Maybe when I'm not wearing half of a cheeseburger on my shirt.

Time to head home.

CHAPTER 7

9:00 A.M.

$\mathcal{I}$t might be the coffee or it might be the full day of sleep I got, but either way I am energized. Yesterday, I didn't wake up until around lunchtime, ate, then went right back to bed. I feel like I could run a marathon right now. Probably the most sleep I've had in a few months. I was the first one at the station for day shift by more than two hours so I made a point to clean my desk up and have a cup of coffee for Davidson ready. I feel it. We are going to make some positive progress today, no doubt about it.

I've been looking on the whiteboard in the office, and it looks like the follow ups have lead nowhere and there isn't any new information about the mystery man. I guess I will be the one to get the ball rolling again. I hear the chime of the front door, and see Chief Marks walking through the front lobby heading my way. Maybe my positivity will motivate him too. I stand up as he opens the glass door. I don't think he will have any interest in a pep talk though, as he looks grim. "What's up, Ch-" He cuts me off by raising his right hand in a "stop" motion.

"McKay, grab your shit and call Davidson, tell him to meet us at the high school. Coach Miller just found a body in the gym."

I grab my bag off my desk and jog outside to catch up with Chief while waiting for Davidson to pick up the phone.

He picks up after the fourth ring, "I know, I know. I'm running a little late, I'll be there in a minute. I overslept."

I tell him the news, and he doesn't respond. "Davidson, you there?" I ask, assuming that he may have lost connection.

"Yeah man, I just…I just knew something was coming," he says, his voice trailing off a little before he continues, "Last night, I told the wife either we are about to make big progress or this was about to snowball."

Holding on to the little bit of positivity I have left, I say, "Let's just hope we have something to work with this time. The gym is a popular hangout spot. Maybe someone saw something and will come forward. Maybe they left something behind… There has to be something that will point us to whoever is responsible."

"Surely. Meet you there, buddy," he says.

* * *

I HATE DRIVING with lights and sirens. The town is too small and people are too nosy. I know that after the first red light I run, I'll see phones going up to take videos and people staring. It also means that there will likely be another run in with Parker Cowan and that damn van in our future. As I head to the school, I wonder what their story will be this time. I can see it now, "Local police department scrambles to the scene of another murder, just as clueless today as they were yesterday. Find out how they are wasting your tax dollars tonight at nine!" Or "Local detective spends more time at the liquor store than trying to keep our town safe!" *Ugh*.

On my right, I pass the large white "Cowboy Country" sign, which means I'm almost there. I can still faintly see the red smears of paint from where last year a group of kids cleverly edited it to say "Coward Country" after a seventy-four to fourteen loss to the East Village Eagles. Coach Miller cleaned it up the next day with the help of the whole team. That man loves his football more than most people love their family, so he took that pretty hard. I can only imagine how hard finding a body in his gym must be on him.

I guess I'm about to find out. As I pull into the parking lot of the gym, I see him sitting on the tailgate of his truck. He has his head in his hands while an officer holds an umbrella over him. I park to the left of him and get out. I wish I had thought ahead about the rain, but getting a little wet won't kill me.

I hear Chief Marks shouting to a few officers standing at the front of the gym door. "Get this taped up, and someone get some cars parked in the entrances so no one comes in, or goes out!"

I grab my bag and jog towards him. He looks to me briefly before opening one of the double doors and motioning for me to go in first. The gym has a small concession area in the front with two large doorways on each side. One for the home team, and the other for visitors. Not seeing anything in this area, I walk around through the home side door. Dead center of the court, there is a large black sheet laying completely over what I assume is the body. It is large and rectangular, almost covering the entire logo at center court. The logo is a cowboy riding a bucking horse, painted with the brown and black school colors. As I approach it, I hear the clicking of a camera. I was so focused on the sheet that I didn't see the Culver Forensics Team or "CFT" as most of us call them, setting up near the bleacher area.

"So, did Coach put that blanket there or…?" I ask Chief as we watch the CFT take their preliminary photographs.

"No. He told dispatch he came in early to unlock the gym and sweep up so the boys could get some indoor cardio in since it was supposed to rain today," he says. "When he turned the lights on he saw all of this. He pulled it back a little and called it in the second he saw what it was."

That must've been horrible to see. Coach Miller is a very emotional man already, I know this is going to devastate him. The CFT carefully remove the sheet by picking up all four corners at once and placing it to one side of the gym. They move a portable light closer and point it down towards the body. They snap a few pictures as we step closer. Now that the body is fully illuminated, chills run down my spine and my face gets hot. I immediately recognize the body… it's…*HER.*

"Relax Detective, I don't think she's going to jump up and get you," says James Scott, wet shoes squeaking as he walks up from the other side of her.

"I'm okay, I just thought it was someone I knew for a second," I say. *I'm glad the coroner broke my train of thought, but my heart is still beating a mile a minute.*

He bends down to get a better look, then looks up at us. "Well, someone knows her. A beautiful young woman doesn't end up like this without her absence being noticed. I really can't definitively place time of death though just by looking. She's as white as a sheet of paper, let's see if there is any pooling on the bottom side."

Part of me knows there won't be. Part of me bets this is just like the other victim with no blood somehow. Part of me is still terrified because I have seen this woman. That same white skin…the black dress and… I glance to her face, half expecting her big smile to be showing, but it isn't. Thankfully.

"Will you guys help me raise her up?" asks James, struggling to carefully turn her on her side.

"Sure," I say as I kneel down beside her, placing my left knee near hers. Chief gets by her head, and after we quickly put our gloves on, we slide our hands under her and begin trying to lift her onto her right side.

"What the…" Chief says as he tries unsuccessfully to lift her at all. I try as well, but all that happens is her knee raises in my hand but she won't roll. I slide my hand higher, under her lower back and try again. She won't budge. I reach further under her back, and I feel something hard protruding from the floor and into her back.

"Hold on, she's stuck on something," I say, grabbing my flashlight out of my pocket. I click it on and place my face firmly against the floor, pointing the light under her. I can barely see it, but it looks like a black bar sticking up from the floor directly into her lower back. "God damnit," I say as I get up, "I bet there are three hooks in her back just like the other guy."

Chief confirms with his light, then stands up quickly. "We are going to have to cut this floor out. I'm not sure how the hell someone did this, but the only way we are going to figure it out is if we take this whole section with us."

He is right. How would she get hooked through her back AND stuck into the floor? This was definitely the work of the same person. Trying to convince myself that I was just making that dream up in my head, I kneel down and look at her again. *It's definitely her, but HOW? Have I seen her before? Was it really a dream or was I really just that drunk, and she actually came to my door asking for help?* There's no way. I stand up and head outside for some fresh air. As I walk out, one of the CFT guys grabs a small cordless saw out of the back of their van. Those guys always come prepared. Hopefully they've sent Coach Miller home before he hears them tearing that floor up. Davidson walks up with a coffee in his hand and a concerned look on his face.

"So we've got a fat man hung up like a puppet and sleeping beauty pinned to the floor under a sheet," he says as he sips his coffee. "Where do we even start?"

"Like I said, there has to be something. The sheet that was used seems to be of the same material that was on the mystery mans head. That might lead us somewhere, it doesn't seem like an every day item. That and those hooks. Surely they aren't something you can get just anywhere," I say as I pull my notebook out. He doesn't reply, and just nods while taking another drink of his coffee.

Staring out into the parking lot of the gym, I notice a few cars pulled over and four people standing together, huddled under a few large umbrellas. I can hear their murmurs over the light rain. I assume they're taking guesses at what we're all doing out here. I'd be willing to bet none of them will have guessed a woman is about to come out along with a large section of wood. I hope everyone can keep this under wraps until we are closer to solving it or the rumors will get out of control fast.

As I make a mental note about the consistencies in the two scenes I realize that both of them occurred in super high traffic areas. Meaning fingerprints and other direct evidence will be a waste of time outside of anything on the bodies, which is unlikely. This rain doesn't help either. Someone smart enough to display the bodies like that is surely smart enough to pull this off without leaving any evidence. *There has to be something I am missing.*

"They said Coach wants a little time before he comes down to the station to talk to us," Davidson says.

"I understand that, but surely he understands the quicker

we get information from him, the quicker we can get moving on figuring this out," I say.

He rubs his face, "Maybe so, but it ain't likely he will give us anything. This is the weirdest shit I've ever seen and it's looking like this won't be the last time I say that."

I feel my phone buzz in my pocket. It's a text from Chief Marks:

> Y'all follow up with Pastor Tim and see if Doc Thompson has any news for us. I'll stay here and wait for the principal to show up so I can obtain the security footage. Meet back at the station before four.

I show it to Davidson, and we decide to split the task. I choose Pastor Tim, so I have to back track in the direction we came. As I drive past the group of people by the road, I make sure to smile and wave. No one returned the favor.

About a mile and a half down the road I pass the infamous baby shit van headed towards the school. As we cross paths, I catch a glimpse of Parker Cowan slicking his blonde hair back while smiling in his mirror, without a doubt more excited to see his own face than he is in providing anyone with any real news or help. What a slimy bastard.

CHAPTER 8

I pull in to Pastor Tim's church around noon. On the drive in I called and asked if he would meet me there for a few questions, to which he happily obliged. He was already at the church, assisting in supervising some contractors who were replacing the beam the mystery man hung from as well as a few minor upgrades. The members of the church and the community had graciously donated to the cause after hearing what had happened. One thing I can say about the community around here is that they may talk shit behind each other's back, but when tragedy strikes they come together like glue to help.

Pastor Tim is talking to a younger man outside of his truck as I walk up to the double doors. I can't help but notice the brand new and obvious camera dead center above the doors, and another on the corner of the wall nearest the parking lot. He notices me approach, and sees me looking towards the cameras.

"Hindsight is 20/20 ain't it?" he chuckles, walking to me with his hand stretched out, "You just never think that a church is a place you'd need security. But, I felt like it was needed for the congregation to feel safe again."

"I understand, sir," I say while trying to escape his handshake, "How are the repairs coming along?"

He motions me towards the doors, "Come and take a look for yourself. Just make sure to wipe your feet off on the mat."

Once inside, it is obvious that the money from the community did not go to waste. The once old and dusty beams that spread across the ceiling are now replaced with thick, stained beams that make the church look brand new. The cracked pews are now replaced with wood of a similar stain and likely a similar price.

"Wow, looks great!" I say.

He grins wide. "What the Devil can do, God can do ten times better! He brought that evil in here and the Lord washed it away with his beautiful gift of love through our community!"

"Well, I'm glad. Have you had anyone come to you with any information that may help find out who this...*devil* may be?" I ask, looking up to where the body hung the last time I was here.

He joins my gaze, "Don't worry son. That wood they hung him on was purely for looks. The roof won't fall in or nothin'. But to answer your question, not really other than a bunch of guesses. I heard something else was going on at the school too, and I'll tell you what. I'm willin' to bet its some dang devil worshipers. Last night on the news, Parker Cowan said these murders were probably some kind of ritual."

If I could roll my eyes right now, they might roll into the back of my head. Any time something bad happens, it's "the devil worshipers" or "some cult". WCDX loves selling fear to this little town and it works for their views but it takes attention away from real possibilities. The only "devil" around here is whoever the hell did this to these people. Sometimes people are just bad on their own.

"So outside of devil worshipers, have you heard any talk around town about anything weird going on?" I ask, pulling my notebook out in case I need to jot something down.

"Naw, not around here. One of the men on the other side of Magnolia had his animals run off is all I've heard. They probably knew what was going on here and took off. You know animals see evil way before we do," he says.

"Well, if you hear anything else, please call me at any time. And make sure you watch those cameras. Whoever did this might come back by. Don't want them to catch you off guard. It might be best to keep the church locked up until we catch them," I say while closing my notebook.

He smiles and lifts his shirt up to reveal a small revolver tucked in his waistline, "Oh they better hope they don't come back!"

Leaving behind the smell of fresh wood and the energized pastor, I walk back outside. I try again to think of how I would get that man in the church had I been the one to put him there. I look around to the edge of the parking lot, and take in the loneliness of the woods that line the area behind the church. The trees are dense and overgrown. Definitely not something anyone could quickly navigate, especially in the dark. The only way in, are the roads themselves. That only leaves two options. Either they came from the back roads to the east of the church, which is the long way towards Magnolia…or they came from the other way, which leads directly back into Culver. Maybe if I retrace each direction I could get an understanding of where they came from.

I decide to head east first. It looks like the rain has let up some, and I dread the post-rain humidity. At least I'll be in my car for a bit driving down the long winding road that makes up Bradbury Road. Around twenty miles of road with dense woods on each side, and a few houses sprinkled along the way. I used to make this drive every day when I first got my license. It made me feel like I was a Formula One driver in my beat up fox body mustang. I was probably only doing five or ten miles per hour over the speed limit but at the time it might as well have been two hundred or more. Looking back, I really wish I'd have spent that time with my mom instead. She would've wanted me to have that fun, but had she known my friends and I would take turns speeding from one end to the other after drinking, she would've killed me.

I come up on the first house, and see a large for sale sign in the yard. I guess no one would be there to help, so I keep driving. A mile or so later, there is a house with a large red truck in the driveway. There is a man pulling what looks to be a bag of dog food out of the back. I decide I will pull in to see if he can offer me any help. The man turns in my direction and places the dog food against the back wheel of the truck as I get out of my car.

"Can I help you?" he asks in a tone that lets me know I will have to work for this conversation.

"Yes sir, I apologize for pulling up on you like this. I am Detective Damon McKay, with Culver Police Department. Just wondering if you or your family might be able to help me out." I pull my notebook out and pretend to flip through pages to break the awkward silence.

"And how exactly would I be able to do that? I ain't breaking no laws that I know of, and even if I was I wouldn't tell *YOU*." He crosses his arms, obviously proud to let me know he isn't the biggest fan of me or authority.

"No worries sir, I'm not here to give you any trouble. Just wondering if maybe you or your family heard or saw anything a few nights ago that maybe could lead us in the direction of the person or people responsible for what happened in Pastor Tim's church," I say as I write down the address of the house so I can look into who this guy is, later.

The man uncrosses his arms, and leans against the bed of his truck. He looks up towards his front door where a woman who must be his wife is standing, throwing a concerned gaze our way. He gives her a quick thumbs up and a head nod, and she shuts the door.

"Look bud, I'll be honest with you. These woods is deep and full of life. There ain't a night that goes by that we don't hear somethin' messing around out there. But anything outside of the few acres we got, we can't hear anything else. That church is bout what, six or seven miles up the road?"

"Yes sir, and I understand," I say, losing hope in any inquiry, "But what about last Thursday night? Anything at all that was different?"

"Naw…well, I'm sure it's unrelated but some dumbass ran over my mailbox last week and it might've been that day but I'm not sure. When I leave in the morning it's still dark so I didn't see it till I got home," he says.

"I'm sorry to hear that. These kids don't pay attention and will fly down the road looking at their phones. That's probably what happened," I say, making a mental note to see if anyone had pulled over any drunk drivers.

"Paying attention or not, that damn sure woke them up, my mailbox was a piece of four by four tube steel and they bent it all to hell. Dumb bastards are lucky I wasn't awake when it happened. I bent it back but I had to replace the box and repaint the whole thing. I had it grey to match the house but whatever they hit it with was black and I couldn't clean it off," he says, reaching down and grabbing the dog food. "If you happen to see a busted up black car or somethin', tell 'em they owe me forty-five dollars for that damn paint!" He walks towards the front of his house, letting me know that he has nothing else to say. I thank him for his time and get back into my car.

Well damn. It seems that this isn't the best method of figuring this out. It isn't like the person or people responsible would stop by anyone's house and let them know what they are doing. I am wasting my time. I think I should go back to the station and see if Coach Miller might be interested in coming by. Or maybe I should show up at Preston Walsh's house unannounced and see if he remembers anything else... It still seems so weird to me that anyone would confess to something so bad, based off of some potentially drug induced premonition. Chief says stuff like that happens all the time on big cases, but I just haven't had enough of them to see it, I guess.

I yawn deeply and decide that maybe heading to the station would be the best idea. I head back west, passing by the church on my left. Pastor Tim is still outside, and I wave to him just as I hear the annoying *BING-BING-BING* of my car telling me I need to stop for gas. Up the road on the right, is the SPEEDY TRAK sign and I decide I might as well stop now. Maybe they have some form of coffee or energy to keep me from yawning so much.

I pull up to the gas pump and pull the gas card out of the center console. Glad this doesn't come out of my paycheck, or I would be broke every week with as many miles as I put on this cruiser. As I pump the gas, I look up the road to the church sitting on the hill. From this vantage point, it looks like a postcard. The trees behind it standing tall above the white steeple. It looks elegant and... comforting. The exact opposite of what it was last Thursday. To think, the same person or people that were hanging a body up in there, could've stopped at this same gas station and grabbed a snack after. The clerk would have no idea he just sold a bag of chips to some deranged murderers…*Wait… I bet this place has cameras. Why the fuck didn't I think of this place that night? Was it even open then?*

I finish pumping my gas and walk inside. "Hours: Five a.m. to ten p.m." is posted on the door. Well, that answers that question. That's why I didn't think of it, it would have been pitch black by the time we were here. I grab a cold coffee from the cooler, and go to the counter.

"Hey man," I say to the clerk, an older gentleman who seems totally indifferent to my presence. "I have a question. Do you have any cameras… like on the outside?" I ask. He doesn't look up from the screen of his cell phone. I ask again, getting his attention this time.

"Yes, why?" he asks, putting his phone down.

I slide my card to him, and pull my badge out. "Trying to get some information regarding that murder last week. I'm a detective with Culver Police Department. I'm hoping your cameras can help"

"Ahh I see. What time would you like to see and I will see what the cameras saw, if anything?" he asks.

I tell him the time frame, and he reaches below the counter and pulls out a flash drive in a plastic container.

"Five dollars for this, buddy, and credit for the info if you see anything that helps," he says, smiling. He scans the flash drive then removes it from the container and walks to the back.

A few moments pass and he returns, handing it to me. "Now, like I said, just make sure that if you find something you tell them I helped so they say my store on the news. I need all the advertising I can get."

"For sure. Thank you so much for the help, sir," I say.

I jump in my car and head to the station. I'm just lucky he didn't give me any shit about asking for it. Support for the police isn't at its highest right now, and I can imagine that won't improve if we don't make some quick progress on this case. Maybe there's something worth at least five dollars on this thing.

CHAPTER 9

3:00 P.M.

*A*s I walk into the station, the sound of a dry erase marker squeaking echoes through the hallway. It's Davidson writing on the large whiteboard in the office. It looks like he's rearranged some things.

"Well, did Doc Thompson have anything helpful to say?" I ask.

"Not really. He only made one real development since he got the body. The only thing that may point us in any direction is the damn hole in his head. He said he didn't notice it at first, but it looks like there was at least *SOME* pressure applied in the surrounding areas of the hole. Like somethin' pressed lightly against both sides," he says, drawing a rough example of what he means on the board. "He also said that the brain matter was still intact, but the vessels that lined the inside of the hole were contracted inward. He said that meant whatever made the hole had to be very sharp, or very hot. But it didn't really look like he was burned. He, like us, is still very confused."

"Odd. I wonder if that means someone may have stabbed him with some kind of long rod. Something like the end of a thumb tack, but bigger if that makes sense. Did he say anything about the girl?" I ask.

"No, not yet. He hadn't even gotten her yet when I left. I decided I would come up here and make some calls to see if anyone has reported her missing, but no luck yet. So I'm doing a little organizing," he says, erasing his drawing. He then draws a stick man, with a huge thumb tack stuck through its head.

"I know it seems silly, but I'm just throwing shit on the wall hoping something sticks at this point," I say. I hold the flash drive up in front of him, "I might have something that *can* help us, though."

I tell him about the gas station, and he shares my hopes that something will be on the footage that will point us in the right direction. We put the flash drive into the laptop that sits on his desk. It shows three separate files. One reads: "Rear." The others read: "Front" and "Front Door." We select the "Rear" file and watch as it begins at eight p.m. on the day the body was discovered. We see nothing but a vacant gravel lot. We speed the footage up two times and watch as a few trucks turn around. Later, we see the clerk walk out and smoke a cigarette. A little while later, a few kids park back there and smoke what we assume to be a little weed, and then nothing until the footage stops.

We then go to the "Front" file. This one looks from the corner of the gas station closest to the road, but furthest from the church. It is angled in a way that you can't see the church, but you can see the road about three hundred yards in that direction. It is overlooking the covered gas pump area. Some of the road on the other side is blocked by that cover itself. We speed the camera up to around the nine p.m. mark and start from there. We see just a few cars pass by on the road in either direction for this segment. Maybe fifteen to twenty go by during the whole footage. Nothing that stands out, mostly because the footage is kind of grainy.

"Damn. This isn't what I had hoped it would be," says Davidson for the both of us.

"You're right, this is shit," I say.

"Well, you gotta think though. How would you transport that big bastard?" asks Davidson, starting the footage over.

"What do you mean?" I ask, wondering if he is on to something.

"Well you damn sure aren't going to move him in that!" he says, pointing at what appears to be a small two door car, "You'd move him in a big truck or SUV, let's look for that. C'mon now, Damon, you're supposed to be the smart one!"

We watch the entirety of the footage again, noting only three vehicles we consider to be possible ways to transport a very large, very dead man. One vehicle that looks like a large, dark truck and two large SUV's. We move the footage to the points where they were, and watch again. We pause on each and zoom in. Unfortunately, the image is very grainy but we are able to make out a few subtle details of each.

"Let's check the front door camera now," I say, backing out and selecting the "Front Door" file. As it plays, we realize this is actually the best view yet. The front door camera is to the right of the doors, pointing towards the road that runs adjacent to the pumps. There is a clear view of the pumps, and this camera has a little higher resolution.

We go to the times we had noted for the three possible vehicles and watch. The first possible SUV drives right in front of the gas station in clear view. It was a younger woman and a child.

"Well that one ain't it for sure," says Davidson, laughing a little.

"You sure?" I ask. "Never underestimate an angry woman. I'm confident my mother could've thrown that man over a fence if he made her mad enough."

"You're right buddy, your momma was a feisty one. Let's assume this lady isn't, though. We can come back to it if need be."

The next SUV actually pulls into the gas station and stops. We sit up in our chairs, hoping that maybe this person will be in clear view of the camera. It was an older man, who gets some trash out of his vehicle and throws it away near the gas pump before backing out and leaving.

"That just leaves the truck, right?" I ask.

"Well I hope so, but remember we didn't get it going up towards the church, just coming from that way. If that one is it, it means they did all that on the way to somewhere else. That seems a little weird. But hell, so is everything else so far," he says.

We go to the last time frame for the truck. Ten-thirty p.m. We see the front of the truck enter the screen, but turn immediately towards a side road and go out of view.

"Hot damn it," Davidson says, grabbing the mouse and rewinding the footage. He slows it down, and we both stare intently at the screen. As the front of the truck enters the footage this time, we can see that this is our first shred of light in the entire case. We can just see the front of the large, black truck as it turns. There is mud up the side of it, all the way to the window that is rolled down. We can make out a figure in the driver's seat and one on the passenger side. The driver is too blurry, but the passenger looks to be a bearded male wearing a black long sleeve shirt and a black baseball cap. For a moment it looks like he glances towards the camera, but quickly disappears with the truck. As the rear of the truck comes into frame, we can see that it has a black cap or cover over the bed. The tag is too blurry to make out, unfortunately.

"Holy shit," I say. "That has to be it. We finally have a starting point."

Davidson jumps up, "Black truck. Silver wheels. Full cab. Mud. Cap on the back. White, bearded male." He vigorously writes in a small box in the corner of the whiteboard. He circles the "Black truck, silver wheels" portion and glares at me. "We have to get every damn black truck with a cap on the back pulled over as soon as possible. If these people are the ones responsible for all of this, they need to be found before they do it again. That's two bodies in less than a damn week. What's next for them?"

He is exactly right. *Who's to say they weren't already headed to give us another body right now?* I pick up my phone to call Chief, when I see him walking our way.

"Oh shit, look who's following him in," says Davidson.

As Chief opens the door, we see a woman in a tailored blazer following him like a puppy.

"Oh shit" is right, that's Chief Hargrove. She's the Chief of Police for all of Union County. Seeing her never means anything good. She was a combat medic for ten years before she decided to get into police work. She is the face of police for not only our small spot on the map, but arguably the entire southern region of the United States. She's been the recipient of every award the state has to offer, and not for lack of reason. She has a legacy of never losing a case in court, and never letting a case go unsolved in any of her area of responsibility. I have a feeling she's here specifically to make sure we don't ruin that for her.

"Find a seat," says Chief Marks, summoning several officers into the office. Once everyone is seated, Chief Hargrove clears her throat.

"I thought we would have a quick meeting to discuss our progress, or lack thereof, in the investigation of the two homicides here in Culver. I know you men have been hard at work, and it has been less than a full week. Deputy Chief Marks has done the honor of briefing me to the best of his ability, but I need the latest and greatest as soon as possible. I have to brief the press tonight at seven and I want to make sure I'm not missing something that could at least make it look like we are on top of this. Any updates?"

She stares at Davidson and I expecting a response. Her eyes are dizzyingly fierce. A light blue-grey that seems to pierce your brain when they meet yours. *Maybe she just looked through that guys head and killed him...*

She is intense, and it's easy to see how she gets people to work hard for her. Davidson jumps up to exhibit our latest finding with the truck from the gas station, proudly high-lighting his neatly written box on the board. I quickly give an outline of the time frame for the first body and explain that the second one is too fresh to really establish a definitive timeline until we can review the footage from the gym.

"That makes sense," she says, pacing back and forth. "Two people answers how they were able to do things quickly, but it doesn't answer *where* they were able to do this to these victims. No way it was in that church or the gym. Primary locations for the murders, secondary locations for the staging of the bodies. How am I to make this community feel safe without even knowing where these murders happened? What is their goal here? It doesn't sit right with me that our victims are a fat man and a young girl that as far as we know, have absolutely nothing in common. Addressing the elephant in the room, do any of you feel that this may be ritualistic in nature? You know they will ask..."

"I don't think any of us really know of any motives, or even possible secondary locations yet since we have so little to work with for now. It's pretty evident that the murders most definitely didn't happen where they were discovered. As far as rituals or cult involvement, I wouldn't rule it out entirely for now, but it's hard to say either way," I say.

"I was afraid you would say that. Marks, you need an action plan for tracking that truck down," She says, turning her eyes sharply from me to him.

Chief Marks stands up and walks to the board. He writes down the names of the three patrol sergeants. Under each, a section of Culver. He points towards Edgar Ricks, the recently promoted young sergeant.

"Ricks, you and your team head out to East Bradbury and pull over any and every damn black truck you see. I ain't worried about wheels or the cap on the back, that could have been changed or removed. Get moving, now."

Ricks and his patrol officers quickly exit the room. Chief Marks does the same for the other two sergeants until all that remains in the office is Davidson and I, the CFT and Chief Hargrove.

Chief Marks then sits down in front of the laptop and observes the short clip of the truck turning. He lets out a long sigh.

"Okay, that road they are turning on leads out to the highway, but we will assume they are still somewhere in Culver, since this was before the second body. Before we look at this footage from the gym, I want to show you two something we discovered about the second body after y'all left."

He pulls a camera out of his bag and begins clicking through pictures that had been taken at the gym. He gets to a picture with a quarter sitting on top of the girl's dress, near her lower abdomen.

"Uhh, what made you do that Chief?" asks Davidson.

"Look closer, notice the indention near where I sat it?" asks Chief as he zooms in to that section of the picture.

Right beside the quarter looks to be an area where her dress sinks in more than the other areas, in a small circle, almost exactly the same size as the quarter. He clicks to the next picture, revealing the source of the indention. A perfectly circular hole, with the same quarter now resting on her skin. Just like in the other man's head, the hole seems perfectly round and all the way through her body.

"Fuck," I say. "So no doubt it's the same people then."

"That's not it," he says. "This is what I *really* wanted to show you..." He clicks to the next picture. In the picture, either his or one of the CFT officers hands is pressed down onto her stomach, near the hole. The hand is pressed way further than it should be. It looks like he almost pushed *through* her.

"Damn she must have been starved, or just skinny as hell," says Davidson before he takes a sip out of a water bottle.

Chief turns the camera off. "No, that's not it at all. James Scott started feeling around and he said it didn't feel like there was a single organ inside of her. He even pressed up under her ribs and he said it was like she didn't even have lungs. The Doc will confirm, but if that's the case these people are getting bolder and we have to figure this out."

How did we not notice that at the scene? I guess her lack of weight was compensated by her being stuck into the floor. Once I noticed the hooks we should've started looking for other similarities... I need to get more focused. I can't afford to miss things like this. I wonder if Chief thinks that I'm fucking up?

Chief Hargrove thanks us for our time and begins to walk out, "I just need you guys to keep this from getting any worse. If we want any chance at better funding next year, we need to get a handle on it and put these motherfuckers where they belong.

I'll mention the truck, and the description of the man from the church and the woman from the gym tonight. Maybe someone will recognize them and point you all in the right direction."

"Chief Hargrove," I say. "Can you make sure in your briefing that you mention that the Speedy Trak gas station is where we acquired the footage that led to knowing about the black truck? I kind of made a promise to the guy in exchange for that."

"Sure thing," she says.

When she makes it to the front of the building, Chief Marks gives the CFT the task of going over every picture and evidence sample from both crime scenes, as well as finding the origin of the fabric and hooks used in both locations.

"I need you both on standby if any of the patrols call in with a black truck we think fits the description. Coach Miller will be here at nine in the morning to talk to you both. After we look at this footage from the gym, I want you both to go home and rest."

We sit together and pull up the file the board of education had sent over with all of the available cameras from yesterday, up to this morning. There were only two working cameras in that location. One that points towards the front parking lot, and another that shows a clear view of the front doors. Neither were of the best quality, but they did have audio. We start with the parking lot camera. Starting at five p.m. the previous day, we speed through a few hours of film with nothing other than people pulling into the lot momentarily and a few loitering teens. At around the five a.m. mark, a vehicle slowly pulls into the front lot and switches its lights off.

Unfortunately, this camera doesn't have night mode, and it was dark. As it drifts through the lot, all we can make out is the silhouette of a large truck, backlit by a light pole at the road that runs behind the gym. I can barely make out the general features, but it looks like a dark colored truck… with a cap over the bed.

"I'll be a son of a bitch. That truck is definitely the one then," says Chief. He speeds through the rest of the video until he sees Coach Miller's truck drive up. He closes that video and goes to the file with the front door camera, and speeds it up until he reaches the five a.m. time frame, then plays it at regular speed. No truck in sight from this angle. He speeds it up again. At five twenty-one a.m. we see a small flicker of light enter the lobby. He rewinds it, then slows it down, and turns up the volume on the laptop. The light comes on again and we can tell that it is some sort of lighting that they are setting up in the gym area. A few moments after, we hear a low whirring noise.

"What is that?" I ask.

"It sounds like a drill of some sort," says Davidson.

After a few more instances of the sound, the light goes away and there is no other sound until Coach Miller walks up to the door.

"Alright detectives. This validates our hunt for that damn truck, but I'm afraid that's about it. Go get some rest and be near your phones. Let's hit this thing wide open tomorrow," says Chief as he shuts the laptop. "Oh and Damon…give that liver some rest too. I need you focused."

I nod my head and grab my bag, realizing my receipt from the package store has been hanging out of it the entire time. *Ugh,* that's all I need right now is for Chief to think I'm some irresponsible shithead. *That's not the case, I am in control of myself. I could stop any time I want to. I just don't want to right now.* Maybe once we have the case figured out and this place goes back to calm, I'll give it a little break. For now though, I think I'll spend the rest of the day on my back porch with Daisy. I'll just have a few drinks, nothing too much.

CHAPTER 10

9:30 A.M.

"*H*ey Coach."

I open the door of the office and point towards my desk, "Just have a seat there. Need a coffee or a water or something?"

"No, I shouldn't be long anyways. I'm sorry I didn't come in yesterday...I just ain't ever seen nothing like that, you know? I needed a little bit of time to get right with myself."

I can tell he is still very shaken up, so I grab him a bottle of water anyway and sit down opposite him at my desk. Davidson had already pulled up a chair and has a notebook ready.

"Okay Coach, do your best to tell us what you saw yesterday," I say.

He leans up and grabs the water and takes a quick, nervous sip before setting it back down.

"I guess I really just saw the same thing you did Damon,

72

only difference is I wasn't expecting it. I came up a little early and was gonna sweep up before the boys ran in there. Hell, I was whistling and having a great mornin'. My old lady made me a plate of bacon and eggs and I was feelin' damn good. I don't reckon I've ever went from that feelin' to such a bad one so fast." He takes another sip from the water, this time staring off into the distance. I know he is revisiting that scene in his head. I feel bad for making him do that, but maybe he noticed something we didn't.

"I understand, and I apologize that you had to see something like that. Outside of the obvious, did you notice anything different about the gym when you walked in?" I ask.

"Not at all. Was business as usual outside of that poor girl. Hell, I thought the boys were playing a prank on me or something. You know how it is."

I do. I think back to when I was one of those "boys" on Coach Miller's team. I had transferred in my seventh grade year, and sports are what really took me from that shy kid to being social and having friends. Coach had always been playful with us, playing pranks and joking. He was definitely the father figure I didn't have growing up. Many men have him to thank for the fundamentals of discipline they were able to apply in their adult life. He's the one that inspired me to go to college, even if it was only a few years before I decided I would pursue other things.

"Is there anyone out of the ordinary who has been hanging around the gym? Anything weird go on worth mentioning?" I ask, sitting up in my chair.

Coach sighs loudly and just shakes his head back and forth. "Some of the parents told me to…told me to ask if this was maybe related to the death at the church, or if maybe uhh… maybe—"

I cut him off, "A devil worshiping cult? No sir. Just

someone who's trying to cause some trouble. We'll get them, though."

He smiles and finishes off his water. "Good. Talk moves fast around here and people are worried sick. Me included. I never in my life thought I would see anything like that other than in a movie around halloween or something..."

I can see he isn't doing well in his head. Unfortunately, what he saw will be with him forever. I hope he is able to cope with it.

"Well, I won't take any more of your time, Coach. just let me know if you hear or see anything worth looking into. I promise we will figure this one out."

He stands up and smiles. I stand as well and go to shake his hand, but he walks around my desk and embraces me in a long hug.

"Damon, I believe in you. I know you will figure this out. You've always been something great and I know your momma is looking down on you proud as can be. You made a damn good man out of yourself. I'll be in touch." He throws the water bottle in the bin by the desk and walks out of the office.

I think for a second about what he said, and I wish I agreed with him. I think my mother would be disappointed in how I ended up. Still in this little town, with nothing more than a dog and an addiction to show for all of the good she tried to build into me. Maybe after this is over I'll look into a transfer somewhere else. Maybe that's what's wrong with me.

"Wonder what *that's* about?" Davidson asks, breaking the silence and motioning towards the front of the station. There is a young man, pacing back and forth having a conversation with our desk officer. She looks towards me and does a "come here" motion with her finger.

"I guess we're about to find out," I say to Davidson, as he

stands to follow me. As we approach the desk, the man notices us and starts to talk loudly.

"Please tell me it isn't Molly bro, please!"

I share a glance with Davidson before asking, "I'm sorry, can I help you? Who is Molly?"

He puts his hands on his head, then runs them over his face, "Molly Baxter, my fiancé man! On the news they had a description and a drawing of a girl who was found dead and…" He groans and puts his hands on his thighs, bending over. "It looks just like her bro oh my god!" He begins pacing back and forth.

"Well, when was the last time you saw her, and do you happen to have a picture we can see?" I ask.

He pulls his phone out of his pocket, "Like 3 days ago, man." He swipes around a few times before turning it to Davidson and I. In the photo, he is with a young woman with long black hair and dark eyes in a bathing suit. They are sitting on a beach towel, throwing a peace sign up for the photo.

"Sir, I'm going to need you to come with us," says Davidson.

The woman in the photo was undoubtedly the woman we saw in the gym. Seeing her made my stomach turn. In the gym, her eyes were closed. But in that picture, her eyes and her wide smile were the same as in the dream I had. *How would my brain know what her eyes looked like... or was she really at my house? Did I have a person in danger at my door but I was too drunk to help? Could I have saved her? I need this to be over.*

"I AM DETECTIVE DAMON MCKAY, and this is Detective Earl Davidson. I am informing you that this conversation will be recorded. State your name for us, please."

"Devin…Stevens."

"Okay, Devin. We are going to ask you a few questions, is that okay? Do you have an attorney, or would you like for us to provide you one?" I ask.

"No bro, why would I need one? I just need to make sure that dead girl isn't my fucking fiancé!" He leans up closer to the table, obviously flustered.

"I apologize, it's just standard procedure," I say, looking to Davidson briefly before continuing, "I just need to know a few things. Where were you yesterday around five a.m.?"

"I was asleep. I'll be honest I drank too much the night before and…and I was just out." He bites his fingernails, then put his hands through his thick, blonde hair.

"Okay, you said you had seen her three days ago. Is it normal to go a few days without seeing each other?"

"No. No. Not at all dude…ugh. We kind of had a fight and she went to stay with her friend. She texted me that day but after that she hasn't said anything and won't answer my calls."

"What was the fight about?" I ask.

"Well, it's kind of embarrassing but…but it was about how I used her credit card to buy a new gaming system without asking. I told her I would pay her back but she flipped and said she was going to Stacy's house." He leans back in his chair, "That wasn't her was it, bro? It can't be her."

I can tell by the panic in his voice that he most definitely won't be a suspect, and is going to come apart when we confirm that it definitely *is* her.

"Who's Stacy?" I ask.

"It's her best friend. Stacy Larson. She's a photographer and she had already planned to go take some pictures with her in Sunridge Valley. Molly does modeling online and Stacy always takes her pictures."

"Okay, do you have a way to contact Stacy?" I ask, hoping he gives us her number so that we can get this closed out quickly. If she is the last person to see her alive, this means she will have more relevant information.

"Yea, but she won't message me back either. I thought maybe Molly told her not to or something. She was super mad when she left. I've never seen her that way bro. If that's her...oh my god if she got fucking killed because of me bro I...I can't...that can't be her, please tell me it's not her!" he says.

I look to Davidson, and I'm pretty sure the same thoughts are in his head, as he looks at Devin and says, "How about we ride down to the medical examiner's office. If it is her, you will be able to positively identify her, and it will hopefully help us catch the people responsible for this. Does she have any family around here?" Davidson stands up, "If it ain't her, we will help you file a missing person report and get some people looking for her. Would you be up for that?"

He takes a deep breath and closes his eyes. He blows out for a few seconds and stands up as well. "Yes please, I would like that. And no, I am all she has around here."

"Okay then, we'll do that," I say. "This is Detective Damon McKay ending the interrogation."

* * *

DEVIN FOLLOWS Davidson and I all the way to Doc Thompson's office, never getting more than a car length away. I can't imagine what is going through that poor kid's head right now. Davidson had called Doc as we left, and he informed us that after identification, he needs us to hang around. He has some information for us that he deems to be "critically important, and alarming." I can only imagine what that may be. This Devin kid is already torn up enough, so hopefully it isn't anything too bad.

We walk in, again greeted by the same staff member as before. "Doc is waiting for you, go ahead."

We walk down the hall, Devin right behind us. I can hear his sniffling over our steps. I know this is about to be horrible for him, as it would be for anyone in this situation. I am really not sure how he's going to react. Doc Thompson stands about ten feet into the room, near the body of the woman. She is covered by a white sheet, and in this moment the room seems very peaceful. The normal smell is gone, and a calming lavender scent fills our nostrils as we pass through the doorway. Devin pushes past us, and walks briskly towards Doc, "Is it her bro? Let me see her!"

Doc nods, and rolls the sheet back to the girl's neck, taking a step back. "NOOO!" Devin wails loudly, "What the fuck Molly, NO!" He lays his head on her chest and begins to sob.

"We will give you a moment, Devin. We are very sorry for your loss," I say. I summon Doc Thompson and Davidson to exit the room. Devin falls to the ground and cries loudly.

Standing in the hallway, Davidson asks, "So what did you find, Doc?"

He frowns, "You're not going to like it, but yet again I am completely baffled. Same as the other victim, but there's something different this time…"

"What's different?" I ask.

"I will just have to show you, after this young man has had his time."

We stand in silence for a few more moments, before walking back inside.

"Devin, again I am so sorry for your loss," I say, walking to him and putting my hand on his shoulder.

He looks up to me, eyes now blood red, "You better find the motherfucker that did this to her before I do, I swear to God." He is shaking now, and I can tell his sorrow has turned to rage. I can't fault him for that, but we don't need some vigilante messing up any progress we may make.

"I understand your anger Devin, but I promise you that we will do everything we can to bring these people to justice. Our next step will be to go pay Stacy a visit, and see what she has to say."

"Well what the fuck do I do now?" he asks broadly to all of us.

Doc steps up, "You can speak to the women in the front office, and they will help you set up arrangements and contact any family members who would need to know. After they have your information and you decide what services you would like, we will provide transport and take care of her. Sorry for your loss."

Devin places his hand on Molly's face, running his thumb across her cheek. He bends down and kisses her forehead. "I will always love you Molly, I can't wait to see you again. I am so sorry. I am so fucking sorry babe..." He hangs his head, and walks out of the examination room.

"Man I tell you, no matter how many years go by, that never fails to break my heart," says Doc, wiping a tear from his eye. "There is far too much evil in this world that takes beauty like that and desecrates it. For nothing more than some horrible thrill. A moment in time for them, a lifetime of grief for everyone else... Anyways, this is what I wanted to show you." He walks to a refrigerator, and pulls out a small container. He brings it to the table where Molly lay, and opens it up. Inside is what appears to be a blob of meat.

"What the hell is that?" asks Davidson, echoing my thoughts exactly.

"More about what it's supposed to be really," Doc says. "This was her left lung. Well, what's left of it..."

I stare at it for a moment and ask, "So how does that happen?"

He places the lung back into the container and closes it. He then pulls the sheet down to Molly's waist to reveal the small hole, and the stitching where he had opened her up. He takes his right hand and places it halfway up her rib cage, right under her breasts.

"From here," he then moves his hand to her pelvis, "To here…there's nothing but bone."

"What do you mean?" asks Davidson.

"I mean exactly that, son. Only thing other than her spine in this area is air. And I haven't even the beginning of a thought as to how they could be removed with absolutely no evidence of any trauma outside of that same damn hole. No burns, no cuts, not an ounce of blood in her whole body. Here, look."

He pulls a printed photo from under the table, showing her chest cavity opened up. Just as he said, there was nothing but her bones, and half of her lungs.

"Boys, I hate to say it again but… I just don't know what's going on. I got a toxicology report back from the first body and there's just nothing at all out of the ordinary. For maybe the first time in your lives, your guess might be as good as mine." He smiles briefly, bringing the energy in the room back from its somber feeling.

"Thank you so much Doc, and just let us know if anything else comes up that might help. I appreciate you," I say, as I begin to walk to the doors.

"Men," he says, causing me to look over my shoulder, "Don't lose hope. I know you two exemplary gentlemen here are going to make sure I don't have another one of these on my table. Go out there and get the people responsible for this."

"Yes sir."

CHAPTER 11

1:00 P.M.

"**A**re we sure this Devin kid doesn't have anything to do with this?" asks Chief Marks. He walks up to the whiteboard, placing a question mark near the name "Stacy Larson." "Do you think this girl is even involved? Is it possible this kid killed the girl, and panicked when he realized we were closer to figuring it out than he thought? Do you think he made that up and is trying to create a distraction?"

I think back to Devin's reaction and how visceral it was. Morbid curiosity taking me to a place in my head where I may have loved someone enough to react to their death in a similar way. I only briefly cried when my mother passed. I *DID* love her a lot, but that's something entirely different... I can't imagine the feeling Devin must have had in that moment. I'm not sure if I'm grateful for that or not, though. Don't they say it's better to have loved and lost than to never have loved at all? I'm not convinced that's true after seeing the pain in his eyes.

"No sir," I say. "You'd have to have seen him. It's one thing to lie, but I've never seen anyone fake remorse like that. I think he's either telling the truth, or missed his calling as a Hollywood actor. We just need to figure out where that girl is and go from there."

Davidson nods in agreement with me before pulling his phone out and calling someone. He sighs as it rings with no answer, "That's the problem though, she isn't answering the numbers we have for her, and Sergeant Ricks already paid a visit to her house with no luck. We may need to consider her a missing person at this point."

"Or maybe she's our next victim. Any local kin-folk?" asks Chief.

"None. All I've found is her website for her photography and her social media accounts. Looks like she moved from Ohio a few years ago. No spouse or kids or anything," says Davidson, crossing his arms.

I am hoping we find this girl alive, and we can get her to help us. Surely she would've seen her friend's attackers. Maybe she was able to run to safety. *All we need is even the smallest thing to work in our favor at this point. Devin walking in was a miracle in itself.*

"Have we looked to see if she has a car registered to her?" I ask, opening up my laptop.

"No, I didn't even think of that," says Davidson.

I pull up her information and see her address and last arrest. Looks like she was arrested a few years ago for having drugs on her when she was pulled over for speeding. *Ahh, there it is.* Her tag number is in the description, and run it through our system. It brings up a 1999 blue Honda Civic.

Chief makes a call and has patrol officers shift their focus away from black trucks to blue Hondas. We just need something to come through. With each day that goes by, we have more and more questions pop up that we can't answer. The forensics team informed us around lunch time that the fabric used at both crime scenes was just standard landscaping fabric that is sold everywhere in town. The hooks are the same in terms of overall uselessness to helping us gain any ground in the right direction. They are meat hooks used by damn near every farmer that lives in the area. No fingerprints. No blood. Nowhere closer to figuring this out.

The rest of the day we call and follow up with everyone to see if there's anything else they have to offer. Just like everything else, no one has anything new. All we can do now is hope that either Stacy, her car, or that black truck is spotted before something else happens. I have a bad feeling that we're already too late. Definitely going to be another night on the porch with a strong drink and some takeout. This whole situation is exhausting me. As I grab my things from my desk to leave, I glance over at Davidson who is just staring at the whiteboard.

"What's on your mind, man?"

He stands up from his seat and looks at a printout of the black truck that he has taped on the corner. "I don't know. I can't say that I've ever seen this truck around before. I wonder if it's someone that is just passing through and this will be one of those things we will never figure out. One of those things that end up on an unsolved mysteries show or something like that."

"No way, we're going to get those bastards behind bars. They have to slip up at some point," I say, sounding as convincing as possible.

I had the same thought he did the night we saw the first body. Nothing like that has ever happened here. I *DO* think that it's possible that someone who's not from here is responsible. I can't imagine anyone in Culver crazy or smart enough to pull this off. I just don't want to say that out loud yet. I hope that if they are gone, we don't have any more bodies to find. I push my phone into my pocket, and head to my car.

As I PULL up to my house, I see Daisy with her head in the window, eagerly awaiting my arrival. She's probably happier to see the bag of takeout than she is to see me, knowing there's always something in there for her too. I probably shouldn't let her eat junk food but oh well, she deserves to be spoiled. Walking in, I go ahead and let her have her prize. A double cheeseburger from the Burger Hut near the station. It's a little cold but she won't mind. Sometimes I think about how lonely I'd be without her. I should find someone to settle down with that would make this house a little more...*whole. Someone that might have even half of the reaction Devin Stevens had if I were to die suddenly.* Not sure what kind of woman would want an exhausted detective with a diet of alcohol and burgers, but I'm sure she's out there somewhere. Not going to find her in Culver though, so maybe on my next off day I'll venture out to Big Lew's again...

Daisy and I eat our burgers and retire to the couch. It's only six and I'm already sleepy. Looking over at the black bag from Lucky's Package store, I make the decision to call it an early night and toss the whiskey I got into the freezer. Maybe if I get some good rest tonight, the search for Stacy tomorrow will be a little easier. I lock up and get ready for bed. I make sure to double check the doors before I go to my room, looking once more at the freezer.

Come on man, just go to bed. You can drink that tomorrow night, relax. I turn off the kitchen light, and go lay down.

. . .

I am jolted awake by a loud knocking sound. I jump up, nearly launching my phone into the ceiling. *What the fuck was that?* I listen intently, waiting for any more noise, but none comes. I must've startled myself awake. I look to Daisy, who is fast asleep on her chair. Surely if there was actually a noise, she would've been barking or at least awake. I pick my phone up off of the floor and see that it's only nine-thirty p.m. Guess I wasn't asleep that long. My body isn't used to sleeping this early and probably stressed itself into action. Then, I hear it again. This time it's more distinct, and I know exactly what it is. Someone is knocking at my door...*again.*

I grab my pistol off of my night stand, and head towards the living room, slowly. I creep down the hallway towards the front of the house, making sure each step is silent. As I cross the threshold into the front room, the knocking happens again. *Why isn't Daisy waking up?* I stay focused on the door, and stop as I get directly in front of it. I wait for the knocking, but there is only silence. My heart is racing, but my breathing is controlled. The second I hear the knocking again, I twist the knob and pull the door inward as hard as I can, planting my feet firmly and bringing my pistol sights dead center of the door.

I see no one. I fall to a knee and quickly look left, then right. Still, no one. The long grass of my front yard is dancing in the full moon to a light breeze. I can see all the way to the tree line across the street. No one is here. If some kids are ding dong ditching me, they are about to learn a valuable lesson. I stand up, lowering the pistol to my side and stepping out onto the porch.

"Alright motherfuckers, better go on home before I call your parents and make them come get you!" I say, as I squint and look towards my car, half expecting a bunch of teens to pop out from behind it and run into the woods. No response. *Should I look around back? Could they have really ran that fast?* I hear a shuffling behind me, and instinctively spin to my left going back down on a knee with my finger on the trigger. I struggle to focus as a small black figure darts towards me from the hallway. I quickly align my sights dead center of the object, and breathe out. Just as the figure passes though the doorway, the moonlight illuminates...*Daisy*.

"Girl! Holy shit, you almost died just now!" I pat her on her head as she arrives to me. She wags her tail and licks my hand, but when she looks up to me her tail stops wagging. She drops down low, eyes pointed up to me and begins to growl. "Daisy what's the matter, it's just me! Sorry I scared you it's just—" I realize now that she isn't growling at me. She's looking THROUGH me, not AT me. I feel the hair on the back of my neck stand up, and cold sweat form all over my body at once. I try to turn to see who's behind me, but I can't. I try to channel all of my strength to at least swing my arm backwards in hopes of landing an elbow on whoever it may be. Daisy's look becomes one of terror, and I still cannot move. I feel a presence directly behind me.

"I WILL SEE YOU SOON." States a deep, guttural voice directly into my ears. It is so loud it seems to shudder my entire body. My chest and back feel an embrace that feels like someone is bear hugging me. I still can't move. I start to feel sweat drip down the back of my legs as my body begins to heat up rapidly. The lights begin to fade from the edge of my vision. With all of my energy I try one last time to break free of whoever is holding me, but I can't. All of the light fades away and my body feels like a furnace. *Am I dying? Did they kill me?*

"I WILL SEE YOU SOON," comes again, this time louder. I try to scream, but nothing happens. I close my eyes and try one last time to break free.

* * *

ALL THE LIGHT crashes back into my eyes as I spin wildly to the ground with a *THUD*. I stand quickly and look around frantically searching for my pistol, only to realize that it's on my nightstand. Daisy throws me a confused stare from her chair and her tail wags, as if I am playing a game with her or something. *What the fuck? Another dream? I wasn't even drunk this time. What is making these dreams so vivid?* I look at my phone.

9:30 P.M.

GOD DAMNIT. I make my way to the kitchen. Looks like it's going to be a long night after all. Reaching for the whiskey in the freezer, I stare into the living room for a moment. I bite the inside of my lip hard, just to make sure I'm still awake.

CHAPTER 12

I arrive to the station about an hour and a half earlier than normal so I can get my self fully awake. I didn't lay down until sometime after midnight last night. I couldn't stop thinking about the voice from my dream. So much more direct than the last. I *WILL* see you soon. More like a threat this time, but I guess my brain is just in overdrive and making me on edge. I refill my cup of coffee and stare at the board. *I really need to focus.* Today is the first day of Davidson's two off days and I need to work twice as hard to make sure I'm on top of any and everything that comes my way. We can't afford any backwards steps. Thinking of where I should start, I hear the phone ring at the front of the station. Our dispatch is ran through a third party company that rings to our line. The front desk phone is for direct calls. Typically non emergency local calls or general inquiries. It's seven-thirty, so it's a weird time for a call. Maybe it's a wrong number.

I walk to Sergeant Hamilton's office to see if he has any good news from the night of searching for the Honda. His light is off. Now that I think of it, I didn't see him in the main office area either. That's weird… Usually he's here typing a report or giving Chief a rundown of the evening. He's been the night shift sergeant for a few years now and I can't remember him ever missing shift changeover. Maybe he's still out following up on a lead. The phone rings again. I really don't want to hear that thing ring until nine when the desk officer comes in. I walk back up the hallway and answer it. "Culver Police Department, Detective McKay speaking, how can I help you?"

"Howdy detective, I'm Officer Steve Adams with the Magnolia PD. I know it's early, but I think I have something you may be interested in."

"Alright, what is it?" I ask.

"Well, our Chief had told us you guys were looking for a blue Honda, registered to a Stacy Larson. We weren't too busy so me and another officer decided we would start driving around looking."

"Did you find it?" I ask, grabbing a sticky note and a pen to write down where they may have found it.

"Naw, but we did find Stacy," he says in matter of fact tone.

"What? How? Where is she?"

"Hell, we had her locked up all night. We got a call early yesterday morning about a drunk walking down the road near the utility department so we went and checked it out. She was wild eyed and wouldn't say a word. When we tried to approach her she got damn near feral and we had to restrain her. She must have been high on some kind of pills or something. We put her in the drunk cell to let her sober up, hoping she'd talk after a while. When we pulled up the info on that car and it showed an old mugshot of hers we recognized. As of this morning she still ain't talkin', but I figure you boys might want to ride over and pick her up."

"Yes sir, we definitely would. Let me get with my Chief and we will be there as soon as we can. Thank you so much."

"Nothin' but a thang, no worries buddy," he says before hanging up.

Well, this makes things easier. If I can get her to talk she may be the closest we've been to figuring out what the people look like that have been doing all of this. Maybe she saw them do it and can describe them, or maybe she was too high to even notice. Either way, I've got to get her here and in that interrogation room. It's good to know we won't be called to remove her body from some elaborate display. I had a feeling she was going to be the next victim, but I'm glad I was wrong.

My call to Chief Marks was brief as usual. He insisted on calling Magnolia and having them transport her to us instead of going there and back. While I wait, I go ahead and prepare to interrogate her. I write down the questions I'd like to ask, but I'm really unsure of where I think she fits into the picture. I wonder if she is actually one of the ones responsible. *Did she lure her friend out somewhere and kill her? Was the guilt of doing that to a close friend too much to handle and she had to go get high to forget about it? Was she involved with the first murder as well? Is the man that was in the passenger seat of the truck her boyfriend?* I guess I'll ask her myself. I pour another coffee and grab a notebook, hoping she's in a good enough state of mind to help us out.

8:45 A.M.

CHIEF MARKS WALKS into the lobby, followed by two Magnolia officers. They all seem a little frustrated and they have a short, plump woman with bright blue hair in tow.

Stacy Larson. I head to the interrogation room as the officers fill out some paperwork at the desk. Several moments pass, then Chief and Stacy enter the room. Chief places Stacy in a chair and removes her handcuffs. He then pulls up the chair beside me, and reaches over to the recorder and hits the button.

"This is Deputy Chief David Marks and Detective Damon McKay. I am informing you that this conversation will be recorded. State your full name for us, please."

"Stacy Renea Larson."

"Thank you. We are going to ask you a few questions. Do you have an attorney, or would you like for us to provide you one?" he asks.

"No."

"Just to clarify, you are waving your right to an attorney correct?"

"Yes."

"As you wish." Chief seems angry at her short, emotionless answers. I look to the first question on my list.

"So, why were you wondering around Magnolia yesterday?"

No response.

"Were you under the influence of any substances at the time they apprehended you?" I ask, this time leaning my head down to her so that I was in her line of sight.

She stares at the table in between us, not acknowledging my question. I ask again. She looks up at me, slides her tongue across her teeth and says, "I wasn't high. I've been clean for six years as a matter of fact. Those rednecks at Magnolia didn't even drug test me. They just assumed, and they weren't smart enough to be corrected, so here I am."

I can tell I struck a nerve, but I continue, "So why were you there, and why would they think you were on drugs?"

She again stares down at the table, "I don't know. I was

just…exhausted. I…" She trails off and shifts uncomfortably in her seat.

"Why were you exhausted?" I ask.

"I…I just…I was running uh… I…I don't know, I'm sorry." She places her head in her hands and begins to cry.

Chief, visibly over her presence already, places his hands down firmly on the table. "Look Stacy, we don't have the time for this. You are the last person anyone knows to have been with Molly Baxter. For all we know, you could be the one responsible for her death. You need to start talking, and fast."

She begins to cry more, but between tears she says, "I didn't kill her! I swear! I loved Molly! I really don't know what happened, I promise!"

"Well you need to tell us anything and everything you *DO* know. You don't want us filling in the blanks for you I promise you that," says Chief, not interested in her waterworks.

"I…I just can't explain it. I really can't." Her tears stop flowing, and a look of dread washes over her. I can tell she's replaying whatever happened in her head.

"Try. This may help us figure out who did this to her, and keep them from doing it again, please," I say.

"That's just it… I…I saw it happen but… It doesn't make sense…" She sits up, and looks directly at me. "I'm telling you both…whatever did that to her is not… uh… it's not normal. We were taking pictures by an old barn near Sunridge Valley and it was going great. The old barn was a great contrast to her black dress. Then when we went to a small clearing on the other side, I made her pose near the tree line and…" She trails off.

"And then what?" I ask.

"He… it… *SOMETHING* grabbed her."

"What do you mean by that?" I ask.

"That's what I'm telling you. I don't know what it was, it was all just a blur. One moment she was leaned against a tree and then through the camera I saw something go around her stomach for a second and I could've sworn I saw a…a face but I couldn't quite make it out. Next thing I know Molly crumpled to the ground and it was like all the sound went away… She never screamed and then I just felt hot and scared. I knew in that moment she was dead… The way she fell was so…unnatural. I panicked and dropped everything and ran. I don't know if it chased me or not but I ran as hard and as fast as I've ever ran… I know it doesn't make sense but you *HAVE* to believe me."

"So, you're saying you didn't see a weapon of any kind? No knife or gun?" asks Chief, his impatience now fading into confusion.

"No…nothing like that. It was only there for a second and if it did have a weapon I didn't see it. I-I really couldn't even begin to describe it," she says.

Chief glances at me briefly and shakes his head, "So, then what? You just ran until Magnolia PD picked you up?"

"I guess so… Like I said I just ran the other way until I couldn't. I never even looked back…I passed out for a while and woke up and ran again. When those cops came to me I thought maybe they found her and thought I did it. I swear I didn't do it…I could never hurt Molly." She looks down at the table and frowns. Thinking of the officer's description of her being strung out, I feel like they very well could have confused her state with someone who was just terrified and exhausted. This woman doesn't look like someone who is used to running.

"Well, what about your car?" I ask after a brief silence.

Her face lights up and she gasps, "Holy shit! I bet it's still there! My camera too! I had to at least have gotten a few pictures right when it happened!" Her realization seems genuine, so maybe she's right. Maybe she was just so scared she couldn't focus, but her camera might have. Maybe we will finally get a look at these sick bastards. Then again, she could just be outright lying. I can't let my optimism cloud my judgement.

"Could you tell us where it is?" I ask.

She nods. "Yes. It's off of Huntington Boulevard. There's a small dirt road you can take after you pass the water tower that goes back into the valley. I'm not sure of what the actual address is, but I can point it out to you on a map."

"No need," I say. "I know exactly where you're talking about."

Chief ends the interrogation and has one of the duty officers take her up to the small holding cell in the back of the station until we can verify her story. I hope her camera didn't get rained on too bad and we have at least a few pictures to work with. Anything that might have captured our perpetrators, especially in the act, would be huge. That's exactly the type of break we need right now.

* * *

MYSELF AND THE officers that are just coming in for their shift gather around the table in the office.

"We need to roll at least four cars deep out there," says Chief, pulling up a satellite view of the area on his computer, and spinning it around to face us. "This could be an active crime scene and since there's so much tree coverage, we won't have any idea what's in those woods waiting for us."

He is right. That road is surrounded by trees, with unlimited options for hiding. Sunridge Valley consists of about sixty miles of steep, winding hills. That road goes right up to the beginning of it, and makes a small loop. It's possible that these people have been using this area as a hideout, and they probably won't be happy to see us when we roll up.

"Make sure you all clean your duty rifles before we head out too. These sons-a bitches already killed two people, so we can assume if they're out there that they won't go easy. We won't know what kind of range we will be dealing with if we have to exchange any gunfire. I don't wanna get caught with my damn pants down, I'd rather be safe than sorry." He points to the water tower on the map, "In forty-five minutes I want all of you at the bottom of this water tower. I'm going to call and see if Magnolia can be on stand by with a few guys just in case." He grabs his phone and exits the office, pausing briefly to look into the still vacant night shift sergeant's office.

I gather my things and head to my car. I don't have to wait and clean my rifle, I do that every week just like our handbook says. I'd be willing to bet it's the cleanest one outside of Davidson's in the whole force. Davidson spent some time overseas when he was in the military, and his weapons are his pride and joy. He'll be pissed when he learns he missed out on today's action, no doubt. I decide to go ahead and head that way so I can stop by and grab another coffee at a gas station. The adrenaline of the interrogation has worn off and my lack of sleep has my head pounding. I pull out and head towards Magnolia.

CHAPTER 13

I don't have to use GPS to get to where we're going, as I know it all too well. When I was in high school that road was called "Lover's Loop", and pretty much all of us have made a few memories down there. Back in high school it was just secluded enough that you didn't have to worry about visitors, but just close enough to the main roads that you could still make curfew if you timed it just right. That's where Brittany Rollins took my virginity on my fifteenth birthday. I still remember awkwardly head butting her on accident trying to get into the back of her Ford Explorer. She was seventeen and I was just too nervous and too young, but she forgave me and we had a good time. I would go on to make several, less awkward trips to Lovers Loop before the police started to take notice and we had to move on to less desirable locations. I hate that the area will probably be forever associated with the death of Molly Baxter when they find out this is where it happened.

. . .

When everyone makes it to the water tower, Chief Marks decides he will lead the way in his cruiser down the dirt road. Magnolia only provided a singular patrol officer who would remain at the water tower location in case we need backup. We start down the long road, in a parade of dust and nervous energy. If the perpetrators are waiting for us, we are at a disadvantage due to our very obvious approach. I reach over with my right hand and pull my rifle closer to me, just in case.

It takes us around ten minutes to finally make it to the long winding turn before the loop. As soon as we make it around the trees and up the path, I'm blinded by the sun's reflection off of the blue Honda. It is sitting to the side, halfway off of the road to the right. We all pull up behind it, and stop. Looking in all directions, it is apparent that no one is here, or has been here for at least a few days. Stacy's car sits covered in dust, almost polka dotted with circles where it must have rained at least briefly since it has been parked. Other than the dust that we brought in, the whole area is still and lifeless.

Lack of presence or not, we exit our cars together, using them as cover from potential combatants. We don't often train for situations like this, and watching officers look wildly up and around in all directions at once is likely a sight to see from a distance. I used to take the training more serious, but it hasn't proved to be very necessary until now. Before I made detective I spent many nights watching videos of combat from overseas, taking note of what I thought were effective strategies and trying to implement them into mock exercises in my house. My stiff joints and raised heart rate are acting as a reminder of just how long ago that was… After we have all scanned the edge of the roadway and determined there are no visible threats, an "ALL CLEAR" comes from Chief Marks.

It's very obvious why Stacy and Molly chose this location for pictures, as the back drop of an old crumbling barn to the right atop the hill provides a serene, yet haunting aesthetic. There is a clearing behind the barn that allows just enough sunlight through to see the beginning of the valley. It highlights just how dense the forest is on the opposite side, as no light makes it more than a few feet in. Easy to see how someone was able to sneak up on the girls as they took pictures. We all lower our weapons, and make our way to Stacy's car.

"No surprise there, huh?" asks one of the officers, pointing to a "Defund The Police" bumper sticker on the car. Moving now towards the barn, I take note of the tree I imagine Stacy was describing. It comes straight out of the hill then abruptly curves to the left, as if the top half is running away from the barn in front of it. I imagine Molly posing, happily anticipating the results of the photos, only to be ripped out of existence moments later. I wonder if she even felt anything. Those last moments for her had to be so terrifying.

Did she even have time to register what was going on? Thinking about her just laying in a pile on the ground makes me feel like shit. I'm sure if she was able to, she would do anything just to have another chance to be alive. Same for the older man. My note I wrote last week seems so silly in these moments. They would do anything to live, and I was trying to just give my life away. For their sake, I need to make sure these sick bastards are behind bars as soon as possible.

I get closer, hoping to see some sort of evidence on the tree, when I hear a *THUD* from behind me. I swing around while drawing my pistol, only to see one of the officers had fallen right on his face behind me.

"You good?" I ask, re-holstering my pistol and helping him up.

"Yea man, I just tripped over this." He reaches down and grabs a lanyard. As he tugs it, he realizes that it's attached to something. He yanks it and it breaks free of the mud it was stuck in. *The camera.* "Oh shit," he says, placing it back down. He quickly puts on gloves before picking it up again. He presses the red power button on the top, but nothing happens. "Hopefully it's just dead, but it looks like it got rained on pretty good. I'll take it back to the cars and see if I have a charger or something," he says, heading back to the loop.

That's good at least. Maybe forensics can get some pictures off of it that we can work with. The other officers and I look around in the grass where he fell and eventually locate Stacy's cell phone, keys and flip flops all within a few feet of each other. I then make my way back to the tree to see if there's something there that can tell us a little more about what happened. Looking at the bark and the surrounding area, I can't see anything out of the ordinary. They either came back and did some cleanup, or the rain did it for them. I sigh, and look towards the barn.

"Anything up there?" I ask to Chief Marks as he walks through the side door.

"Nah, nothing but some spiders and old wood." He puts his hands on his hips and looks back down towards the loop, observing the other officers now congregating by their cars.

"Well, I guess this is a bust huh?" he asks.

"Not really," I say. "That camera could very well be the break we need in at least identifying one or both of these people."

He nods in agreement and turns back to the other side of the barn. He walks around the opening of the barn towards the clearing, and I look around and make out what used to be a hay loft, left to rot and fall apart. I wonder whose barn this even is? I can't imagine having something that I owned fall into disrepair like this. It seems like in its prime it was pretty functional. Looks a little too far gone to try and save now, though. *Maybe I should work on myself a little harder before I'm in the same state as this thing.*

"Damon! Come here!" I hear Chief say in a whisper. I turn to see him crouching back by the opening of the barn. I jog over and he whispers again, "Look around that corner and tell me you see what I see…but don't go sticking your whole body out."

I slowly crouch down and pull myself around the opening. At the end of the clearing, about three hundred yards or so, sits a large house. I squint to try and make out the details. It's the back side of a two story, southern victorian style home, with a wrap around porch. I pull back into the barn.

"Oh shit…that house wasn't on the map," I say.

"Must've been a while since they updated the maps. Did you see what's in the front yard?" he asks.

I look around the corner again, and sitting to the right side is a large black truck with a cap on the back. There appears to be some deep scratches down the left side, and mud caked up in the wheel wells. *I'm willing to bet this is who hit the mailbox of the guy I talked to... looks like he's lucky they didn't decide to stop. He could've been the next victim. It also doesn't look like he'll be getting that forty-five dollars anytime soon, though.*

"I'll be damn," I say.

"Yep. Let's call this in to Magnolia. They'll know how to get to that house from the other side, and have more resources closer. Let's go back down to the cars and be ready for when they can assist. Try not to cause too much alarm walking back down. I ain't sure if you can see all the way down here from that house or not. I guess if they could see us they would've already taken off by now, though," he says as he begins to walk out of the barn. I take another look towards the house to see if I can see any movement. Nothing. I walk back down to the cars, stepping around the two officers who are putting up the crime scene tape. I walk to see if they have made any progress with the camera.

"Things fucked, but the memory card seems to be okay, we'll have to see what's on it when we get back," says the officer who fell earlier. I inform him that it won't be anytime soon and tell him and the other officers to be ready to head towards the house behind the barn. Chief comes over to inform us that Magnolia PD would be ready to approach from the other side of the home in roughly fifteen minutes. He also told us that he has already arranged for a warrant to search the property. *Damn, that was quick. I guess the district attorney and judge are just as ready to get this over with as we are.*

I decide I would rather use my rifle for this, since we will have to cross such a large distance before reaching the house from this side. I pull the charging handle back a little to verify there is a round in the chamber, then join the rest of the team. We walk up to the barn, being sure to stay out of the line of sight of the house. We gather inside the barn, and wait for Chiefs direction. It's been a while since we've had something this tense. I can tell the other officers are wishing they could've been off instead of Davidson. Not me though, I actually hope the people are in there and we can get them to come with us peacefully. They owe us too many answers to risk a gunfight. After several silent minutes pass, I see Chief's phone light up, and I know it's time to start the approach to the house. I take a deep breath, and fall in line behind him as he steps around the opening of the barn.

Hugging the tree line, we stay low. We make sure to be as swift and quiet as possible. My knees are burning and sweat is beginning to form on my brow. The flash of blue and red lights reflecting off of the windows indicate the Magnolia PD is already at the front of the house, near the truck. I look from window to window on our side of the house. No movement. As we get about fifty yards from the back of the house, we hear the other officers announcing their presence at the door.

"This is Magnolia Police Department! Open up!"

We pause, listening for movement. Nothing. We move closer. They announce their presence again, this time finishing with, "If you do not reply we will break this door down!" Chief makes his way up the back porch steps as we hear the loud crack of an officer's boot on the front door. Either the officer had a damn good kick or the door was weak, because from the back we can see Magnolia officers pouring into the home.

"Clear!" We hear from the living room, followed quickly by another "Clear!" from the kitchen. Chief reaches for the back door and slowly turns the knob. It's unlocked. He swings it open and darts to the right as I pull my rifle up and swing to the left, looking from center to the left wall. Nothing but a side table and a small lamp in my quadrant.

"Clear!" says Chief. It looks like we are in an entertainment room that backs up to the living room area. We then hear an, "All rooms clear!" From the front of the house. We breathe a sigh of collective relief and frustration, and walk into the living room area.

"No one in the whole spot. Looks like they must've known we were coming," says a Magnolia officer, walking up with his thumbs tucked into the arm holes of his vest. Looking around I notice the home is unusually clean. Freshly vacuumed carpet and only a light layer of dust on the furniture. Maybe someone was about to sell this place. Looks like they'll need to replace the door first. Chief Marks falls into conversation with the other officers, as I begin to look around. If this house is for sale, maybe someone knew that and was using this place to hideout. Maybe they thought

Molly and Stacy were on to them, or taking pictures for the police and that's why they killed her. If that's the case they surely got the hell out of here once they let Stacy get away.

There is a stairwell at the edge of the living room, and I decide I'll head up there to look around. There are only two rooms up here that are separated by a shared bathroom. I choose the one on the right. Inside is nothing but boxes lining the entire wall. Some labeled "Glassware", some "Christmas" and the like. I see a small closet that is unobstructed, so I decide to look in it. Nothing but more boxes. I'm sure whoever is selling this place put them all in here to keep them out of the way and to make their move easier or something. I enter the other room. There is a bed pushed up against the far wall, with a single night stand beside it. It's neatly made and appears to be indented in the center, indicating someone has been using it for a long time. I wonder what they'll think when they find out some sick fucks murdered someone at the back of their property.

Looking around it appears that there isn't much of anything in here either. No pictures or clothes in the closet or anything. Just a big empty house backed up to the woods. Nowhere closer to finding these people than we were when I woke up this morning. Maybe the camera will turn up something. I sit on the side of the bed for a moment to gather my thoughts. I reach over and open the drawer of the nightstand. Empty. I try to shove it back in but it comes off of the track. *Great, we broke their door down and now here I am breaking their nightstand.* Trying to line it back up to push it back in, I notice a small white corner protruding from the left side of the drawer. I remove the drawer entirely to reveal a small, white rectangle, pressed against the side. This is likely what made it come off of the track in the first place. I pull it out, and turn it over.

It isn't just a piece of paper, it's a photograph. In it, a

younger couple at what looks to be the edge of the Grand Canyon, arms wrapped around each other in a loving embrace and smiling. The woman is wearing a floral button up t-shirt, and white shorts. The man is fit and shirtless, wearing cut off blue jean shorts. They must've missed this in their packing up since it was lodged. I squint at the picture trying to see if I recognize either one of them. They don't look familiar… *Wait*…on the man's right shoulder in plain view is a tattoo. It is a bright red heart, surrounding the name "Gina." My mouth opens wide as I realize where I saw it last. The man in the morgue. The unidentified man hanging from the ceiling of the church. *This is huge. This explains the connection between the two victims. It looks like Molly was just in the wrong place at the wrong time. I'll bet the man was murdered on the property too.*

"Find something?" asks a voice from the doorway behind me, causing me to jump.

I turn to respond, "Yea, this picture!"

The voice belongs to that same Magnolia officer who had delivered Stacy earlier. "Well, what is it?" he asks.

I turn to show it to him, "Recognize these people?"

He looks intently at it for a moment and shakes his head, "Nope. Can't say that I do."

I walk past him and quickly down the stairs to find Chief. I find him in the kitchen talking to one of our officers. I shove the photo to him, "Look! I found this upstairs!"

He looks back at me confused.

"Look at the tattoo!" I say.

He pulls a small pair of reading glasses out of his pocket, and re-examines the photo. "Well, I'll be a son of a bitch. That's our John Doe right there, well at least fifteen to twenty years ago." He pulls out his phone and takes a picture, then sends it to someone. "Magnolia! Do any of you recognize the people in this picture?" he asks, walking to the group of the Magnolia PD gathered in the living room. They all shake their heads.

"This must be his house. Let's get some info on this address and let forensics do a sweep to see if anyone left anything behind. We didn't help anything by trampling around in here, but at least with that camera and this place we are a little closer," Chief says, pulling his phone out and calling someone as he walks out the front door. I walk out as well and begin to look around the yard. This is a very nice home, and it's *so* secluded. I wish I had something like this. I think of how our killers must have somehow snuck up on this poor guy when he was asleep or something to be able to kill him like that, but that really doesn't explain the lack of blood, *or literally anything else for that matter.*

Chief walks back towards me, "Hey, does Lewis Parley ring a bell at all?" he asks.

I think for a moment, "No, why?"

"That's who this property is registered to. That damn truck too." He points to the large black truck in the yard.

I had almost forgotten about the truck entirely. I walk over to it, noting the mud all up the right side. Walking around the back, I decide I'll open it up and see if anything is inside. I go to grab the clasp for the back glass when I read the personalized license plate…

BIG LEW.

"No fucking way," I say. Lewis Parley is "Big Lew." The woman in the photo is his wife before she died. This is the house in the valley the bartender talked about… *Big Lew was our first victim.*

CHAPTER 14

8:00 A.M.

*D*riving into work, I can't stop zoning out. My brain is working just enough to keep me between the lines, but not much else. Yesterday was such a blur I hardly feel like I slept at all. For the first time in at least a few months, I didn't need to drink to fall asleep. *I might as well have based on the way I feel...* After we turned the house over to the CFT, we spent the rest of the day trying to locate next of kin for Lewis Parley. I ended up having to call the tavern to find out the names of his business partners, who were also of no help. Eventually, we convinced one of them to come identify him via a few respectfully edited photos. By the time I got home I just passed out. Now I wish I had stayed up just a little so I wouldn't feel so groggy. I pull into a gas station to hunt down an energy drink. Maybe that will get me a little more focused so I can make as much progress as possible before I'm off tomorrow.

I make my way to the front of the store, and am greeted with a large smile by the man behind the counter.

"No worries about the cost today sir, I thank you for the free advertisement!" he says.

"Not a problem. I don't mind to pay, I promise," I say.

"No, no. I insist. More people have been in this store since they showed that footage on the news than in the last six months!"

I oblige, and take my free energy drink to my car.

PULLING into the parking lot of the station, I see the dreaded green WCDX van parked to the side and a small camera crew huddled around the front door. Great, exactly what we need right now. There's no telling what story they've concocted since everyone knows who the two victims are. I drive to the back, and sneak in through the side door. When I make it in, Chief is sitting on top of a desk in the office on the phone with someone. He waves me over, then points up to the whiteboard. There are several printed photographs that I assume are from Stacy's camera aligned on it.

There are about 20 total, and they have been organized in order of the time they were taken. On the top left, a picture of the old barn, with the sun pouring through the trees around it. The bottom right has several blurry pictures that can only be the result of Stacy running away. I look at them in order to try and paint a picture of the event in my head. It looks like the first few were just Stacy making sure her settings were right, and were of no importance. The ones that followed, were of Molly in various poses around the barn. Some she was smiling and happy, others were more aligned with the energy of the backdrop. In those she would mimic the haunting aesthetic by glaring into the camera as if she was auditioning for a role in a horror movie where she was the villain.

Now for the last row of pictures. I can see a picture of just the tree, then one of Molly looking over her shoulder as she walked up to it. The next photo, which was three before the last, showed exactly what Stacy had described. Molly had leaned her body against the tree where it bends away from the barn. She had her arms over her head, which she had turned away from the barn. It was truly a great picture. The light pouring around her was a great contrast to her pale skin, and black dress. Had this not ended how it did, I'm sure she would've used it as her profile photo on all of her social media, or at least framed it. The next photo was a little blurry, but I can clearly see Molly now staring directly at the camera, eyes wide with fear. Her arms now down to her side with both hands holding her lower abdomen, covering what appears to be a black object that wrapped around her left side.

It almost looks like…an arm, but I can't really see it clearly. The next picture made the hair on the back of my neck stand up. This one is more blurry than the last, but I can see Molly has already fallen. She lay crumpled on the ground, and where she once was on the tree, sits a hand. I can barely make it out, but it looks like it's solid black. Maybe it's a glove or something, but it looks like the fingers are slender and very long with pointed ends. My eyes follow the slender wrist attached to it, hoping to see a figure of some sort, but it wraps around the back side of the tree. *Damnit.* The last picture was just too blurry to see anything, clearly from when Stacy had dropped everything and ran.

"Weird as hell right?" asks Chief, who I didn't realize had ended his phone call and now was standing a few feet behind me.

"Yea, this doesn't make any sense. What did he stab her

with? It doesn't even look like she bled, or at least I can't see any blood in the pictures," I say.

He walks up and puts his finger on the image of the black hand, "Has to be this…glove or whatever it is. Doesn't really make sense for the size of the hole but it's all we have to work off of for now. Could be some type of blade on the inside. Hard to tell."

I stare back at the picture of her right before she was killed, trying to see if maybe I could catch a glimpse of the person, but I don't see anything. *I wonder how long it took her to die? Did she even feel whatever it was that killed her? The look on her face seemed to be one of horror, not pain. I don't understand how it happened so fast.*

"I just wish she could've gotten a better picture so maybe we could recognize who this is," I say.

"I knew you'd miss it!" Chief says, moving over and pointing to the first row of pictures, "Look back at this row, tell me when you see it."

I look back through the initial pictures, scanning each one until I find what he meant. It's in the second to last picture in the first row, just barely visible at the side of the barn on the far right. About 6 feet up, a part of the wall of the barn is broken, creating a small opening. Through the opening, a pair of grey eyes on what looks to be a black face is visible, but I can't see anything else. "What th—"

Chief cuts me off, "It's gotta be contacts or something. But still, we absolutely can not let this picture get out. I'm sure the black face is like paint or somethin', but right now WCDX is out there in the front reporting that people think this is a damn vampire and this picture would make the whole town go crazy."

"A vampire? Huh?" I ask.

"Yep. Somehow it got out that neither of them had blood in them and they shifted their opinion from Satanic rituals to a vampire. Craziest shit I've heard in a while. I was on the phone with Hargrove when you came in and she's sayin' she will have to do another press conference today to put those rumors to bed."

Crazy is definitely right. This town is all about the rumor mill and drama, but *vampire* wasn't even in my top ten guesses on who is responsible. Whoever this is, is definitely scary and admittedly strange, but not *VAMPIRE* strange.

Chief looks at his phone and frowns. "On top of all of this, Sergeant Hamilton hasn't been in for 2 days and I'm worried. He's never missed a day in the last 5 years."

"Isn't he going through a divorce?" I ask. "Maybe he just had too much to drink and is sleeping it off."

"That's what I thought too, but I drove by his house this morning and his truck isn't there. His patrol car wasn't there either. He could be at a friends house and I'm over thinking it, but I'm just on edge," he says.

"Understandable. I'm sure he'll turn up and you can give him hell for being a no call no show," I say.

As the day shift officers come in, everyone begins talking about the way Parker Cowan is scaring the whole town with the "Vampire of Culver" theory. This is exactly why I never watch TV. I can't imagine how much better of a place the world would be without the media telling everyone what to be afraid of. On one hand though, I'm glad he's made up some scary alternative to reality. It means that people will be less likely to go out at night, which might keep everyone a little safer until we can find these people.

"Any luck with the house or the truck turning up any evidence?" I ask to one of the CFT members that had just walked into the office.

"Yes and no," he says. "Whoever they are, cleaned up the house damn good." He takes a set of keys from his pocket and unlocks a small filing cabinet beside his desk. "Same goes for the truck. Not a damn thing in there that's worth noting, except for *this*." He pulls a ziplock bag from the filing cabinet and hands it to me. Inside is a pack of cigarettes.

"Any fingerprints?" I ask.

"No. They were wedged down in the drivers seat, unfortunately."

"So what makes them noteworthy then?" I ask.

"Because they're Strada 308's! I guess you're not a smoker then?"

"No, are they expensive or something?"

He types quickly on the keyboard of his computer, then points at the screen. "Strada 308's, an Italian cigarette brand made famous by actor Marco Pancholi in the 40's. They are still really popular out West. Just not something you see around here," he says, scrolling through pictures of Marco Pancholi smoking in old advertisements on his computer.

"That's something then. Surely Lewis Parley wasn't the type to smoke those. I'll keep that in mind, thanks," I say before going back to my desk. I need to make sure to pay attention to what other people are smoking now, I guess.

I can't stand being around cigarettes. They always reminded me of when I was a kid and my dad would smoke in the house, and in the car. I was so glad when my mom left him and brought us out here. The fresh air was like drugs to me back then. Going from the middle of a big city as a little kid, to out here with all of the farmland and wilderness was the best thing that could have ever happened to me. If I could find a way to regain that clarity now, I might be better at this job…or maybe have a different career entirely. Maybe I wouldn't be writing suicide notes to myself every few months. I've always thought I was good at this, but this case has me really re-thinking everything about my ability. *If we can just get a name…or a face, I believe we can close this thing out quickly.*

10:00 A.M.

CHIEF MADE the call to release Stacy and recommended she see the psychiatrist that the department keeps on call for traumatic events. Things like shootings, fatalities or in this case…vampires that just so happen to be out in the daylight with black face paint and contacts. I laugh to myself imagining Count Dracula himself descending on Culver to scare rednecks. As if it was that simple… The locals would have that thing hunted down and mounted over their fireplace before the end of the day. Hunting season here is more important than politics and sports. If we put a five hundred dollar bounty on the "Vampire of Culver" I'd be willing to bet he'd be in the bed of a lifted truck in no time… Now that I think about it, I wonder how much hunting happens near the part of the valley where Molly was killed…

"Hey Patrick, you still hunt?" I ask to the patrol officer Patrick Turner, who happened to be refilling his coffee cup at the back of the office.

"Every year!" he says.

"You ever hunt out in Sunridge Valley?" I ask.

His eyes light up, "Oh yea! When I can. It's mostly public land so it gets pretty jammed up with youngins' since that's where all the big bucks go to hide."

Damn. Public land means that it isn't likely that there would be any trail cameras. Sunridge Valley is a big place though, maybe some of it is private property.

"Any clubs or private spots out there?" I ask.

"Oh yea man. The Fosters have damn near a thousand acres out there. They lease part of it to some hunting club, but it's too expensive for me. Plenty of green fields, shooting houses and even a lodge that's nice as hell. I think that kind of hunting is for pussies though. It ain't really the same if you're baiting them like that. Why, you lookin to bag you one this winter?"

"Nah, I'll let you do all that and I'll buy some jerky from you, though," I say.

I grab my keys and walk out of the office. I know just what I need to do today. I need to get with the Fosters, and hear first hand about the story I heard at the bar the other day with their animals. Maybe they'll have some trail cameras or at least security cameras at their lodge. I type a quick text message to Chief, explaining my plan. He responds:

> Okay, I'll let Magnolia know you will be out
> that way. Be safe.

I wish Davidson was working today. It's normally not that big of a deal to be alone, but nothing about this is normal and I can't help but to feel like that person with the grey eyes may just be out there in the woods somewhere. I check my pistol and my rifle before heading towards the valley.

* * *

ON MY DRIVE, I give Doc Thompson a call to see if he has made anymore progress.

"Sorry Son, but it appears that I have nothing of use for you as of yet. I took as many photos as possible and sent off all the samples I could to a couple university labs in hopes that I would have some type of breakthrough here. A few have returned as inconclusive, and I foresee the same result from the rest... The poor girl's fiancé has decided that he wants her cremated, and the funeral for Lewis is tomorrow. Without the bodies, I fear we will continue to be clueless unless this "Vampire of Culver" leaves us something to work with."

"Damn Doc, I had hoped you had this thing solved so I didn't have to go play in the woods," I say. "Should I stop and get some holy water just in case?"

He laughs, "I'm sure you will be just fine. If this was a vampire, he's definitely different from any vampire I've ever heard of. Maybe just pick up some garlic to be safe."

I laugh and hang up. I briefly think of stopping for garlic to place with a wooden stake on Davidson's desk when he returns tomorrow, but quickly abandon that thought when I consider what the locals would think if they saw me purchasing that. Especially when the news is telling them we were out vampire hunting.

I pull onto the road that runs parallel to the Fosters farm, and slow down as I approach a group of men repairing a section of fence. I pull over and roll down my window.

"Any of you guys wouldn't happen to be Mr. Foster would you?"

A younger man with a large brimmed cowboy hat on walks to my car, and leans towards my open window. "Well that depends on which Mr. Foster you want. I'm Mr. Foster, and that's my brother Mr. Foster. Hell, my daddy is Mr. Foster too, who's askin'?" he asks, as his brother chuckles behind him.

"Detective Damon McKay," I say. "I just had some questions for you all."

The man looks back to his brother, then asks, "What else could you need to know? Magnolia PD was already out here twice. Animals are weird man, sometimes they get freaked out and do dumb shit like this. Are they wantin' to press charges or somethin' since they all shit in town?"

"No sir, I'm not even with Magnolia, I'm from Culver," I say. "And I'm more interested in your hunting lodge." They both look at me with the same confused expression. I explain to them about the event that happened at Lewis Parley's property, and that I just wanted to see if they had any trail cameras, or lodge cameras that might point in that direction.

"That man's property backs up to ours about 2 miles into the woods here," he says pointing over his shoulder, "But there wouldn't be any trail cameras out now cause it's too far out of season and we don't allow them just yet. The earlier you let people put cameras up the more likely they are to put corn or somethin' out and we don't like that. A man that baits to hunt ain't no hunter in my book. The lodge is pretty close to that area, but it stays locked up till about a month out. It does have some security cameras on it, though. They record to a hard drive inside. They keep about a months worth before it deletes itself."

"Any chance I could go see it? It's a shot in the dark really, but if there's a chance any of them happened to catch a glimpse of our killers, it would be huge. You think your dad would mind?" I ask.

"Hell naw, I'll take you up there myself. But you ain't gonna make it up there in this thang," he says, slapping the side of my car. "Hop out and we'll take you up there on a side by side."

I get out and follow the men through the yard to a small barn. Inside sits a few four wheelers and a large side by side with big lights on top.

"Hop in this one and get your back ready, it's about as bumpy as a frogs ass heading up that mountain. Lot easier coming down though I promise," he says, smiling. I get in, and we pull across a large, rolling field. We pass dozens of beautiful horses, cows and even a small herd of goats grazing near an island of trees that protects them from the sun. As we approach the edge of the woods, the opening of a narrow dirt road becomes visible. It leads directly into the sea of dense trees. I prepare myself as the road appears to be rough and uneven. He speeds up, and we begin the climb to the lodge.

I place my hand on my pistol as a form of reassurance, briefly thinking of the possibility that the people responsible could still be in the woods somewhere. *I wonder if they fled through this way after killing Lewis and Molly? Maybe they are what spooked the animals...*

CHAPTER 15

$\mathcal{A}$scending the hill is in fact "bumpier than a frogs ass." By a substantial amount. I know I'll pay for this tomorrow, but I think it will be worth it. On one hand if I turn up with nothing, I'll get to say I went trail riding while getting paid. Can't beat that. I haven't really done anything adventurous in years. On the other, if any of the cameras caught even the slightest glimpse of something, it might be the difference in this entire shit show. The rain has taken its toll on the trail, leaving ruts on either side several feet deep in some places.

The Foster brother driving makes some calculated, likely unnecessary, maneuvers in a few spots that has covered my pants with a mist of mud. I'm sure they'll love telling their buddies about how they made sure I left looking like a swamp creature. I really don't mind it. I spent a good bit of time in the woods growing up, and I feel like part of it never left me. Sometimes my friends and I would camp out and have a few drinks, and sometimes I would come out here just to get some time to myself. I should do that again. I'll need to find some friends first, though.

Slowing as we come to a small clearing, the brother looks to me. "So, do y'all really think it's a vampire doin all this mess?" His question seems genuine.

"No, do you?" I ask, doing my best to listen over the roar of the vehicles.

He looks to his brother, who has now pulled along side us, then back to me. "Well Cain does, b—"

His brother interrupts. "No I don't, motherfucker!" They exchange a few cuss words in a progressively thicker country accent, then we pull to a stop. "Well, I mean I ain't sayin I *DON'T* believe it but hell, what else would it be?" Cain asks.

"I'm not sure. But I think it's safe to say it isn't a vampire, and is more likely just a few people who are fucked up in the head," I say. I turn to the brother who was driving me on the side by side and ask, "So if your brothers name is Cain, does that mean your name is…"

"Yes," he says. "My name is Abel. Daddy calls me Abe though. And if I can ever save up enough money to move outta here, I'm gonna change it to something else."

"You'd make a damn fine Misty, why don't you change it to that or like… Rebecca?" Cain asks through a smile. The two devolve into more cuss words for a moment, then we move forward again.

"Lodge is up here to the right," Abel says as we make our way up a steep incline.

I laugh to myself thinking of some proud parents naming their sons Cain and Abel, likely never reading, or at least understanding, the story about them in the Bible. *Specifically the part where Cain killed Abel then lied to God about it.*

We make a right turn, and there sits the lodge. A large single story, wooden building sitting atop a raised platform. Underneath looks like storage for four wheelers or equipment, and a wide stairway leads to a black door that I assume is the main entrance. A covered porch wraps all the way around. Immediately after the lodge, the mountain shoots straight down into the valley. Surely a great spot to hunt, and hopefully a great spot to look across to Lewis Parley's property.

"There's a camera right above that door, and another one in the back. We'll grab that hard drive and see what's on it," says Abel as he turns off the side by side. We get out and walk up towards the steps. As I am halfway up, Abel abruptly stops in front of me and I run into him.

"My bad," I say.

"Naw you're good, but we got us a problem," he says, looking sharply towards Cain.

"Whats it?" Cain asks.

"The fucking lock is busted. Somebody's been up here," Abel says.

"Aw shit, wonder if it's Keith's stupid ass," says Cain. "You know Daddy kicked him out last season."

I look up to Abel, who has now produced a small pistol that he must have had tucked into his pants.

"Hold on now Abel," I say. "If anyone is still in there, we would've seen four wheeler tracks or something."

He puts the gun back into the front of his pants. "Yea, you're right. Dumb bastard probably did it months ago." Cain chuckles behind us, and touches his face, pulling at what looks to be a spot of razor burn on his chin.

In this moment I realize that I may have been too confident in my assumption that the Fosters would be of help. Looking back at Cains strong frame and black hair, I am reminded of the man in the passenger seat of the black truck in the security footage, minus the beard. There is a possibility that Abel could have been the driver. *There is also a possibility that the Foster brothers were the killers.* They have basically back door access to Lewis Parley's property, right where we know two people have been killed. And now I'm standing in the middle of the fucking woods with them, miles from anyone who could help me. *As if they would even get here in time.* I hide my suspicion, and take a step around Abel.

"Let's take a look then," I say, wiping the sweat from my forehead. I walk to the front door, removing the broken padlock from the hasp that was bolted to the door frame and turn the knob. As soon as it swings open, we are hit with a foul odor that erupts from the lodge as the wind from the door moves the air around.

"Holy shit boys, I bet Keith threw a dead animal in here or some shit and it's just been cookin' in this heat," says Cain.

I knew that wasn't the case, as the unmistakable smell of death filled my nostrils. I cover my nose with my shirt, and look forward. To the right is a small kitchen area. It looks like it hasn't been used in a few months other than a dripping faucet that has sprinkled water onto the counter. Straight ahead is a small hallway with a door at the end that is cracked open just a little.

"What's in there?" I ask, doing my best not to breathe in.

"Main room. Has a fireplace and a big TV," says Abel between breaths.

I pull my pistol from my holster and walk towards it. I push the door hard and take a step back. It bounces off the wall, revealing the origin of the putrid smell and my heart begins to beat wildly.

"What the hell is that?" asks Cain.

I stare up at a large black sheet, hanging from the ceiling, draped all the way to the top of the fireplace. Below it lays a pile of what looks to be excrement.

"I need you to call 911 and tell them there's been another body found. Do it now. Don't touch anything on your way out either," I say to Abel.

He sprints outside, and Cain follows him repeating "What

the fuck!" several times in a frantic tone. I pull out my phone to call Chief Marks, but I see that I have no service. *Shit.*

I walk up, and examine the pile at the base of the fireplace. Definitely feces. I look to see how the sheet is being held up, and it appears that small hooks have been screwed directly into the high, vaulted ceiling. I pull on it firmly, and hear it begin to rip. I decide to take a few steps back, and take a photo of the hooks, the feces and the entire scene. I don't want to make the CFT's job any harder. I hear Cain's four wheeler start up and tear down the mountain.

Abel walks back in the door, holding a phone to his ear. "Hey man what'd you say your name was?" he asks. I tell him, and he repeats it into his phone.

"Tell them to inform Chief Marks of Culver Police Department immediately," I say.

He steps back out, and I look back to the sheet. I grab the bottom corner, and carefully try to pull it back to get a glimpse of what was underneath. It is held in with either some kind of staple or nails. I can tell from this angle that there is a large lump in the center, about three quarters of the way up the wall. *I wonder who it is this time?* Whoever it is, I don't want to just sit here alone with them until the CFT arrives. Once they're here, we can pull this sheet down. I step back through the door, and back outside.

I walk around the side of the lodge until I reach the back. Looking from this angle is a clear view into the valley. I can make out "Lovers Loop" by the absence of trees where the road is. I can also see the top of the old barn, but I can't get a good view of anything below the tree line. Cameras wouldn't be of much help, I guess. *Oh yea, I completely forgot that's why we're even up here.* I walk back around, and see Abel is now off of the phone, and is just sitting at the top of the steps.

"Hey man, I'm sorry this happened here. I understand if you want to go back down to the bottom and be with your brother. No point in waiting around and seeing what's behind that sheet, I promise I'll be fine up here by myself," I say, placing my arm on his shoulder.

"Why'd they have to do that here man? My dad loves this place he's gonna be so upset. We built this thing bout fifteen years ago with a few of my uncles. Some great memories here just to prolly be torn down after this," he says.

I apologize again, and ask, "Where's that hard drive for the cameras?"

"In the pantry on the back wall of the kitchen. There is a small screen above it."

I walk back inside, and open the pantry. I see a small computer monitor, sitting on a shelf about four feet up. It's off, so I click the small power button at the bottom. Nothing happens. I kneel down, and see a cable hanging below it that isn't connected to anything. *Of course*. It looks like they made sure to take the hard drive with them after they left us this...*surprise*.

I walk back out and inform Abel.

"Ah hell. This ain't good. This ain't good at all," he says.

"You're right. Do me a favor," I say. "Go back down to the bottom so that when the officers arrive, you can give them a ride. Just be careful."

He stands up, glancing at the doorway of the lodge. "You sure you're okay up here by yourself?" he asks.

I reassure him, and he gets on to the side by side and heads down the trail. I take his place sitting on the steps, and think back to the images we saw from Stacy's camera. The long fingered gloves, the black painted face with grey eyes, burned into my mind. I scan the tree line, half expecting to just see him standing there looking back at me. The wind blows, and I hear leaves rustling in the distance. The hair on the back of my neck is standing up as I imagine that person running towards me through the woods... My phone vibrates several times, startling me. I have one bar of service now and all the text messages are coming through. The most recent one is from Chief Marks, and I quickly reply:

> We're on the way. Wait for forensics. Hang tight.

> Yea, I'm not going to stay in there alone. Just from the way it looks from the outside of the sheet, this one is going to be worse than the others. Not even going to send you the pictures…

> Jesus Christ.

Ironically enough, the closest thing to Jesus Christ here now is whoever is behind that sheet, likely hung up in some impossible way. *Is that what all this is about? Are the bodies some type of religious offering or maybe just a ritual? Should we have taken the cult approach more serious?* I've never even heard of murders like this. Whoever these people are, they want us to see their work, and I have to figure out why before it's too late and the whole city freaks out and starts a witch hunt or something. I guess a *VAMPIRE* hunt would be more appropriate. Not many vampires take security camera hard drives into consideration but I guess there is a first for everything. I lean back against a post of the porch and breathe out. This is going to be a long wait for everyone to get here.

ABOUT FORTY MINUTES later I hear the first four wheeler making its way up the trail. Thinking back now, if someone was here when we made our ascent, they would have had plenty of warning to get out of dodge before we made it. After a few moments, a small parade of four wheelers and side by sides erupt from the trail, all piled up with muddy police officers. The first to greet me is a member of the CFT, with a large camera bag and a bottle of water that he hands me.

"Show me the way," he says, obviously not happy about the mud that covers the side of his pants. I walk him into the lodge and through the door at the end of the hallway. He takes several pictures, and shines a blacklight towards the floor. "Were any of y'all bleeding?" he asks.

I look at my hands, unsure if I had maybe gotten cut by a branch or something on the way in. "I don't guess so," I say.

He points to a few small droplets of dried blood on the bottom corner of the doorway. "Good." He smiles and takes a picture of it before scraping it into a small vial. He takes several more pictures, then sets his camera down. "Wanna help me pull this sheet down?" he asks.

I nod my head, and walk to the right side and grasp the corner tightly.

"On three, pull down and back so it doesn't fall on us," he says. "One... two...*THREE.*"

We pull on the sheet in unison, and hear it rip off of the hooks, and the small staples that affixed the sheet to the wall. As it falls, we step back and it lands on the floor in front of the fireplace in a crumpled pile. Before I can process what I'm seeing, I hear an officer behind me gasp loudly, and various cuss words echo from the hallway. Looking back at us, hanging from the ceiling by a long steel cable, is Sergeant Hamilton. His eyes are wide open and hazy, and arms are limp and hanging down to...where his sides *should* be. About halfway down his chest, his skin is hanging loosely, and his lower half is completely detached. His lower limbs lay over the antlers of a large mounted deer, with his intestines spilling from his lower abdomen on to the top of the fire-place. Now the feces on the floor makes sense...*but nothing else does*. As I try to fully take in what I'm seeing, I hear an officer vomit behind me near the doorway.

"Okay y'all, step outside if you can't deal with it. I understand," says Chief Marks, walking through the hallway into the room. He takes a long look at Sergeant Hamilton's remains, and hangs his head for a moment before looking at the CFT member. "I want every damn inch of this place looked at, even if it means taking it apart board by board." He nods, then begins taking more pictures. "Damon, now who in the blue hell would do this to him? He was a damn good man. Why is this one so much worse? They tore him in half for Christ's sake."

I glance back to Sergeant Hamilton, then to Chief. "I wish I knew, Chief. This is horrific. This isn't just randoms anymore. These people are bold enough to do this to one of our men. They must know we found their hideout and are teaching us a lesson."

He doesn't respond, only takes a step closer to Hamilton, and shakes his head. He then speaks up to him, "I'm sorry we couldn't get em' sooner, brother. But I promise you they are gonna pay for what they did to you, so help me God."

CHAPTER 16

8:00 P.M.

I sit in the side by side, as the motor idles and the lights illuminate the front of the lodge. I am exhausted. Chief made the call that no one was to leave until the body of Sergeant Hamilton was out of the cabin and could come back down the mountain with us. None of us protested, and would have stayed regardless. It isn't often an officer is killed, especially here. That hasn't happened at all in our department, at least since I've been here.

"Alright, let's get the hell out of here boys," says Chief, sitting down in the drivers seat of the side by side. He stares at the lodge for a moment, then we turn and head down the mountain with the rest of the team following behind on the four wheelers. The Foster family gladly let us borrow them, as they weren't interested in assisting with the cleanup of any remains. We slowly make our way down the trails, being careful not to allow Sergeant Hamiltons remains to be damaged more than they already were. He had just barely fit into the small dump-bed of the side by side, and the last thing we want to do is to have to pick him up out of the mud somewhere along the way.

"You think those boys had somethin', to do with this?" asks Chief, staring intently at the trail.

I think back to the tense moment when we first arrived at the lodge, "I wouldn't write them off entirely, but I don't think so. I had that thought before, but their reaction to seeing even just the sheet seemed real. They seemed terrified."

He let out a long sigh, and gripped the wheel tightly. "It ain't possible for no one to see this shit happening. Somebody's gotta know something," he says.

I nod in agreement, but I don't really think that's the case. There are so many places out here that you could be twenty feet from someone and not even know, especially in the dark. The woods are impossibly dense and hard to navigate. I think the only people who likely know anything, are the ones that hung him up there in the first place.

As the hum of the four wheelers drone through the forest, I think about how anyone could have possibly put Sergeant Hamilton up there in that lodge. Like Lewis Parley, he was suspended by cable with a hook into his back. Except this time it was only one, and he hung more vertically. I'm guessing just because he had less available body to hang. *But HOW?* The cable was hanging from the center of a beam at the top of the high vaulted ceiling. I just don't understand why they put this much effort into displaying the bodies. It isn't for no reason, but I just can't comprehend it. I'm confident every other officer is asking theirselves the same questions as I am after seeing that.

We reach the bottom of the trail, and see the display of lights that awaits us at the other side of the hill. There are two ambulances, several patrol cars and of course...the baby shit WCDX van. I wish we could've gotten off the mountain before they got here, but nothing moves quicker than bad news in a small town. They must have someone permanently assigned to listening to a police scanner. We pull towards the back of the closest ambulance and turn to back up to it. As we step out, a bright light swings around the side and a large camera is shoved forward to the back of the side by side.

"Chief Marks! Parker Cowan h—" Before he can finish his sentence, Chief Marks shoves him so hard in the chest that he is flung backwards into the ditch at the side of the road. He makes a horrible gasping noise as he lands, as it is evident he has had the breath knocked out of him.

Chief then points directly into the camera, face wild with rage. "And you get this God damn camera out of here before I throw it over that fuckin' mountain! Have some respect for the dead you slimy bastards!" I pull him away as the man complies and places the camera on the ground. He then goes into the ditch to retrieve Parker, who has now sat up. It looks like some horse shit had softened his fall.

The ambulance crew helps move the black sheet that held Sergeant Hamiltons remains into the back and close the door. Chief sits down in the seat of the side by side again and puts his head in his hands.

"I really shouldn't have done that. Hargrove is gonna kill me," he says.

I place my hand on his shoulder, "No worries Chief, we've all wanted to do that at some point. Maybe she will understand when she finds out who it was."

"Hell I hope so," he says. "Thanks for following up on this. We might not have found him for months if you hadn't. Now go on home and take in those off days. Davidson's gonna shit when he comes in tomorrow to all this. I'll call ya if something comes up." I pat his back, and walk towards my car. *What a fucking day.*

CHAPTER 17

1:00 P.M.

The sun pierces through the darkness of my room, illuminating a framed picture of my mother and I on my wall. I look to the window, and see that Daisy has poked her head under the blinds and blanket I use to black out the room to get a look outside. I glance at my phone, and see that I've slept all morning. Just as I had planned. The trail riding and stress of yesterday has set into my bones and I feel like I've fallen out of a tree. I stretch at the end of the bed, and head to open the door for Daisy. She happily bounces outside and finds herself a spot in the yard to do her business.

Making myself a quick sandwich for lunch, I decide I'm going to call Davidson to see how his day back has been for him. He doesn't answer. A few moments pass and my phone vibrates. It's a text from him that reads:

Sorry man, Hargrove is here and we are
about to meet. I will fill you in when I can.
Enjoy your day off!

Damn. I imagine that meeting won't go well. She's probably tearing into all of them now. She went from having some unsolved murders to having a dead police officer AND a horrible PR issue all at once, and I'm sure Chief will have to pay for it in some way. To be fair, it isn't like it is anyone's fault really. The only luck we've had so far is bad. That doesn't seem to be getting any better. Our best hope is that something turns up when forensics sweeps the place today, but I'm not holding my breath. I need to do my best to not even think about all of this today, and make my days off count. I definitely need to go to Big Lew's and have a drink in his honor tonight. My liver is probably reenergized after not drinking last night anyways. I was just too tired.

6:00 P.M.

AFTER SEVERAL HOURS OF LAUNDRY, cleaning and playing with Daisy, I decide I should start getting ready to go out. I look into my empty closet hoping that maybe someone broke in and provided me with better clothing options. I ultimately decide on the same blue jeans and black shirt I've worn out 50 other times. Looking in the mirror is like looking back in time at my dad the way I remember him before we left. *Gross.* I put some food in Daisy's bowl and grab my keys. My stomach growls as I begin to imagine "The Lew" meeting its demise when I arrive in Magnolia.

"Need anything while I'm out?" I ask to Daisy. She tilts her head and wags her tail, which I interpret as "A big hamburger, *duh*." I head to my car, and start my journey to Magnolia.

* * *

FIFTEEN MINUTES INTO MY DRIVE, my phone rings. It's Davidson.

"Yessir?" I ask.

"Just now heading out, thought I'd call. You got a minute?"

"Of course, what's up?" I ask, slowing to a stop at a red-light.

"Nothing really, but has Chief called you?"

"No. Was he supposed to?" I ask.

"Well, I don't guess so," he says, sighing loudly. "He just made it pretty clear that we all need to be on our toes and to watch our backs at all times. You know; lock your doors, don't be out doing anything stupid and just be careful I guess."

I wonder if he's implying I shouldn't be drinking too much while a couple of cop killers are out and about.

"I understand. Anything new?" I ask, deflecting.

"Not really, just kind of recovering from the ass chewing Hargrove gave everyone. She really made sure to let us know we'd better be figuring this out or everyone's job is on the line, including hers. Hell, she even said the Governor had called her saying that the FBI had made an inquiry about everything going on. Been a pretty grim day, which is to be expected, considering…"

I think briefly about Sergeant Hamilton's body hanging from the ceiling, and shudder.

"Oh damn. That's not good. Any word from the Doc?" I ask.

"He said he needed some time to process the remains, but he was pretty confused still. He said there were bones and organs missing...he wondered if maybe they were keeping them as some sort of trophy."

"Let's hope not," I say, pulling into a gas station. "Any luck on your inquiries?"

"Well that Mr. Foster spent damn near two hours talking to me and Chief. He had a lot of interesting things to say, but nothing that is of much help really."

Thinking back to my conversation with the brothers, I ask "You mean the dad right... Not one of the brothers?"

"Oh yea, definitely the dad. He said the boys are tore up about it all and haven't left his house since yesterday."

"So what do you mean by interesting then?" I ask.

"Just a lot of mess about how those woods aren't holy, and hold a bunch of bad energy. That God was the one that told him he should build that lodge so during the hunting seasons men with guns would be there most of the time in case uhh... I guess in case the Devil decides to come out? I'm not sure man it got too churchy in there for a bit, even for me. Stout ol' cat though. He has to be pushin' eighty years old."

"So basically he's on the same page as Pastor Tim huh?" I ask, jokingly.

"Yea I guess. He seems real sure about it though. Says that he knows that there is more to come, but if we all pray and ask God to step in, that we'll be aight."

"Well I guess you better give God a call then," I say sarcastically.

"He ain't answered in a while, but I'll see what I can do. Stay safe out there man and get you some rest. Looking forward to getting this over with. I'll keep you posted." He hangs up as I get out to grab me an energy drink before finishing my trip to Big Lew's. I want to use all of this night that I have, and this drive is always boring enough to make me sleepy. *Maybe the energy will keep my mind from slipping back to the scene from last night.*

* * *

I COMPLETE THE DRIVE, and park in the same place as last week. I look towards the front of the tavern, hoping that little to no one is here since it is so early. Maybe I can talk to the bartender Jacob about Lewis Parley before I get too drunk to focus. I get out and make my way to the door. Just as I had hoped, only two people are inside. There is an older man at the bar, engaged in conversation with Jacob. I wonder if they are reminiscing about Lewis Parley, or if he was just being the man's therapist for the evening. The other patron is at the pool table. He must be practicing, because even though it's just him, he seems intently focused. He didn't even notice me walk in. As I approach the bar, Jacob and the older man pause their conversation and turn to me. Jacob extends his hand and leans forward to shake mine.

"I knew you'd be back, good to see ya," he says, releasing my hand. "Same as last time or are you in the mood for something else?"

"I'll at least start off the same, and we will go from there… just whenever you get a moment though. No rush," I say, nodding to the man who was now facing directly to me, grinning slightly.

"Sure thing." He pulls a small notepad out, and scribbles down my order and frowns.

"Something wrong?" I ask.

"Well, I know I wasn't close to him by any means, but it's still kind of weird writing his name down and seeing it everywhere after hearing about his passing. It'll pass in time I'm sure."

"Of course. It may seem a little morbid, but it's part of life. I'm sure he'd be happy to know his memory will live on in at least a few people here," I say.

"You're right, man," he hesitates for a moment, "Oh man, I apologize. I heard about there being an officer who passed away. Sorry for your loss."

He makes my drink quickly, then walks to the back with the notepad. I take a long sip, feeling the cold whiskey hit my stomach. *Exactly what my body needed.* I breathe out a sigh of relief. I didn't realize how bad I was needing that until now, I guess. I take another quick sip before being interrupted.

"I seen yew on the news this mernin' ain't I?" asks the old man. His words are followed by a hot foul beer smell that would've pulled vomit from my stomach had I already eaten.

"I doubt it, but then again I don't watch the news, sir. You may have me mistaken," I say.

He scoots his stool a little closer and leans in towards me. He closes one eye, and squints the other. His smell, movements and his one visible glazed eye tells me that he is most definitely more intoxicated than I had imagined.

"Nawww Naw, buddy. I seen ya. You's with that feller that pushed ol' Parker Cowan in some horse shit!" he says, throwing spit halfway across the bar before slapping his leg and cackling. "I woulda paid a hundred dollars to have been there for that! Good stuff!"

"Oh yea, that was me. It was an unfortunate circumstance, but sometimes things happen in the heat of the—" He puts his hand on my shoulder and stands up quickly, almost knocking his empty beer over.

"No need to apologize' son, I loved it. Anyways I gotta hit this pisser for it hits me ye know what I mean?" he asks, cackling again and stumbling to the restroom. I use this opportunity to move myself to the far end of the bar, just as Jacob is bringing out my burger.

"I'll go ahead and get you another drink ready. Sorry about that old man. His dog died a few days ago and he's been in here every day. Don't worry though, he leaves at eight thirty sharp," he says.

"Good deal. Not the dog dying thing, but the 'leaving soon' thing," I say, pulling the "Big Lew" to me.

He chuckles and heads to clean up the old man's mess at the other end of the bar. I'm glad he will be getting out of here soon. However, I imagine whenever the day comes when Daisy passes away I will be equally devastated. Maybe I won't harass a stranger and will be in a better place than a bar by then. Hopefully she'll outlive me so I don't have to worry about it. I finish off my first drink and the burger quickly, as Jacob brings me another glass.

"So, Mr. Detective, what's the latest and greatest? Any luck in finding out who's doing all this?" he asks.

"Not really to be honest. A lot has happened since I was here. I'd like to say we are a lot closer than we were then, but I'd be lying."

He grins, and asks, "You'd tell us if it was a vampire right?"

I smile, and take a long drink. "Yea I think it would be easier if it was. At least we would know how to stop it."

"True. True. Well if that's what it turns out to be give me a call, I've always wanted to hunt them like those two dudes on that one show where they drive that badass Camaro," he says chuckling and walking to tend to a patron that had just walked up.

I really wish that was how easy the case was. I just hop in some cool car, drive around until I find the "vampire" and kill it in some knock down drag out fight then drive off to fight another one in some other town. Rinse and repeat. *As if.*

Instead, I'm out here searching for some team of assassins that are smart enough to perplex the smartest man I've ever met with their displays of…whatever you would want to call these crime scenes. I'm so out brained here and I need everything to go back to the way it was before. *I have to stop thinking about this.*

"See y'all fuckers later!" I turn just in time to catch a glimpse of the old man stumbling towards the door, middle finger proudly displayed to the whopping total of five other people in the bar. Must be eight-thirty. I smile, and finish my drink.

"Surely he didn't drive here right?" I ask Jacob as he grabs my empty glass.

"No his wife drops him off and picks him up, I figure she lets him grieve this way to keep him out of her hair," he says.

"Good," I say, as Jacob leans in closer to me.

"Look, I don't have any problems with you guys, but I would be careful with any cop like behavior tonight. Whole town is pretty angry with how things have been going. Last night I heard some guys saying they were going to organize a group to go out hunting for the uhh… 'vampire' since the police couldn't get anything done," he says in a whisper.

"I understand, good looking out. I appreciate it, I'll be right back," I say. I walk outside and jog to my car. Fumbling around in the backseat, I find the hat I was looking for. It's solid black, with a United States flag on it. Maybe no one else will recognize me from the news now. I pull it down low, and walk back inside. Noticing now that the bar is beginning to fill, I make sure to secure my spot in the corner.

9:30 P.M.

HAVING RAN through four drinks now, I'm right where I need to be. Buzzed enough to feel it, but not drunk. In talking a little more to Jacob between patrons, he let me know that the owners of the tavern were pretty devastated at the news of Lewis's death. They had closed the tavern down that night, but decided that he would've rather it stay open so they opened back up the next day. They had planned to organize a special "Holiday" where drinks were half price and people would win prizes and stuff, they just hadn't nailed down a day yet.

"This seat taken?" asks a man who couldn't be over twenty-five. I shake my head no, and shift my seat a little to give him more room. "Come sit right here babe!" he says to a woman who had just walked up. They sit and order themselves some drinks. With the man's back to me, I overhear their conversation.

"A little less stressful in here I think…more people makes me feel a little safer. Thanks for coming out with me," says the woman.

"Of course babe, always. Definitely a more chill vibe than making sure the doors are locked every few minutes. I'll be glad when the cops stop all of this."

"Damn right," she says.

I wish I would've thought ahead and went to a different bar further out of town so I could make it more than a few hours without hearing about these murders. When I go back in to work I need to lock myself in with all the information we've accumulated and try to make some sense of all of it. I don't know how much longer I can take all of this pressure. I get Jacob to pour me another drink, and decide I'm going to try some of their loaded fries as a snack. As he walks to the other end of the bar to put my order in, I make brief eye contact with a woman who is leaned up against the bar near the register. I look away. Something tells me to look back at her, but when I do, she isn't there. Damn. Must've been closing out. *Was that the woman I saw the last time I was leaving here?* I lean up to look for her, hoping maybe I can get a glimpse of her moving through the crowd of people, but can't find her. *Damn.*

I feel a hand on my shoulder, then hear a soft voice in my ear.

"Looks like I'll have better luck getting a drink over here, mind if I squeeze in?"

I turn to see the woman I was looking for, and lose my voice a little.

"I…yea, uh…sure," I say.

She smiles and leans up against the bar as Jacob comes to get her order. He quickly makes her a vodka soda, and slides it her way. She looks back to me, moving her long black hair out of her face.

"Told ya," she says, winking and walking away towards the back of the tavern. I watch her move through people like she's ice skating, never touching anyone.

"Pick that tongue up Pepe Le Pew," says Jacob from behind the bar.

"Sorry, she's just uhhh gorgeous," I say, turning back to him.

"Yea she's a knockout. She's been in here pretty frequently this month. Never really talks to people other than anyone brave enough to approach her. Kind of like you in a way, I guess. Stays to herself," he says.

"Only difference is she looks amazing and I'm having a tough time keeping whiskey off of my shirt. She'll have forgotten about me before she sits down."

"Speaking of, let me go check on your fries. It'll give those butterflies in your stomach something to eat," he says, walking away shaking his head.

Butterflies is right. When she looked at me it was like all

of the alcohol I've drank left my body and the room slowed down. I'm glad our interaction was brief since I forgot how to speak, but damn I wish she would've stayed a while. I'll go look for her after I eat. Maybe we can talk and she'll be what finally takes my mind off of all of this negativity.

CHAPTER 18

I let Jacob give me another drink, and I decide I'm going to try and sneak in a game of pool. I haven't played in years, but it might get my mind right for at least a few moments. I snake my way through the crowd of people and go to the back corner where the fewest people are standing. There are two men who are close to the end of their game.

"You got next?" asks one of the men.

"Sure thing."

I look to the wall and grab one of the pool cues that looks the least damaged and wait. I scan the room, trying to keep my eyes busy as the whiskey is finally laying claim to my brain. Not too drunk, but I definitely need to slow it down if I'm planning on leaving anytime soon. The men finish their game, and the loser heads to the bar to grab the victor a beer. The man sets us up a game, and breaks the balls violently. Several striped balls go in, indicating that he will likely defeat me just as quickly as the last man. Oh well. I get lucky and he misses his next shot. I line up a corner shot with the solid yellow ball, and miss it horribly. It banks off of the side and knocks one of his striped balls in.

"Preciate' it big dawg," says the man, smiling.

He proceeds to knock all but one of the striped balls in before he misses again. I guess this was the real reason there weren't many people at this pool table, this guy is great. I manage to knock a few solid colored balls in before accidentally letting the cue ball follow one in.

"Damn, it's all you now dude," I say.

"Yup, nuthin but me and a nother' free beer after thissen'," he says, moving some dip around to the front of his lip.

He knocks his last striped ball in with ease.

"Front pocket. I'll call it 'the pussy' just like y'all dipshits," he says proudly, pointing towards the front corner pocket. He stretches gracefully over the edge of the table and strikes the eight ball, sending it flying directly into the front pocket. He puts his pool cue down, and bows dramatically. I shake his hand and head to the bar to grab him whatever the cheapest beer is.

On my way I notice two men out of the corner of my eye pointing in my direction and shaking their heads. I wonder if they were pointing at me, or someone I happened to pass by. I make it to the bar and order the man his beer. As I bring it back to him, he thanks me, turns it back and drinks it all at once. He lets out a monstrous burp, and beats his chest like a gorilla before falling back into character for the game of pool he had started when I left. Truly a sight to see. I turn to find a better spot to watch the game, when I accidentally bump into a man.

"Hey bud, you gotta open your eyes when you're walkin'," he says in a serious tone.

"Sorry man, just trying to see a little better, I wasn't paying attention."

"Well you'd prolly see a little better without yer damn hat

so low like that," he says, reaching and pulling my hat up to the top of my head.

"You're right, my bad man," I say, trying to move away from him to avoid the confrontation.

"Now hold on a minute buddy, you look like that damn cop that was on the news the other day. Why the hell you in here drankin' and not out there finding that damn vampire?" he asks loudly, causing a few people to turn towards us.

He raises his hand abruptly to point at me, accidentally knocking a beer out of a man's hand who was just trying to walk by. The glass bottle shatters on the floor and beer spills over everyone's feet.

"The fuck's your problem, cocksucker?" asks the man, stepping to the other.

"Hell I guess you're my problem now that you wanna be tough!" says the first man. The first man swings wildly at him and misses. They begin trading punches and cuss words, then a few men jump in to try and break it up. I feel a hand grabbing my wrist and pulling me away. I turn to see who it is, and it's the woman from earlier.

"Close one! Come with me!"

She pulls me towards the bar as the men now take their fight to the floor, each hurling a creative insult at each other between blows. We make it to the bar and she turns to me. "What are you drinking?" she asks.

"Uhh whiskey…just whiskey and coke," I say.

She turns and orders for us as Jacob hangs up a phone, that I'm assuming was just connected to a police officer. "So you're a cop? You don't look like a cop to me."

"What do I look like then?" I ask.

"You look like you would be a lawyer, but one that rides horses to court to be different," she says, laughing.

I'm not sure whether to take that as a compliment or not.

"I could never be a lawyer, but I'd be willing to ride a

horse to work as long as I got to wear a cool cowboy hat," I say.

She smiles, and takes our drinks from Jacob. We see a few Magnolia officers come through the door, and quickly remove the two men who had been fighting. I'm glad too, because I am confident that man was not going to have anything good to say to me and I'm in no condition to fight right now. I made sure to stare down at the floor as they were hauled out so that none of the officers would recognize me. I'm sure they'd have similar things to say about me being here in this tavern and not trying to figure this case out.

The woman takes a long sip from her drink and asks, "So why *are* you here? Just curious."

"It's one of my off days and I like this place. They have good food and I don't know anyone. Perfect combo for me," I say.

"Well now you know me," she says, tilting her head to the side a little.

She stares into me with the greenest eyes I've ever seen, causing me to forget what she even said. *Maybe my butterflies need some more to eat.*

"Uhh… thank you for the drink. I can buy your next one."

"No need. I never drink more than a few when I know I have to drive home. I had a few shots in my car before I came in to get the most out of my money. Don't tell on me officer," she says, fluttering her eyes at me and smiling again. "Looks like you'll need to drink a gallon of water and eat some food before you leave though."

"You're right. I should probably do that now," I say.

I get beside where her stool is and wave to Jacob. I place mine and Daisy's order, and he walks to the back. As I'm going to step back away from the bar, she grabs my arm.

She points to the scar on the outside of my forearm. "What happened here?"

"Fell off of a tree when I was a teenager and got cut up pretty bad. My friends had dared me to climb a huge one out in the woods and I was too proud to back down. Learned my lesson."

She puts her hand over it, causing chill bumps to cover my whole body. It was like she touched my soul. She just stared into me for a few moments then moved her hand. "There, that will be healed right up in no time." She giggles and finishes her drink.

I try to remember the last time a woman touched me, and draw a blank. A few years ago I had a short "situationship" with a woman who had transferred in from Texas for some kind of an audit, but it had fizzled out as soon as she went back home. It turned out that I was an extra marital fling that was only there to pass her time. *She wasn't even half as beautiful as this woman is, on her best day.*

We exchange a few injury and funny stories from our youth, and I realize I hadn't spoken like this to anyone in years. Even the short moment with the auditor didn't include this level of comfort. Everything just seemed...*natural*. Words were flowing out of me, and I was smiling and laughing like I've known her for years. *I wish I had.* It was relaxing to the point that I must have missed when Jacob brought me my food.

"So, you gonna eat that or...?" she asks.

I pull the bag to me, and pull out the burger.

"Want to try some?" I ask, presenting it to her.

"No thanks, I have leftovers back at my hotel."

"Hotel? So you're just passing through? Here to flirt with me and then disappear forever?" I ask, sarcastically.

"Sort've. I'm in town visiting family. I'll be leaving in a week or so if I had to guess."

It seems I am cursed to interact with women who are temporary. *Does she have a husband at home too?* I don't see a ring, but maybe she left that at her hotel. Maybe I should back off from her since this won't have time to go anywhere.

"That's unfortunate. Maybe I'll see you again before you go," I say, closing the bag of food.

"Wait are you about to leave?" she asks, frowning.

"I really should, it's getting late. Plus my dog will probably break out of the house and come looking if I'm not back by midnight," I say.

She leans in and squints her eyes. "Or are you just afraid of the sun coming up…seems like you might be the vampire all along!"

I laugh and stand up, wobbling a little as I grab the bag.

"Maybe I should give you a ride home," she says, noticing that I'm not sober just yet.

"I'll be okay, plus it's like thirty minutes away," I say.

"I really don't mind, silly. Not a good look if you get pulled over like this, especially with everyone already on you guys about catching the…vampire."

"Okay, sure. Let me get my house key out of my car first," I say. I close my tab and walk out to my car. I realize now that this is definitely the right call. My vision is hazy and my head is swimming. I make it out to my car and grab my keys. The woman has walked over to the end of my car, cigarette in one hand, and my bag of food in the other. I must've forgotten it when I got up.

"Thanks, Daisy would've been pissed!" I say, reaching for it gratefully.

"No worries. I like the name Daisy. Is that your—"

"I'm so sorry," I say, interrupting her. "Daisy is my dog! Uhh, I haven't even asked what your name is and I'm about to get in your car. I apologize."

She smiles, "Once again, no worries. I'm Evelyn, and it's nice meeting you!" She extends her hand to me.

I grab it gently. "Damon, and same to you."

Her happy expression falls flat, and a look of worry covers her face. Her eyes shift from mine to behind me. I turn around to see what she was looking at, but I get dizzy and can't focus on anything. She grabs me to keep me from falling.

"What is it?" I ask.

She smiles, guiding me towards a white sedan. "Nothing, I just thought I saw someone."

I get into the passenger seat and she pulls out onto the street. I tell her my address and she puts it in her phone, then places it on a mount on her dash. The road noise makes me sleepy, and I rest my head on the door.

I AWAKE as the rough road leading up to my house bounces my head off the side of the door.

"Wake up sleepy head, we made it," she says, putting her hand on my knee.

I look up as her headlights hit the front porch, illuminating Daisy's head in the window. We pull to a stop, and she walks me to my door.

"I hope to see you in the sunlight soon, so I can at least know you're a real man and not...Count Dracula or something," she says.

"Trust me, if I was a vampire I would have a way cooler house than this."

I open the door and Daisy flies out onto the porch, sniffing Evelyn up and down.

"Oh! Hello Daisy, nice to meet you!" She extends her hand down for Daisy to sniff, to which she replies with a few licks and an extra sniff. Daisy then runs down the porch and into the yard to pee.

"What a nice lady," says Evelyn, wiping the slobber onto her jeans.

"Yea she's a go—" I'm interrupted by Daisy barking wildly at Evelyn's car door. "Daisy hush!"

I jog over to her, and see that she's barking at what looks like the sleeve of a jacket hanging out of the back seat.

"Chill girl, its just a jacket!" I grab her by her collar and see that all the hair on her back is standing up. I pick her up and walk her into the house, and shut the door as I step back out onto the porch. "I'm sorry, she must've thought that was a snake or something. She's usually not like that I promise," I say, as Evelyn opens the door to shove the jacket back inside.

"It's okay, maybe she doesn't like flannel," she says. She grabs my wrists and looks up to me.

"You want to come in? I've got some drinks and I'm sure Daisy will be alright as long as you leave that jacket in the car," I say.

She bites her lip, then smiles. "Nah, I think I've excited her a little too much. Maybe next time when it isn't so late. Get you some sleep."

"Yes ma'am," I say, wishing she'd reconsider.

"Let me see your phone and I'll put my number in so we can arrange that."

I hand her my phone, and she calls her own phone number. She then saves her number as "Evelyn" with two black hearts.

"I'll let you know when I make it home, okay?" She reaches up to the back of my neck, and pulls my head to hers. She kisses me quickly on the lips, smiles then turns to walk to her car. My stomach flutters and I can't do anything but smile as she gets in her car and drives away. I can't wait for her to get back with me so we can arrange to spend some time together. She seems amazing. I can only imagine what time with her outside of a bar will be like. Maybe I shouldn't be so hopeful, but fuck it. If she's only going to be around for a little while, I can at least make the best of it. I walk back inside to give Daisy her burger, and see her staring out the window intently as Evelyn's taillights exit the driveway. It isn't until Evelyn is out of sight that she shows interest.

"Sorry about that jacket girl. I guess I won't be buying any flannels for the winter." I rub her head and hand her the burger. Time to get ready for bed.

CHAPTER 19

11:15 A.M.

I rub my eyes and sit up. I don't see Daisy in her normal spot, so I call for her. She comes trotting into the room and looks at me with an "about time you woke up" expression before trotting back out into the hallway. I look to my phone and see that I have a few text messages, and a missed call from Davidson. Looking at the text messages, I see where Evelyn had text me last night:

> Just letting you know that I've made it back home!

> Let me know when you'd like me to take you back to your car. If you even remember who I am! 😅

> Of course I remember you, how could I forget?

And you can take me back whenever you'd like, I'm off today.

I go to the other message and see that it is from Davidson.

Call me when you can. Got our lucky break, sort've.

What does he mean by SORT'VE? Of course a major break-through would happen when I'm out all night drinking. *I had hoped to be the one making the big moves in this case, but as long as it gets solved I guess I don't care...*

I walk to the kitchen to grab some headache medicine and a glass of water. Daisy is staring out the front window, just like she was last night when Evelyn left.

"She's gone, girl, you can relax," I say. She just wags her tail a little and continues looking out. I finish off a glass of water and go to let her outside. She runs to the yard to pee, then starts sniffing around in the driveway where the car was the night before. "Relax Scooby Doo it was just a shirt," I say as I walk back inside. Now I'll Call Davidson and see what our "lucky break" was.

"Just now waking up huh?" Davidson asks.

"Yea I didn't get in till early in the morning."

"I figured. You just wait till you're my age. Only late night activities you'll be doing is getting up to piss and that'll feel like a hangover in itself," he says.

"Maybe so, but for now I'll enjoy it while I can," I say.

"Understand that, buddy. Anyways I thought I'd let you know that we have a suspect," he says, raising his voice at the end in an excited tone.

"Who? Is it one of the Foster brothers?"

"Not even close. If you aren't too busy you could swing by and I can just show you," he says.

"Well, I can't really do that. My car is in Magnolia right now. I'll have to explain tomorrow," I say, hoping he won't be too inquisitive.

"Ahh. You ain't in any trouble are you?" he asks.

"Not at all. You'd know by now if that was the case."

"You've got that right. Well since you can't come here, I'll just tell ya. Our suspect is a man named Grant Lungston. Ring any bells?" he asks.

"No, not at all. I'm assuming he isn't local? I don't think I know anyone named Grant at all."

"Yup," he says. "Washington state believe it or not."

"Huh?" I ask, confused. *Why would a man from Washington state come all the way down here just to do all of this? Is he a serial killer? Has he done this across the whole United States to get here? Surely we would've heard of something like this if that was the case.*

"Yea it's wild. Remember that blood that they found at the lodge?" he asks.

Thinking back to the scene, I recall the CFT officer noticing the dried blood at the bottom of the door. That must be how they are linking him to the murder.

"Yea I remember," I say.

"Well, that was his blood. There was also a shit ton of it in the sink drain in the kitchen there. He must've got himself cut up pretty bad. They ran the samples of it against everyone in our state database and came back with nothing. When they ran it in the Federal Database, it came back to Mr. Lungston. He's been arrested three times. Breaking and entering twice, then theft and assault," he says.

"So was he down here trying to start a new life or what? It's a big jump to go from those crimes to murdering people and hanging them up. Doesn't really make sense. Any chance he had just used the lodge to hunt like other people? Maybe he comes down and is a part of the Foster's club."

"Nope," says Davidson in a matter of fact way. "The Fosters say he ain't registered, and they've never seen him before. Only other way to that lodge is up that mountain from the other side near Lewis Parleys property. So if he got there, that's where he had to come from."

I think back to the steep mountainside behind the lodge and try to imagine someone getting Sergeant Hamilton up that, then being able to hang him up that way. This guy must be super strong and an expert woodsman. That definitely won't make finding him any easier. I open the door to let Daisy back in.

"So what's the plan then?" I ask.

"Find his ass and bring him in! Maybe he'll spill who his accomplice is too!" says Davidson. I hear someone talking to him and his tone changes. "Well I'm gonna have to go but you know the drill, we'll put his picture out everywhere and maybe that'll point us in the right direction. I'll send it to you too, so you can be on the look out. I'll holler at ya later if something else comes up. See ya." He hangs up the phone.

My phone vibrates. It's a text from Evelyn:

Can I pick you up at twelve-thirty?

Of course!

I put my phone down and get into the shower.

As the warm water hits me I can't help but to think about the suspect. I try to align it in my head in a way that makes sense. *So this guy who is a pretty regular criminal, jumps across the entire country just to end up in this little town? Then he starts killing?* I just don't get it. I'm glad we finally have a name but I just feel more lost. I'm willing to bet his partner is the brains behind the operation. Whoever it is probably has a history that makes more sense. How do you even get into something like this with a partner?

"Hey man you seem cool, want to go to the South and kill some people?"

"Sure thing man!"

Seems like we're missing something huge here. Maybe we will get lucky and someone has seen him. I get out of the shower and throw some clothes on. I look to my phone and see that Evelyn has text me.

Be there in ten minutes!

I refill Daisy's water bowl, and go to wait on the porch.

* * *

She pulls into the driveway, sun glaring off of her window. She comes to a stop about ten yards from my steps. She rolls her window down.

"Step into the sunlight, if you dare!" she says, pulling her sunglasses down and motioning for me to come join her. If I was a little less shy I might have faked like the sun was burning my skin, and I was the "Vampire of Culver" all along. Getting into her car, I realize that she is just as pretty as she was the night before. Her long hair is now put up into a messy bun, and she's wearing a tank top and athletic shorts.

"How you feeling?" she asks.

"Not too bad. Thanks for giving me a ride home…and a ride back."

"No worries. I needed an excuse to see you again anyways." She smiles as she cracks the window. "Do you smoke?" she asks.

"No ma'am. Never have."

"Do you mind if I do?" she asks, cigarette already in hand.

"Not at all. Your car, your rules."

I think back to the many car rides with Davidson, where

he would go through no less than four or five cigarettes at a time. We turn out of my driveway and head towards Magnolia. I think for a moment on how to break the awkward silence as the gravel breaks free from her tires and bounces down the road.

"So what do you do for work?" I ask.

"I'm in management at a marketing firm. I work mostly from home. It gets super repetitive but I can't complain. The money and freedom are nice," she says, flicking her ashes out of the window.

"Not bad. You said you're visiting family right? So are you from the area originally?"

"No," she says firmly and pauses for a moment before continuing, "I'm from Oklahoma. My parents got divorced when I was younger. My mom came down here to be with her friends and I stayed with my dad."

In gauging her response, it seems like that isn't a happy memory for her, so I'll change the subject.

"What kind of music do you listen to?" I ask.

"This," she says, turning the cars stereo up.

My ears are filled with the unmistakable sound of Mozart.

"Wow, I didn't expect that," I say.

"It just relaxes me. Nothing beats ending a stressful day with a drink and some classical music."

"I agree. My mother used to play this in the house when I was younger. I loved watching her pretend to play the piano on the counter while she was cleaning," I say.

"Is she still around?" she asks.

"No, she was killed by a drunk driver about ten years ago unfortunately."

"Well I'm glad I gave you a ride home last night then, she probably wouldn't be a fan of you drinking and driving," she says, patting my leg reassuringly. *Even the smallest touch from her wakes those butterflies back up. I feel like a teenager again.*

"You're right. Thanks again."

We spend the rest of the drive listening to a playlist of symphonies, and taking in the scenery.

We arrive to my car, and she pulls into the space behind it.

"Hungry?" she asks.

I'm not sure why I hadn't considered spending more time than just getting this ride from her. She insists that we go and eat at a Mexican restaurant up the road, ensuring me that it's as close to authentic "Tex-Mex" as it gets.

* * *

WE ARRIVE AT THE RESTAURANT, "Los Marcos." The parking lot is pretty much entirely empty except for a few people standing outside smoking.

"I assume that's the staff?" I ask.

She looks up at them and waves, and they return the gesture. "Yea they are all nice. I've eaten here no less than five times since I've been in town," she says, getting out of the car.

We head inside and they seat us in the very back. I order a burrito, and she orders something in Spanish that I can't understand. I really admire her. A single, attractive Midwestern woman with what I assume to be a great job and a level head. *What's the catch?* There aren't any women like this around here. As much as I would hate to be involved with something long distance, she might be worth trying it for. I mean who else would I even try to be involved with at this point?

My phone vibrates loudly on the table. It's Davidson. It was the picture of Grant Lungston that they would be using in the news.

Here's the guy, interesting fella to say the
least. Meant to send earlier but was busy.
We're about to release the picture to the
press any minute now.

Thanks. I'll be on the lookout.

"Work?" Evelyn asks.

"Yea, we actually have a suspect now and believe it or not…no fangs or pale skin," I say.

She looks back to me intently, not reacting to the joke. "So have they…arrested the person yet?" she asks in a concerned tone.

"No, we don't even know if the person or their accomplice is still around. Not a local by any means," I say, eating a tortilla chip.

She shifts in her seat and looks to her phone. "That's just kind of scary to me you know? Someone like that just out and about. The news channels around here make me feel like the people are just everywhere all of the time and it really stresses me out."

I look around the empty restaurant, "I think we're good here at least."

"True," she says.

We get our food and begin to eat. She was right about the food being good, but it is way too much for me so I go ahead and ask for a to-go box. Daisy is going to be really excited to have half of a large burrito to eat for dinner tonight. As we finish up, Evelyn gets a text message and stares at it for a moment before typing briefly and setting her phone back down. It goes off a few times and she looks to her screen frustrated.

"I need to make a quick call, is that okay?" she asks.

"Of course," I say.

She steps out. *I wonder if that's her boyfriend or husband.*

Surely a woman as beautiful as that isn't single. Unless she's crazy or something. Or like me and just...lost. The waiter comes with the check, and I go ahead and pay for it. I sit for a few moments before deciding I'll just meet her outside. I grab my bag and exit the restaurant.

Outside I see her leaned against her car on the phone. I hear her say, "Do whatever you need to but I'm telling you that you're just going to fuck it all up. Think of how far you have come!" Seems like a pretty intense work conversation so I give her some space. "Look, I've got to go. I'll talk to you later," she says before hanging up.

"Sorry, some people are just too stupid for their own good," she says, smiling and opening her door.

"I understand that completely," I say.

"Thanks for the food, you didn't have to pay for that silly," she says, grabbing my hand.

"It's the least I could do," I say. "I really appreciate you looking out for me last night."

"No worries!"

* * *

SHE DRIVES me back to my car, and we depart. No kiss this time, unfortunately. Maybe when she was a little buzzed she was more comfortable. Or her call with whoever that was ruined the moment. It could be that seeing me in the sunlight has turned her off to the idea of me. Our difference in attractiveness is noticeable to say the least. I would understand. I don't really have much to offer someone like that. *At least I'm not a vampire...* I hop in my car and head back towards home. I think I'll go ahead and stop by the store and grab me something to drink for the evening and make sure I'm in bed at a decent time tonight. I dread going back into work but at least now we have someone to look for that will make it more interesting than just chasing our tails.

8:00 P.M.

I FINISH my glass of bourbon and begin to clean up my mess. Seems like a good time to call it a night. I place my clothes for the next day out, and I hear Daisy bark.

"What is it, Girl?" I ask, walking into the hallway to investigate. She's at the front window again, with her tail sticking out. She barks again. I walk up to look out of the window, but when I get close, she turns and barks at me.

"What the hell Daisy, what's going on?" I ask. She growls at me and turns back to the window, barking again. I jog into my room, stumbling once before catching myself in my doorway. I grab my pistol and head back to the living room. I hear a loud crackling sound, as if a tree had just fallen outside. *What the hell is going on out there?* I try to look out the other window but can't really see anything. I go to open the door, and again daisy barks at me.

"Hush girl, I'm alright."

I swing the door open and step out. Laying in my yard, is a large tree that has fallen. It goes from one side of my yard, all the way across my driveway. *What the fuck? I don't have any trees in my front yard.* I look around and now there are fifteen to twenty large trees throughout my yard. I rub my eyes, trying to focus as the bourbon has me too drunk to see clearly. I stumble forward, tripping on my steps and falling to the ground.

"Fuck," I say as I pull myself up. I look up and there are

MORE trees around to the point that I can't even see more than a few feet in front of me. I turn back to the porch but… it's gone. No porch, no house, no lights. I am surrounded by dense forest. *What the fuck is happening?* I look down to see my bare feet in the dirt. I reach to my pocket but I must've left my phone in my room. I look to the ground and can't find my pistol either. I must have dropped it when I fell. *Fuck.* I squint to try and see but I can just barely make out my hands in front of me. I feel around and find a large tree to lean against, and sit down at its base.

What the fuck have I gotten myself into? Did I get so drunk that I wondered deep into the woods? Am I going to have to just wait until sunlight before I can find my way out of this? I hear a loud cracking again, and cover my head as I hear branches snapping closer and closer to me. A loud *THUD* emanates from the ground near me. It couldn't have been more than ten feet away. I stand up to run, but I feel something grab me from behind. I turn to see what it is and all I can see in the darkness are two grey eyes staring back at me. I try to scream, but nothing comes out. I try to break free, but I can't move anything anymore. I feel like I'm stuck in concrete. The eyes look into me and we stare at each other in total silence for a moment. *Fuck. They must've seen the news and did some digging to find my address and they're going to kill me before we can arrest them. Where is the other person? Will they kill Daisy too? How will they display my body?*

"*SOON!*" Thunders from all around me, almost deafeningly loud. I shudder violently. The eyes get closer to me, and I close my eyes, expecting pain at any moment. I feel a wetness on the bottom of my face, that slides all the way to the top. I'm too scared to open my eyes… I hold my breath.

. . .

ALL AT ONCE, all the sounds crash back around me and I feel a pressure on my stomach. I open my eyes, and Daisy is sitting on top of me, licking my face. *Huh?* I push her away and sit up. I look around and see that I am laying in my kitchen floor, along with my turned over bottle of bourbon, my phone and half of the sandwich I had made. I glance at my phone for the time. Eleven-forty-four p.m. *God damnit.*

CHAPTER 20

8:00 A.M.

*L*ooking into my mirror as I brush my teeth, I realize I have a black eye. I assume from my fall to the floor last night. *Embarrassing.* The second we have this case wrapped up I'm taking a break from drinking. *If that time ever comes anyways...* Maybe we'll have some luck locating this Grant guy and that will put an end to all of it. *We'll see.* I text Evelyn and see if she would be up to meeting during the week for some food or something, but she doesn't respond. She's probably sleeping in. Last night she had text me all the way up until I took a dive in the kitchen.

I recall the vivid dream I had as I pull out of the driveway. I take note of the absence of trees, and make my way down the road. Each one of my wild dreams lately has been followed by something bad happening, but I hope this one was just a dream and nothing more. This time the feeling was...*stronger.* I can't really wrap my head around it. It was overwhelming. I can't let it ruin my focus though, today is important. I pull into a gas station, and forage for an energy drink.

"What's tha other guy look like?" asks a familiar voice from the end of the aisle. Raymond Stokes. He looks a little more put together than I remember.

"I slipped in my kitchen, unfortunately. Turns out my counter is a little stronger than my face," I say, placing the cold energy drink to my eye.

"Hell, I'd say that too if I lost a fight," he says.

I notice that he has work boots and is wearing a shirt with a logo and a phone number on it.

"You get you a job?" I ask, making my way to the counter.

He follows me with his candy bar and bottle of water, "Yes sir. Got me a job with Harry Montgomery. Making some good money now, just gotta bust my ass for it. He's got us out here working on the weekend, and I'll take all the overtime money I can get! But uhh, you know man, that whole…situation at the church scared the shit outta me. I figured I'd make me some money and get up outta here, you know? Find somewhere a little safer and start taking things a little more serious."

Harry Montgomery is an older gentleman who made his money doing off shore welding, then moved to Culver and started a contracting company that was an overnight success. Pretty much anything built after the year 2000 here was in some way a part of his operation. It is good to see Raymond have things going his way.

"Happy to hear that," I say. "I bet it'll work out just fine for you, man."

"Thanks. See ya later."

. . .

Walking into the station, I notice Davidson standing in the threshold of the office with a big smile on his face.

"Before you even say it, I fell. I promise. No fights or anything," I say.

"Oh I know it buddy. Your scarecrow lookin' ass would be a lot more beat up than that, if that was the case!" He laughs and steps aside as I walk in.

I place my things down on my desk and look to the whiteboard. The name GRANT LUNGSTON is written in bold letters across the top with a few bullet points below stating his description and a few pictures and reports held up by magnets to the side. With a height of six foot three and a weight of two hundred fifty-five pounds, it isn't surprising that he was able to lift Sergeant Hamilton and carry him through the woods.

"Big dude huh?" I ask, looking at his mugshot.

"Big and weird," says Davidson, pulling off one of the reports and handing it to me. He points to one of the paragraphs. "Read this."

I squint my eyes, and read it:

"Suspect detained after a security officer observed him breaking into the archives of The Native American History Preservation Center. Suspect tried to flee but was easily apprehended after he tripped over one of the books he was trying to steal. Security officer stated he was not showing any signs of being under the influence of drugs or alcohol, other than ranting about how it was his destiny to find "them" and he would never stop. Did not resist."

"Okay so by 'THEM' I guess he means some lost tribe or something? Or does he mean the people here that he has found and killed?" I ask.

"Not really sure," says Davidson, sitting down in a chair at the front of the room and leaning back, "They must have a lot more crazies up there than we have cause they really didn't ask him much. They drug tested him and made him pay restitution for a door he broke but that was pretty much it. Prolly some history nut that wants to have the next TV show about finding lost peoples or some wonky shit."

"I guess. That doesn't really explain why he would travel over two thousand miles to kill a couple of people here. It's not like we have much Native American History here anyways," I say.

Davidson sits up quickly as if he'd just been electrocuted. "Not much? Boy did you even go to school? There's more Native American bones around here than there are trees."

I think back to history class and draw a blank. During school I was too focused on girls to care about history, much less the history of a town as small as this.

"My bad man, I don't guess I paid enough attention to Mr. Pratt," I say, picturing the very short and round Arnold Pratt waddling to write on his board.

Davidson stands up and goes to a small supply closet and begins sifting around until he produces a large rolled sheet. He lays it flat on a desk, placing his coffee on one corner to keep it from rolling back up.

"Aha!" He says, pointing to the corner of the map. "Culver Historical Society Native American Territory Map" was written in a large, swirling font. The map had color coded different areas of Culver based on what tribe had claim to it during specific time periods, with small boxes detailing major events.

"Look here, we even had a major war!" says Davidson, pointing to a small area I recognize to now be where the co-op sits. The small descriptive box stated that there were 400-600 casualties, and that it was considered the bloodiest battle that had ever taken place in the entire area.

"Wow, I guess I never knew. So wouldn't it be possible that this guy was in the wrong place at the wrong time?" I ask, pointing to the area of Sunridge Valley on the map, "See, there are three different tribes that were in this area. He could've been looking in the woods for artifacts or something and got hurt, then stumbled into the lodge and cleaned himself up."

Davidson puts his hand on his chin, and stares at me intently. He leans back down to the map, and points to a spot, a little deeper into the valley. "Look at this."

There is a small information box that reads: "Intersect of Coalition Treaty" with a small, shaded triangle that none of the territories touched.

"So what's the Coalition Treaty?" I ask.

He raises his eyebrow, "Hell, I don't know. I've never heard of that."

"Come on now Davidson, I thought you were the expert!" I say, patting him on the shoulder.

"Well I guess not. I'll do some diggin'. That gives me something to do today," he says, pulling his phone out. "My brother loves this typa stuff. I'll holler at him." He takes a picture of the map, then rolls it back up.

"Meant to tell you," he says, placing the map down beside his desk, "Doc Thompson said Sergeant Hamilton's death was… different."

"How so?"

"Well he said it was the same as the girl on the inside and all…just worse. But this time there was definitely signs of trauma," he says in a hushed tone. "Said his head was beat up a little and his hands had scratches like he was in a fight."

"What the hell… maybe he put up a good fight before they overpowered him," I say.

"It's a damn shame, man. Hope he at least hurt em a little."

I sit down at my desk to finish off my energy drink as Chief Marks walks in.

"Mornin," he says, looking as if he hadn't slept at all. He does a double take and glares back at me.

"Fell in the kitchen, no fighting I promise," I say, assuming his look was directed at my black eye. He shakes his head and walks to the board. He writes the word "sightings" under Grant Lungston's notes. He scribbles a couple of locations on the board, with a rough estimate of time beside them.

"These are the places people have called in and said they've seen this guy or at least someone that looks like him. Doesn't do us any favors that he looks like any other mid thirties man around here," he says, looking to the mugshot.

He was right. With a baseball cap on, Grant looked like he'd be any other man in town. He chose the right place to try and fit in.

"I want you boys to split up today and spend some time driving around these areas. I want y'all in marked cars too. Make sure you're seen. If I hear another damn comment about us not doin' anything I'm gonna lose it," he says, walking to the copier with his notebook.

I think back to my interaction at the bar, with the angry man and how I could have ended up with a black eye worse than the one my counter produced. Maybe it will ease everyone's mind seeing a bunch of police cars roaming around. Chief brings Davidson and I two sheets of paper.

"Here's the names of some people who called in saying they've seen Grant and their addresses. We couldn't write everything down. In between y'all's stops at the other locations, pay them a visit and see what you can come up with. Maybe he has a frequent spot he likes to hang out," he says.

"Chief, you ever heard of the Native American Coalition Treaty? asks Davidson.

"Sorta. Not sure why it happened, but I know at some point there were several rival tribes that decided to stop fighting each other or something. My grandaddy loved telling stories about that type of stuff," says Chief. "What does that have to do with any of this?"

Davidson explains the map, and how it's possible that the Grant guy just happened to be in the wrong place at the wrong time.

"It's possible, but we'll let him explain that when we find him," he says, walking out of the office, "Now y'all get out there and find him and his accomplice before they have a chance to do any more harm. Hopefully if we grab him we can put this all behind us. Be safe out there. It ain't like he's just gonna walk in here with his hands up anyways. Be prepared for the worst when he's pinned in a corner."

Davidson and I gather our things and head to the parking lot.

"I call dibs on the Dodge!" he says, referring to the newest patrol car we have, courtesy of a donation from Magnolia. Usually it's used by Chief or for parades since it stays the cleanest. We depart from the station and head into town.

I DECIDE my first stop will be "Lux Boutique" in downtown, where one of the employees had sworn that Grant had came there several times. Unfortunately, they don't have cameras but if I know what kind of clothes he may be wearing, it could help with identification. Lux Boutique is one of way too many in Culver. About ten years ago, a wave of them opened up and they never went away. It's kind of an inside joke that they are all money laundering schemes since they are rarely busy yet take up the most expensive commercial lots, but no one's ever cared to do any digging.

I walk in, and see a few teenage girls gathered at the counter on their phones. I walk up to them, and it isn't until I'm almost right beside them, that they even notice me.

"Uhhhm can I help you?" asks one of the girls, not even looking up from her phone.

"Yes. Were any of you the one who happened to call in

and report that you'd seen the man on the news we are looking for?" I ask, handing them a printout of Grant's mugshot.

"Ohhh yea that's farmer John," says one of the girls.

"Farmer John? Is that what he told you his name was?" I ask.

"Nah," she giggles, "he just looks like he would work on a farm or something…he really gives me the ick."

One of the other girls gasps, "Yaaaas, that man is the CEO of ick."

"What's the ick?" I ask.

The girls all laugh. I guess I'm behind on the slang.

"Like when someone is weird or makes you feel uncomfortable," she says.

"So what did he did he do that…gave you the ick?" I ask.

She looks at the other teens and laughs again, "He just came in and wandered around on the phone a while one time and didn't even buy anything. The next time he like… stood in here for a long time then just bought a few hats."

"When's the last time he was in here?" I ask.

"It's been like four days I think, is he uhh the 'Vampire'?"

The girls giggle again, except this time one of the girls says, "Shut up! That's not funny. That's literally so scary what if he is and now he knows us…" They fall silent.

"You're right, it is scary. He may not be a uh…vampire but he is potentially a very dangerous man. If you see him again, call us immediately. Thank you girls for your time," I say.

I walk away to leave the store, and the girls go back to their phones as if I was never there. Little do they know, they had encountered a person who might be a serial killer. A little more creepy than just the "ick" I'd say. Thankfully he had decided on someone else and spared them.

I pull out and head to my next stop, a small coffee shop. Using this more as an excuse to grab some coffee than actually investigating anything. The owner of that place is known to be a scumbag, and I wouldn't doubt he lied about seeing Grant just for the attention. He owns some apartments too and really fits the "slum lord" stereotype.

As I go to get out of the patrol car, my phone rings. It's Chief.

"Yes sir?"

"I know y'all are busy but be finishing up whatever you're working on and head back to the station. Hargrove wants to brief us within the hour," he says.

"Got it."

* * *

I WONDER how rough this situation must be for someone in her role. The political element of this is something I've never been fond of, and I'm glad I have no interest in ever becoming something like that. I walk into the coffee shop and see Ross Southard, the owner. He smiles and heads over to me.

"I'm guessing you heard that I've seen the suspect in my store and you're here for my statement?" he asks loudly, so the few people in line can hear.

"Of course," I say, walking to the counter. I order a coffee, and turn to him.

He tells me a very obviously inflated story about how Grant came in and haggled him for the price of coffee and sat around using the wifi for too long. He said he eventually complimented him on the taste of the coffee and shook his hand. *Sure, because if was a serial killer on the run, that's exactly what id do... Yea right.* I realize that his sighting is of no significance and my coffee is getting cold. I decide it's time that I go ahead and get back to the station. He writes his cell phone number on the back of a napkin and tells me to give him a call if he can help in any way. I make sure to toss it in the bin outside before getting into my car. I imagine the only "help" he could provide is trading coffee for free advertising. I'm sure he doesn't care about anything other than profits. *Fucking scumbag.*

* * *

PULLING BACK INTO THE STATION, I have to pass up my regular spot, as the entire lot is full. Every patrol car lines the front, with several other cars filling up the exterior lot. I pull to the very back, and make my way inside. The entire office area is filled with officers of both night and day shift along with Chief Hargrove and several individuals I don't recognize. One of which is wearing a polo with "FBI" written on the chest. *Oh shit.* I bet they're going to take this whole thing away from us. Now that technically this can be categorized as the work of a serial killer, it would make sense for them to at least take note of it. As I find a place to sit, Chief Marks walks in, shutting and locking the door behind him.

"That's everyone," he says to Hargrove.

She walks to the front of the board, and clears her throat.

"I'd like to start by saying I appreciate everyone who was able to donate to Sergeant Hamilton's family, and everyone who volunteered to be a part of his arrangements. He was an exemplary officer, and his contributions to this region did not go without notice. The Mayor has teamed up with the art department of Magnolia's community college, and they are commissioning a piece to add to the park in his honor. That being said, I am asking that you all respect his family's wishes and do not speak to any affiliates of the media about his passing. That goes for any of this for now, as this town is up in arms about what they perceive to be a lack of action. Chief Marks has caught me up on where we are overall. I'm here today to inform you of a few things."

Everyone in the room collectively tenses up, bracing themselves for whatever news could have warranted this type of meeting.

She continues, "Firstly, Stacy Larson, the woman with Molly Baxter when she was killed...is dead of an apparent suicide."

I quickly cut my eyes to Davidson, who is staring intently at Hargrove.

"She drove to the mountains of Gatlinburg, Tennessee and took her own life after writing a very long note, detailing her struggles with what she saw that day. I will have Chief Marks let you all read it in your own time. But in one part of the note she says she also had a vivid dream where she saw a police officer in danger, and felt like it was a sign of things to come. I need all of you to make sure you DO NOT let this part get out to the public, understood?" she asks.

All of us nod our heads and continue listening.

"That's all we need is this vampire bullshit to now include the premonition of a random suicidal woman adding to the chaos. If that leaves this room I'm coming for someone's badge. It's important we control what the people hear until we can get this wrapped up," she says, scanning the room for compliance.

"Second, this is Mike Banner, with the Federal Bureau of Investigation. His team has been monitoring the happenings here, and he has a few things to say. Give him your undivided attention." She gestures to a fit younger man, who walks to the front of the room. He stands at least a foot taller than Hargrove. He shakes her hand, and she steps to the side.

"As your Chief stated, I am Mike Banner. My team is tasked with checking into murders that exceed three within a certain time period to evaluate whether or not our physical presence is needed to assist in any way. It is evident that this case fits the criteria, so here I am."

I hear a few murmurs between the officers as Mike pulls a flash drive out of his pocket. He looks at it for a moment, then continues, "However, after reviewing the data your team has so graciously provided me, we will not be coming on site to assist. There is a good and bad element to this determination. On the good side, you won't have to have myself or my team looking over your shoulder. On the bad side, it is very unlikely that you will be successful in your search for the perpetrator of these crimes."

The murmurs in the room fall silent, and a wave of confusion hits me. *Why would the FBI come all the way here just to tell us they aren't going to help?* I look to Chief Marks, and he wears the same confused look as the rest of us.

CHAPTER 21

Mike Banner walks up to Chief Marks and hands him the flash drive.

"I can give you this, though. It holds all the evidence of similar cases we currently have. You will see that yours has been added. Not giving it to you so that you can go out and try to solve this, but more to help you understand the scope of it. I don't want you to think your team here isn't able to figure it out due to lack of ability, as we have also not been able to for a long time," he says, walking back to the front of the room.

"What do you mean similar cases?" Chief Marks asks.

"This may be new to you all, but it isn't a new phenomenon. Over the last twenty-five years, there have been a total of seventeen bodies like this discovered in varying stages of degradation. What is unique to this area is the addition of displaying the bodies in this way. Every other one we have found before has just been in the woods or in the water. We believe this is due to your suspect. He must be an accomplice to the real perpetrator of these heinous acts. He might have been a witness that was coerced along the way, a deranged individual who has been just finding the bodies and displaying them in this fashion for his own personal reasons, or someone who wants to continue these… acts when the original suspect passes away. Based strictly on the timeline of the first bodies found, he she or IT would have to be getting too old to continue," Mike says, drinking from a large hydro flask.

"What you mean, *IT?*" asks Davidson.

Mike looks to Davidson for a moment. "We like to consider all options. It could possibly be an animal or something similar. We have yet to be able to recreate the damage caused to the bodies after years of testing different poisons, weapons and methods. Whatever is causing the deaths in this way has no similarities with anything we've ever seen. In each event we observe, the bodies are progressively worse, then it ends within a few weeks. In seeing your last victim, it would appear the deaths are close to being over. I would assume one to two more before this moves to a different area. We definitely will need to obtain any audio or video recordings Grant Lungston provides when or if you are able to locate him. I will leave your Chief my contact information in the event that something new comes up. I wish you all the best of luck, and I commend the work you have all done. Thanks." He nods to Hargrove and exits the room.

After what feels like an eternity, she stands up.

"I know this seems overwhelming, frustrating and frankly confusing…but I need you all to keep your heads down and continue to work on finding Grant. He is the one thing we have that can help us potentially solve something the fucking FBI can't. Let's do our best. Like I said earlier, not a single word to the media about Stacy, or about the FBI being here. Got it?"

The room is filled with a multitude of "Yes Ma'am's." She and a few other men exit the room. Chief Marks dismisses the night shift crew, with the understanding that they could come in two hours later than normal. He starts directing other officers, and tells Davidson and I to continue working down the list we had started, and to be sure to report back to him with anything noteworthy. I exit the office and walk back out to the parking lot. I get a text from Davidson that reads:

> Meet me at the Food Mart parking lot.

> Okay, on the way.

* * *

ON THE SHORT drive I recollect the last hour or so. Firstly, the suicide of Stacy wasn't much of a surprise to me. Most people struggle with the aftermath of traumatic events, but this one was pretty unique and to be completely honest, Stacy did not seem like she would carry the weight of something like that well. Of course it is unfortunate either way, but the news hitting me wasn't something that took my breath away. Maybe I'm growing cold to that type of thing, or maybe it's just because of the information that followed. I've never been around an FBI agent before so maybe that interaction was normal, but it just seemed so odd. It seemed like he really wasn't interested in even trying to figure it out. Almost like he was intentionally discouraging us from trying to proceed. I pull into the Food Mart, and park beside Davidson.

"So what the fuck was that about?" he asks out of his window. He must have been thinking along the same lines as me on the way over.

"Was just thinking the same thing."

"I bet they almost got this shit figured out, and they don't want us taking the credit for it. They've been tryin' to figure it out for two and a half decades, they'd look dumb if some little ass city cops closed it for them," he says, lighting a cigarette.

I hadn't even considered that as a possibility, but it makes sense. I imagine a press briefing where the FBI admits that after their unlimited budget and resources had been exhausted trying to figure out this case, it all came to a close when two random detectives in a no name town figured it out.

"Well I guess we need to get on finding this guy then. Let's see if we can beat them to it," I say.

"Yea. Let's haul ass and bring him in. I hate that about that girl though. Wish she could've pulled through it," he says, flicking his cigarette to the ground. "Holler if you hear something useful."

He rolls his window up, and takes off. Turning out of the parking lot I catch a glimpse of the the WCDX van passing by, heading in the direction of the police station. I'm sure they are hoping to add just a little more fear to the hearts of the community with the station as a backdrop. At least they weren't there earlier listening in. I can't imagine what they'll do when they figure out about Stacy. Especially the dream… *I know it's likely unrelated, but what if her dreams were like mine?* It would honestly make me feel a little better if I wasn't the only one experiencing them.

* * *

THE NEXT THREE and a half hours were wildly unsuccessful. Everyone's story was the same. "Oh I just think I saw him walk by at the store." Or, "Yea I think it could've been him, but I was going the other way." I get Chief's reasoning though, as just being out and about garnered mostly positive interactions. Only a few people remained angry or seemed genuinely mad after my conversation with them. I just feel like I wasted a lot of time driving around instead of…well I'm not really sure what I would even be doing. I decide I'll take a break and call Evelyn and see what she's up to. It rings several times before going to voicemail. She must be busy. A few moments later, my phone vibrates and it's a text from her.

> Sorry, I'm really busy right now. Is everything okay?

> Yes, just bored. No luck at work today. Hope you aren't busy later and can give me a call.

She doesn't respond. I guess she's decided I wasn't worth her time. Maybe she'll have a change of heart. Either way, I understand. I briefly consider running her name when I get back to the station to try and understand who she is a little better, but decide against it. *Don't be a fucking creep Damon.* How would I explain it to anyone if they saw me looking her up? "Yea don't worry it's totally normal I'm just doing a background check on a woman I met at a bar. She seems nice but I'm looking for red flags while doing something everyone would also consider a red flag!" *What if I learn something about her that sucks? What if she's married? What if she has a whole family and this is her little fling that she'll keep a secret for the rest of her life? What if I just do my job and stay out of this hypothetical loop of events that may never even happen?*

I shake my head quickly, trying to fling the "what ifs" out of my brain.

* * *

I LOOK to my list that Chief Marks made for us, and cross out the final name. I'm sure other people have called in since then with the same, useless statements. I hope we don't have to follow up on all of them the same way we did today. This seems more like a dog and pony show now anyways.

What was it that the guy said again? We have one or two more murders before it's...gone? What did he mean by that? Does the person ever stop? Have they been doing this for twenty-five years, or is this a copycat? Is there some magic number where they decide that they'll take a break for a while? I should've asked more questions, but I didn't want to bring any unwanted attention to myself with this black eye and all. I wonder what's on that flash drive they gave Chief. Maybe if I get back before shift is over he'll show me. I put the patrol car in drive, and head to the station.

* * *

ON THE DRIVE in I realize that Evelyn has text me back:

> Sorry! I'll call you when I have a little time. If
> not, want to hang out tomorrow night after
> work? I can bring some food and we can
> hang out at your place if that's okay?

I smile. *That's exactly what I want.* I think that would clear my head a little and allow me to get to know her a little better in a more comfortable place. I feel the weight of the disappointment I felt earlier slip away. I go to respond when I see brake lights in front of me light up. I slam my brakes hard, sending my phone flying into the floor board.

"What the fuck!" I say, as the tail lights dim and the car pulls forward. I now notice that the car was just stopping at a stop sign, and I was too distracted by my phone. They were probably stressing because a cop car is behind them and I'm back here texting. *Wait...*

I realize that the car in front of me is also a patrol car, but it's very dirty. Must be a regular officer heading back to the station as well. I wonder where they'd be to get it so dirty. Their day was likely more fun than mine. We come up to a red-light and I let off the gas, but the car in front of me doesn't and goes right through the light. *What the hell? Why would they do that?* No lights on or anything so they aren't responding to a call. I turn my lights on and go through the intersection. At least now if people noticed that they'll think we were headed to something serious. We approach a stop sign and the patrol car again blows right through it. I look in the back window of the car and see its identifying number. I grab the radio mic in my car, and squeeze the button.

"Forty-seven, what's the emergency?" I ask. No response. "Forty-seven, what's going on?" Again, no response.

My phone rings in the floor board. I slide it back with the heel of my boot, and grab it. It's Chief Marks.

"Yes sir?"

"What the hell are you talking about on the radio?" he asks angrily.

"I'm behind car forty-seven and it has ran three intersections now with no lights but he isn't speeding. Trying to figure out what's going on," I say as the car runs through another light.

"You gotta be fuckin' kidding me. Are you sure it's forty-seven?" he asks.

"Positive, why?" I ask.

"That's Sergeant Hamilton's car is why. Put your God damn lights on and don't let it out of your sight!"

Chills run down my spine and my hands start to sweat. I switch the lights on, and get closer to the car.

"Looks like he might be on his way to the station. We're

about a mile out. Get everyone outside, just in case. If this is Grant there's no fucking telling what he's planning," I say, wondering if I should prevent him from making it there in case he plans to ram into it, or worse. *I'm willing to bet that if I spin him out he will come out of that car shooting. He's killed one officer and I doubt he'd just let me take him in without a fight.*

I unclip the pistol on my hip and take a deep breath. *I hope this goes smoothly.*

"Play it smart, Damon. Everyone will be watching. Get ready for whatever he's got." Chief hangs up, as the patrol car makes a left turn onto the road that leads to the station. As it turns I catch a glimpse of the driver. It's definitely Grant Lungston, and he has a frantic look on his face. He speeds up, and I speed up to his rear bumper, ready to spin him out if he tries to run into the building. I see several officers taking up position outside the station, weapons drawn. I pull up quickly to the rear quarter panel as we get around fifty yards from the parking lot. Just as I'm about to bury the front of my car into the side of his to send him spinning, he puts the flashers on and slows down. He rolls his window down, and puts both of his open hands out into the air. *I guess Chief was wrong about him turning himself in. Unless this is a set up.*

He slows to a stop, roughly ten feet from the curb at the front of the station. I stop right behind him.

"PUT THE CAR IN PARK AND GET OUT WITH YOUR FUCKING HANDS UP!" Yells Davidson with his gun drawn.

He complies and is on the ground and swarmed by a sea of officers in seconds. I look in all directions, scanning the surrounding buildings to ensure this isn't an ambush involving the other person…or people. *We have only estab-lished that it was AT LEAST two people. I never thought to rule out a group. This seems shady...* I walk up as an officer is reading Grant his Miranda Rights. They have him sitting on his butt on the curb. He looks like he hasn't slept in a week, and the beard he had in the security footage is gone.

"I'M SORRY! I'M SORRY! PLEASE JUST PUT ME IN JAIL, PLEASE!" he says, tears falling onto his shirt.

"Oh we'll put you there you piece of shit. Don't worry bout that," says Chief Marks. A few officers pick him up by his underarms and carry him into the station. I look again to everything around the station to ensure that this isn't a set up. *This seems too good to be true. Why would he just offer himself to us like this?*

CHAPTER 22

6:30 P.M.

"I am Detective Damon McKay, and this is Detective Earl Davidson. I am informing you that this conversation will be recorded. State your name for us, please."

Grant shakes and leans forward. "Grant. Grant Lungston. Look, I don't give a fuck about the formalities, just please put me in jail."

Davidson and I look up to the two way mirror behind Grant, where most of the entire department waits eagerly to see what this man has to say.

"With what you've done, we aren't skipping any process or procedure. We ain't letting you get out on some technicality here. Sorry bud, you have to do this our way. Do you have an attorney, or would you like for us to provide you one?" asks Davidson firmly.

"Whatever then, I don't care. I'll talk to you but I'm not

doing it today. I know you have to hold me at least twenty-four hours. So for now, I'm not saying shit. I'll talk till my lungs give out tomorrow, though. I just need sleep and I need to be safe. I have been up for at least two days…or three I don't even fucking know. Just please give me some water and throw me in a cell, I'm begging you," Grant says, then pantomimes zipping his lips shut and lays his head down on the table.

Chief Marks calmly walks into the interrogation room. He reaches over and clicks the recorder off. He makes a hand motion to the two way mirror, then squats down beside Grant.

"YOU'RE FUCKIN' STUPID IF YOU THINK YOU CAN JUST TROT IN HERE AND TELL US HOW IT'S GONNA GO AFTER WHAT YOU'VE DONE. I OUGHT TO KNOCK YOUR ASS OUT RIGHT NOW!" says Chief, startling Davidson and I.

Grant raises his head momentarily and glances at Chief for just a second before burying his head back into his arms on the table.

Chief then puts his left hand under Grant's chest and his right foot behind the leg of his chair, then violently flips his entire body backwards. The chair and Grant hit the ground hard. Grant groans and rolls over onto his knees and starts to get up. Before he can stand fully, Chief pushes him backwards against the wall, holding both of his shoulders. I jump up to try to pull him off before this gets out of hand.

"BOY WE COULD'VE PUT SO MANY GOD DAMN HOLES IN YOU OUT THERE THAT YOU'D GET CONFUSED WITH FUCKING SWISS CHEESE AND NO ONE WOULD'VE BAT AN EYE. YOU'RE LUCKY YOU'RE STILL BREATHING, YOU HEAR ME? YOU OWE IT TO US TO TELL US WHAT HAPPENED. YOU BETTER GET TO FUCKIN TALKIN!"

Davidson and I manage to pull Chief off of him and hold him back for a moment. Grant seems totally unfazed, and calm other than his ruffled hair and bloodshot eyes.

"I understand your anger sir, but hurting me solves nothing. I am not afraid of you, or any of you in fact. Scream at me all you'd like, but that won't bring anyone back. I will tell you everything you need to know, I guarantee it. It just won't be today. I have to get rest. You are right, I owe you much more than an explanation, and you will get every bit of information I have. Just please, let me sleep," says Grant.

Chief Hargrove bursts into the room.

"Marks, go to your office, NOW!" She points to Davidson and I and commands, "You two, get him in a cell ASAP. Then tell every day shift officer to go home. Nights will watch him all night long. He will be waiting here for you in the morning. Be here at seven with your heads on straight. Not a word about this, okay?"

"Yes ma'am."

Davidson and I grab Grant and lead him out of the room. Walking down the hall, we see all the day shift officers walking out of the listening room. Looks like we won't have to tell them anything, as they likely were watching the entire situation unfold. A night shift officer meets up with us at the holding cell. He will be the first on watch for the night. As we remove Grant's handcuffs and lock the cell door, he begins to sob. He flops down on the small cot in the corner and looks up to us, hands clasped together.

"Thank you! Thank you both! You have no idea how fucking happy I am to be in this cell!" he says, burying his face into the small pillow and sobbing harder.

"What a fucking mess," says the night shift officer, sitting down in a small chair a few feet away from the cell.

"Glad I don't have to do that," I say, looking back to the

officer as we walk away. Grant's sobs echo throughout the entire main hallway.

"Damn right. I can't believe Chief went off like that. Never seen that from him. Scary as hell," says Davidson.

We walk through the main office and can hear Chief Hargrove's muffled yelling from back where Chief Mark's office is.

"Yea, and it sounds like he's paying for it now," I say, grabbing my bag.

"Let's get the hell outta here, see ya at seven," says Davidson, darting out of the side door. I follow him out, and head home.

8:45 P.M.

FINISHING UP MY DINNER, I look to Daisy for advice.

"What would make him come to us, just to then not say anything? Maybe he overestimated our efforts to get him and decided he had no chance? I just don't get it. What kind of freak says that they are happy to be in jail? What do you think?" I ask, putting my plate on the floor for her to lick clean.

I rack my brain with scenarios that would explain Grant's reasoning for delivering himself to us. It's possible that it's a diversion for his accomplice, or maybe he plans to rat the other person out for a lesser sentence. If it was to buy his accomplice time to escape, they could be halfway across the country by now. Either way, I guess I'll find out in the morning. I take a swig of the small whiskey bottle I picked up on the way home, and burp loud enough to distract Daisy from her scraps for a moment. Best case scenario, he spills everything on his involvement, who the accomplice is and everything we're curious about so we can close this out. I feel good about it. I do hate the thought of a sick fuck like him getting some type of lesser sentence for that, though. I hope he gets the death penalty, or life in prison. *I'm not sure which is worse.*

Even the FBI agent had doubts we would get him, and now we will get to interrogate him. That's at least a win, even though he turned himself in. I'm just ready to get some answers, and get it over with. I might see if Chief will let me take some vacation after the dust settles so I can decompress. I feel like I've been running on fumes since the day this started. I wonder if Evelyn could provide a little perspective. I would ask her, but she never called back. I guess whatever had her too busy earlier was enough to take over her night. I wonder what she could be doing.

I text her:

So can I expect to see you tomorrow night?

I finish off my bottle and toss it in the garbage, along with the now cleaned paper plate from my food. I pat Daisy on her head, and head to my bedroom. My phone vibrates. It's a text from Evelyn:

Of course! Drinks on me! I'm going to sleep soon though. I hope you have better luck tomorrow! Goodnight! XoXo.

I smile at the thought of her walking up to my door, drinks in hand and that same messy bun from the other day. Hopefully tomorrow's interrogation will go smoothly, and I might be able to sneak out a little early to be able to spend as much time as possible with her. I decide now is a good time to lay down, and lock up for the night.

7:00 A.M.

DAVIDSON and I sit patiently in the interrogation room, awaiting Chief Hargrove to bring Grant in. She decided that she would fill in for Chief Marks for the day. I'm guessing after his outburst yesterday, she didn't give him a choice in the matter. Hopefully she will understand, and not punish him too harshly.

"He better not be bullshittin' about telling us everything. If he made that whole scene yesterday just to lead us on this ain't gonna go well for him," says Davidson, sipping his coffee.

"Surely he wouldn't go through the hassle of turning himself in just to lay down on us. I'm holding on to hope that this is the home stretch," I say.

"Anything to get those damn vultures out of our parking lot," he says, referencing the WCDX crew who beat us all to the station this morning.

I bet those guys camped out all night after they announced Grant was in custody.

Hargrove and another officer walk in, leading Grant to the seat opposite us. She removes his cuffs, and gives him a bottle of water.

"Ready to talk?" she asks.

"Yes," he says, drinking half the water at once.

"Hang tight," she says to Davidson and I. "I'm going to lead this one. I just want you both in here as witnesses so you can testify if need be. Don't take it personally."

I don't take it personally at all. As a matter of fact I really just want him to spill what he's got so we can all stop stressing about this.

She exits the room, and quickly returns with a rolling

188

chair from one of the offices. She begins with the standard formalities and Grant complies to answering our questions. His posture is different today, he seems a little more together and confident. He is sitting straight up, and appears to be in the right mind for questioning.

"So now that we have that out of the way, and you've chosen to waive an attorney for whatever reason, I'm going to ask you a few direct questions before allowing you to tell your side of everything, is that okay?" she asks Grant.

He nods.

She continues, "Did you murder Lewis Parley?"

"No."

Hargrove rolls her chair closer to the table. "Did you murder Molly Baxter?"

"No."

"Did you murder Sergeant Walker Hamilton?"

He pauses for a moment, confident gaze fading slightly.

"No...No I didn't," he says.

"Are you sure? It seems like you hesitated there. Why is that?" she asks.

"I -I didn't murder anyone. I would just have to tell you everything first," he says.

She looks to the two way mirror.

"Marcus, bring me the box I gave you," she says loudly. An officer brings in a large bankers box and sits in on the ground beside Hargrove. She opens it up, and pulls out a small piece of black fabric in a clear bag. She slides it to him.

"Do you recognize this?" she asks.

"Yes."

"Explain to me what it is please," she says.

"It's just a piece of fabric barrier I got from the co-op. I used it at all of the crime scenes."

"Why? So you're saying you *WERE* at the crime scenes, but want me to believe you didn't kill them? What do you mean when you say you *USED* the fabric? In what way?" she asks.

"Yes. I was there… But…I really would just have to explain it all before any of it will make sense, I'm sorry."

"Okay. What about this then?" She produces a large black hook, and places it on the table.

"I bought a bunch of those at a yard sale the first day I was here. I also used those at the crime scenes."

She stares at him for a moment, then pulls another item out. It's the box of cigarettes found in the truck. She slides them to him, "And these?" she asks.

He picks up the bag and stares at them a moment. He closes his eyes and breathes in deeply. "Yes, these are mine."

Hargrove takes the bags and places them back into the box. She then pulls out a large manilla envelope, and pulls out a stack of laminated pictures. She grabs the one on top, and slides it over to him. It's a picture of Lewis Parley hanging from the ceiling of the church.

"Did you do this? Did you hang him up like this?" she asks.

"I hung him up there… but again, I did not kill him."

"How'd you get him there?" she asks.

"I used one of the ladders from his property to get up to the ceiling. I anchored three pulleys into the joist, then pulled him up. Once I got him up there, all I had to do was remove the pulleys and clean up. I plugged the holes with a plastic cap that was the same color as the ceiling. I assumed, correctly it appears, that you never found them," he says.

I think back to the scene. When we were there, I never even looked anywhere but the body, and the beam it was hanging from. Those pulley holes are likely what weakened the beam to the point of failure.

She slides another picture towards him. A picture of Molly Baxter on the floor of the gym.

"What about her?" she asks, leaning back in her chair.

"I drilled holes in the floor with a hammer drill from Lewis's house, then used anchor bolt epoxy on the back of the hooks to secure her to the floor. I already had the hooks in her beforehand."

"Why? Why go through all that trouble? Why even show us? Why not leave them lying in the woods or wherever?" she asks.

"To cause confusion. The more confused you were, the more time I had," he says, leaning towards the table.

"More time for what?" she asks.

"Time to… Well you'll just have to let me start from the beginning really…"

"Okay. I'm assuming Sergeant Hamilton was hung up in a similar fashion as Lewis Parley?" she asks, sliding the last picture to him.

He leans back in his chair, and looks away. "Yes, mostly. I had to use a smaller ladder that was already there, and it was more difficult. Due to…his *condition*."

"Can you at least tell me where the three of them were killed?" she asks, putting the pictures back into the envelope.

"Sure. Lewis was killed in his home, in his bed. The girl was killed in the backyard near the barn. The cop…The cop was killed in a lodge up in the woods."

Hargrove stares across at him, as if attempting to read his mind. The energy in the room is intense, and I exhale. I don't know how long I had been holding my breath. I'm not sure what I expected him to say, but listening to him coldly respond with these details was not it. He didn't seem to be remorseful, but I could tell that something was more troubling to him about Sergeant Hamilton's murder. Maybe it was the state of the body, or how hard it was to get there, but something was different about his reactions. He still hasn't explained HOW they were killed yet, though.

"Okay. Thank you for providing that information. Your compliance will be noted in your trial. Now I need you to tell me, did the same person murder Lewis, Molly, and Sergeant Hamilton?" Hargrove asks.

"Yes."

"If not you, then who?" she asks, leaning forward.

I hold my breath again, mind racing with possible names. *Would it be someone we knew? What if it was Preston Walsh this entire time and we just let him walk out?*

"It's not that simple. I have to tell you everything first," he says. His leg begins to tap under the table.

"I believe that it is that simple. Just tell me the name. They won't know you told right now. We can have them taken to another jail and they won't see you until your trial. Your assistance in bringing this person in can be the difference in a lengthy prison sentence and something shorter and more manageable. Might even be something short enough that you can still have a life after you're out," she says, leaning her body hard against the table.

"No. No it isn't. First of all, there's no way you could ever bring …uh…him in. Trust me. Second, he…he doesn't have a name. This is too complicated to begin with, and there's no way I'll be able to explain it any other way than from the start. None of you will probably understand it at that point anyways, but at least I will have said what I need to say." His leg tapping stops and he sighs.

"Okay. I will let you start from the beginning then. To clarify you did mean HIM right? The murderer is a man?" she asks.

"Yes. Well…kind of. Not like a man like me or them," he says, glancing at Davidson and I for the first time since the interrogation started, "More like in appearance… but not *LIKE* us. Again, I have to tell it all first, please."

"Have there been any other murders besides these three?" She asks.

"No… Well, I-I I'm not really sure… Again I NEED you to let me tell you everything for anything to make sense."

Hargrove looks quickly to us, finishes off her coffee, and stands up.

"Okay first, I'm going to the restroom. When I come back I expect you to tell us everything. From whenever the beginning is, up until yesterday. I don't want to leave this room until I know everything there is about this…man. Understood?"

"Yes. I can't make you believe me, but I promise I will be as detailed and concise as possible without keeping you here all day… Can you bring me some more water please?" he asks.

"Oh, don't worry. We have plenty of time."

CHAPTER 23

Grant twists both ways in his chair, popping his back. He breathes in deeply, then exhales for an uncomfortably long time. He sits up straight in the chair, and clears his throat.

"Well, as I'm sure you know... I'm from the Northwest. Washington specifically. I was born and raised there."

Hargrove interrupts, "By the beginning you don't mean the beginning of your life, right? What you're saying will provide context to the crimes and not just act as your vocal autobiography...correct?"

Grant reaches for the water and takes a sip, wiping his mouth before saying, "No no. I am telling you only what's relevant."

"Proceed, sorry."

"So, I'm not sure if you all would be aware, but there is a rich history of Native American culture in Washington. Most people don't think of it when they think of that state, but it's a reality. Thirty or so federally recognized tribes, and more that were either too small to be noteworthy, or too old to figure out," he says.

Hargrove shifts uncomfortably in her chair. I'm willing to bet her patience is wearing thin and she's thinking that he's going to drag this out far longer than necessary.

He continues, "Growing up, my father always told me the amazing stories from the different tribes. The stories they used to scare the young into compliance, the ones to explain their religions, weather, and so on. The ones that used to interest me the most, were always the stories of things that they were afraid of, or couldn't ascribe a certain god or energy to. Their mysteries and questions about things was always so fascinating. I took so much of an interest in them, that when I was older and got a car, I'd drive to different reservations on the weekends and hang out. When kids my age were out drinking and getting in trouble, I was learning about the ceremonies and culture of whatever reservation would allow me in."

"Are you of Native American lineage?" asks Hargrove.

"Aren't we all, just a little?" he smiles and leans back, "But no, not really. My father was born in France, and my mother was from Montreal. Dad used to say I was 'French and a half'."

"Okay, so what does all of this have to do with murders on the other side of the United States?" she asks, obviously not interested in any of the quirks of his upbringing.

"Well." He leans forward and his smile fades. "In spending all of this time on reservations, I heard thousands and thousands of stories, and got to see many ceremonies depicting different Gods, seasons, etc. For each reservation most of them were similar themes, which makes sense due to their location. As far as the things they feared, it was the same. Each tribe had their own twist on different monsters depicting different mysteries to them that could now, be easily explained away with weather phenomenon or things from western culture that they hadn't had time to adapt to...

except for one. One of their monsters was exactly the same. No matter how far I traveled within the state, its depiction was EXACTLY the same, as well as its story."

"And what…*monster* was that?" she asks.

"Some tribes call them *Feyollocuani* or just *Feyo*. Some refuse to speak of their name, and only show their likeness in the form of body paint and costume. They don't really know much about their biology, but they believe they are somewhat of a male counterpart for the female *Teyollocuani* in indigenous Mesopotamian culture."

"Okay, and what makes the *Feyo* so special?" she asks, sighing to indicate that she is not interested in folklore.

Grant's expression grows colder. "Feyollocuani is a soul eater. All of the tribes knew of the existence of them. Like I said, there was no difference in their depiction either. Each tribe I went to depicted them as solid black, slender and with grey eyes. The ceremonies would have the Feyo come and dance around the young, then the old would come and pretend to lead them away. In talking to elders of the tribes, this represented the only way they could keep them away which was to sacrifice their old or injured to them. I obviously became very interested. I saved up money to travel to other reservations outside of the west, to see if they had similar stories."

"Did they?" she asks.

"Yes," says Grant. "Every single tribe as far east as Virginia has their own tales and ceremonies dedicated to the Feyollocuani, and every time I've seen them, they are exactly the same. They all say that way back in earlier years they would come in groups and erase entire populations almost in an instant, leaving nothing behind."

I think back now to my dreams, and the pictures that Stacy was able to take. That's what it showed, and that's what I saw. The black body, and grey eyes. I am becoming more confused the longer Grant speaks. *Is he saying someone was inspired by the stories of this monster to play dress up and kill people?* I glance to Davidson who seems the be sharing the same thoughts. I can tell that he really wants to ask questions, and is having a tough time keeping himself from interrupting.

"Okay so evil Native American monsters that killed a bunch of people hundreds of years ago…got it," says Hargrove in an annoyed tone.

"The Feyollocuani aren't Native American. The tribes all say they were here long before us."

"Well where did they go? Why do they speak of them only being in the past? Did they kill them somehow?" she asks.

"They don't exactly know. Some tribes claimed to have killed some, and some trapped them in caves. Some tribes said they all just went away one day. If they can't feed, they become too weak to move and go dormant. They usually either burn or bury them if they are trapped so that they could not escape. Some tribes said that if you found one and freed it, it would spare you and give you eternal life, and others said it would turn you into a Feyollocuani yourself," Grant says, then finishes his water.

"Okay, that's an interesting campfire story and all, but how is that relevant?" asks Hargrove, visibly frustrated.

Grant leans towards the table and squints his eyes, picking up on Hargrove's mood. "It's relevant because Feyollocuani is what has killed the people in your town, and that is what will continue to kill until it gets tired. Then it will rest, and then it will kill again, as long as the buildings stand, and long after we are dead and forgotten. With each kill, it becomes stronger and more capable."

A silence takes over the room. All of us simultaneously trying to process what Grant has said. Hargrove lets out a long sigh and puts her head in her hands. She stands up, and motions for Davidson and I to exit the interrogation room with her. We walk to the end of the hallway.

* * *

"This is shit. The whole thing is shit," she says, putting her hands on her hips.

"What do you mean?" I ask.

"The media has these people thinking we have a vampire on the loose. Now we have a man in there telling us it's actually an ancient monster or something. If this gets out, Culver will be the laughing stock of the entire country. This might be our jobs if we can't figure out what is actually going on here," she says.

"I believe him," says Davidson, putting his hands up, "Not the part where a dang Feyo…uh Feyo…loo coo or whatever is doin' it, but prolly some psycho dressed up like one. He prolly saw how fuckin' fired up about that thing Grant was, and found a way to convince him to help kill those people. Bet he thinks since he helped it, it will make him immortal or somethin'."

Hargrove bites her fingernails for a moment. "You know, that actually makes sense. He's interested enough about this that he's traveled across the country for years. It isn't too far out to assume he would be willing to believe it was real. He seems just deranged enough to want to try and pull it off. I bet he finally saw through the bullshit and that's why he's here now, to turn the guy in. I'm going to the restroom again and we can let him finish up."

She walks down the hall to the restroom, so Davidson and I take this opportunity to do the same. While at the urinal, Davidson asks, "I know it's just a story and all… but what if that shit he's talkin' bout is real?"

"I guess we're fucked then, but it's more likely that I'll be the next president of the United States," I say.

Davidson laughs and we head back to the interrogation room. Just before we make it in, we hear a loud "HEY!" Come from the lobby. We turn around, and standing in the doorway is Devin Stevens. He has a revolver in his hand, and begins to walk our way.

"TAKE ME TO HIM!" he says, closing the distance.

I put my hands up slowly, as I hear other officers taking note of what is happening. "Take you to who, Devin? Put the gun down please," I say.

"TO THAT FUCKING COWARD THAT KILLED MOLLY, BRO! I KNOW HE'S IN THERE!"

"Devin, trust me man, this isn't how you want this to go. Molly wouldn't have wanted this," I say, hearing a few officers murmur behind us, likely attempting to posture theirselves for a clean shot if Devin were to advance any further.

"YOU DON'T KNOW WHAT SHE WOULD'VE WANTED BRO, TAKE ME TO HIM SO I CAN BLOW HIS FUCKING HEAD OFF!"

"You know I can't do that, Devin. Just put the gun down. Let us make sure he spends the rest of his life in prison," I say.

"Sure, bro… What about me though? I have to fucking deal with this forever. WHAT ABOUT ME?" Devin puts the revolver against the side of his head and closes his eyes before falling to his knees.

I use this opportunity to slowly walk forward. "Devin, don't go out like this. You're right to say I wouldn't know what Molly would have wanted, but I promise you it would not be this. You have a long life to live. Live twice as good, for her. Just because she isn't here anymore, doesn't mean she's not with you. She needs you to carry on."

Devin begins to cry, "But it's just not fair bro. I'm so

fucking lonely. I miss her so fucking much bro I can't deal with this pain…"

I kneel down in front of him, hearing the officers shuffle behind me. *If I can just get my hand on that revolver…* "Listen, man. We have great resources here to help you get your head back right. I promise we can help you. Just please, give me the gun."

He looks at me, tears pouring down his face. I see his finger twitch on the trigger, and I wince. He lets out a long breath, and hands the revolver to me. Officers pour around me and put him in handcuffs. I take a deep breath and unload the revolver, placing all six rounds on the receptionist's desk.

"Thank you, Devin," I say as the officers take him to the holding cell.

"Good job, buddy," says Davidson, patting me on the back, "Now let's get in here and finish this interrogation."

We walk back into the interrogation room to Grant, who has no Idea how lucky he is that Devin wasn't able to get to him. My heart is beating out of my chest. *I'm lucky too. I'm not sure how much more death I can take seeing. I'm glad Devin didn't pull that trigger.* I focus on my breathing to get my heart rate back down.

* * *

"Okay, Grant. You can continue now," says Hargrove.

He runs his hands through his hair, and leans back. "Doesn't matter really, does it? You already don't believe me, I can tell."

"I believe that *YOU* believe that this thing is real, and that's all that matters right now. Tell us how you ended up here, and how we can stop it," she says.

"Okay. Just trust me though. It *IS* real. I've seen it. It's why I am even in this tiny ass town to begin with. I was with a

Chesapeake tribe in Virginia six months ago. Their Chief told me about a story of a trapped Feyo in northern Texas. I asked him if I could see it, and he warned me against it but I was curious. He told me there was a keeper of stories in Oklahoma I would have to consult first before I could be shown. I went to her, and she refused to let me see it. She said it was too close to their tribe to risk it, but that there was another that could be viewed in the south. I was pissed, having traveled so far to be told no. I tried to find it on my own, and she found out and banned me from their reservation. I did some digging and found out about a Choctaw reservation in Mississippi that might help. So I went there. They told me about three different ones, but would not guide me to it for fear of cursing their tribe. They did give me the rough location of two of them though," he says, rubbing his eyes.

"Did you see them?" asks Hargrove.

"I couldn't find the first one. Either it had been buried, destroyed, or freed. But when I came here, I found out about the Coalition Treaty."

Davidson and I share a quick glance, remembering the triangle on the map he had discovered.

"What's that?" asks Hargrove.

"It took me a while to figure out, but there were three major tribes in this area about three-hundred and fifty years ago that constantly disputed over land and crops. Several large scale battles happened over things as simple as who would be considered the owner of specific trees or creeks. Then, they formed a coalition. Went from hating each other to shaking hands overnight," he says.

"Why's that?"asks Hargrove, now leaning forward.

"Feyollocuani. It was pretty well detailed in one of the books I had uh.. stolen from a preservation center that had some literature on things like that...Anyways, a Feyo had begun to terrorize this area. Killing dozens of people, taking out entire families. The Chiefs of the tribes got together and had their best warriors go into the forest to try and kill it, but they were unsuccessful, and lost many men. They made a council to try and find a way and kill it. They consulted with other tribes and finally devised a trap where a fast young man would lure the Feyo to a specific spot in the woods, where a small group would trap it with ropes and tie it to a tree."

"Did it work?" asks Davidson, obviously no longer able to keep his curiosity at bay.

"Yes. The trap worked, and they used several horses to pull the ropes tight, then filled it full of arrows and sat the tree on fire. For a few days they repeated this process until the Feyo was no longer moving. Then they put the Feyo into the burned tree trunk, and bound it with ropes so he couldn't come out. They then planted a cluster of trees around the burned one. They labeled that area in the woods off limits to all tribes until the end of time."

Davidson shifts uncomfortably in his chair. He must be superstitious, as he seems bothered by the story.

Grant continues, "So, I went looking for it. I went through someone's farm, the next town over. Where it was at on the map was almost impossible to get to. When I finally found it, I had to leave and go back to a store and get a saw. I could see the old, burned tree in between two other trees that had grown up around it. It was like the trees twisted themselves together around it in an odd dance. Almost like the trees knew they had to keep the Feyo trapped. The next day I went and cut some of the dead tree away and was able to look down into it, and I saw it. It was bound with ropes, and had a sack over its head. I realized one of his feet was actually sticking out of an opening at the bottom. I started to cut the trees away at that spot, and I was able to easily reach it then. I was able to cut the ropes away, and when I removed the bag... Its eyes were open."

I look to Davidson, and he is starting intently at Grant, as is Hargrove. I close my eyes for a moment and try to imagine what meeting something like that, alone in the woods would be like. As I imagine walking up to that tree...that tree that seems familiar for some reason. *Have I seen it before? Was it the tree from my dream?* Grant speaking dissolves my train of thought.

"It didn't move though. Even after I poked it with a stick. So I thought it must be dead or too dormant to move. I stared at it for a while and thought about maybe taking it out of the tree somehow, but I just didn't have the equipment. It was getting dark so I decided to just abandon it. I thought I might come back the next day and take some pictures when it was sunny so I could show a few tribes the next time I was there. I walked back into the field that I came from, and as I walked past some cows I heard one of them make the craziest noise... I turned around and saw the Feyo with his hands around a cow's head. He was crouched awkwardly, but staring directly at me. After a second I realized it had killed the cow, and it stood up a little straighter and just stared at me for a moment. It walked slowly towards another cow and did the same thing. It touched its head and the cow just...fell."

"Hold on, you're saying you watched this thing kill two cows with its hands? How?" asks Hargrove.

"Yea. Thats just how they...*feed*. Some of the tribes say the Feyo have to eat with their hands because they were cursed for speaking against the gods. They really don't know why they do it that way outside of the stories. It isn't like they could just ask them... Anyways, with the first cow it was just a tiny hole it left behind, but with the second it was a little bigger," he says, using his pinky to represent the size of the hole.

"Then what? You just stood there?"

"Yes. I was terrified, but I didn't know what to do. All of the stories the tribes told never were from first hand accounts so I didn't know if running was an option, or if since I had freed it, if it would follow me around. All of the animals on the farm were going crazy, and I turned around because I heard a horse running nearby. When I turned back, the Feyo was gone. I decided then was a good time to get the hell out of there."

"So you're sayin' this is real like… for *REAL*? That don't make no damn sense!" says Davidson.

Hargrove reaches over and puts her hand on Davidson's wrist, and shoots him a scolding look. "Sorry," he says, slumping down a little in his chair.

"I didn't believe it at first either," Grant says. "But the next day I wanted to go back. I went back near that farm but there were a ton of people, so I went further down the road and saw that there was another road that leads directly to the woods. As soon as I got out of my car though, an older man saw me. His name was Lewis. His house was right by where the road was and he asked what I was doing. I told him I just wanted to explore the woods a little. He told me to come up to his house and he would give me a good flashlight to use, since the woods were super dark. He was a really nice man."

"So what, you lead him to the uh… Feyo in the woods?" asks Hargrove.

"No. I took the flashlight he gave me and went looking for it. Lewis went back up to his house. I looked all day, but couldn't find him. Nowhere near the tree or anything. When I came out of the woods it was in the late afternoon. I went to go return the flashlight, but when I knocked on the door… he didn't answer. I assumed he had went to sleep, or just didn't care to interact with me again. So I left the light on his back porch and walked back down the yard. About halfway down, something told me to turn back to the house. When I looked back, I saw the bedroom light on upstairs…and the Feyo looking out at me. I ran inside, screaming for the man but he didn't respond. I ran upstairs, expecting to see the Feyo looking back at me, but all I saw was the man laying down, with a hole in his head." Grant shifts uncomfortably in his chair.

"What did you do then? Why didn't you call the police?" asks Hargrove.

"As if anyone would believe that. I was already in the man's house, and he was dead. It wouldn't look good for me, so I went out front and decided I would put him in the back of his truck until I could figure out what I was going to do. It took me a while because he was so heavy. I looked all over the house but never found the Feyo. I decided I would clean the house so that if anyone showed up, it was like he was just gone somewhere. I don't know what I was thinking but honestly I was just sort of panicking. That's when I decided that maybe the Feyo was trying to like… I don't know…repay me for freeing it. Like it was trying to do like the tribes said and make me… immortal somehow or something. So I uhh… decided I would do something to throw everyone off while it got stronger. I just—I just figured that would be the best possible scenario so that it wouldn't hurt me." Grant's leg begins shaking under the table.

"What made you think that's what it was doing?" asks Hargrove.

"I don't know. The tribes had been right about everything else, so I figured that was what was happening. Plus, it didn't kill me and had now seen me twice. I felt …*connected* to it. When it looked at me, I felt like it was trying to communicate somehow."

"Alright then. You already told us how you put Lewis into the church, tell us about Molly. How did that one happen?" asks Hargrove, throwing away an empty water bottle.

Grant sighs. "I swear that wasn't my fault. I wasn't even there. I came back from getting some food and just so happened to notice that car in the back. I went down to check it out, and saw her…laying there. I knew I had to act quickly, so I used his truck again and got her out of there."

"So you were staying in Lewis's house during this time?" she asks.

"Just for a few nights. I was going to see if there were any apartments in the area, but I didn't have any luck," he says.

"So you didn't feel bad for any of this? Staying in a dead man's home? A man you hung up from a ceiling of a church? You didn't feel bad for taking the body of a poor girl who did nothing wrong and sticking it in a gym for children to potentially see? And what about my officer? Tell me how he was killed," says Hargrove in a demanding tone.

Grant puts his head in his hands for a moment, and wipes

his eyes. "Yes. I did care and I felt horrible. But you have to understand... I've lived my life with no purpose or desire to be anything or really have a career of any kind. Every dollar I've ever made has went into looking into Native American culture. I'm a nobody. I thought that maybe if the Feyo gave me...whatever, I would be something. It felt like my calling..."

Hargrove stares at him a moment as she braces herself for the story of Sergeant Hamilton's death.

"And the officer..." Grant swallows hard. "When I was getting ready to leave, really early in the morning the next day, I planned on moving the girl's car. I walked down there, and as I was about to get in it he pulled down the road and stopped behind it. I hid behind the car, and when he came over beside it, I jumped out and hit him in the back of the head as hard as I could. It didn't hurt him too bad and we fought for a moment. I was able to get the best of him and knocked him out. I knew people would probably come looking for him, and remembered an abandoned lodge in the woods from when I was looking around that first day. I put him on my back and carried him up there. I really didn't want him to die, honestly. I was hoping putting him up there would just give me enough time to get the hell out of town for a few days."

"Well, how did he die then? How did you do that to him?" asks Hargrove angrily.

"I didn't. When I finally got him into that lodge... he started to wake up. I was going to try and knock him out again, but before I could get to him ...the Feyo did. It came out of nowhere and put his arms around him... and right in front of me part of him just like...*dissolved.* It was terrifying. I started throwing up on the ground, and I couldn't look at it for a moment. By the time I collected myself, it was gone, and I was alone up there with that officer. I did the best I could to get him hung up there and get cleaned up and leave. When I got back down to the house, I bailed and went to a hotel a few towns away to lay low. Threw that security camera shit off of a bridge on the way too. Seeing it happen scared the hell out of me. It had gotten so much stronger in such a short period of time, which meant it had killed animals or more people that I wasn't aware of. I knew I couldn't continue to be a part of whatever it was doing, I was just way too scared after seeing it kill that man."

Grant begins to cry, but continues, "Then I had a dream that he killed me. It was so real and it was like I felt it. It's like I knew it was out there looking for me, and was going to track me down and do to me what it did to the officer, but worse… That's when I decided that I definitely needed to get away from it. I couldn't sleep, expecting it to come in at any moment… Then I saw my face on the news and knew I fucked up somehow and this was over. I went and got his cruiser that I had hid near some storage units a few blocks from my hotel… and here I am."

Hargrove sits in silence for a moment, with her hands clasped together, thinking. She looks to me and Davidson, then to Grant.

"So who was with you this whole time? You keep speaking as if it was only you, but we are fully aware you did not act alone," she says.

Grant looks to the floor, not responding.

"Don't tell me you're gonna stop talking now after all of that."

Grant looks up and frowns, "Someone was around me, but trust me…they had nothing to do with any of it. They knew what was happening, but didn't do anything."

"You expect us to believe that? That someone came across

the whole U.S. with you just to hang out on the sidelines while you hung people up like puppets? I'm not buying it," she says.

"I understand, but it isn't like that. It isn't someone who came with me. I'm not going to get them in any trouble. I will take all the repercussions for hanging those people up. It was all me. I'll spend as long in prison as you need me to. That keeps me away from the Feyo and safe," he says.

"What about those damn cigarettes?" asks Davidson,

Grant looks confused, "Huh?"

"You said those cigarettes were yours, but you ain't asked to smoke even once since you been here. Somebody that cares enough to get cigarettes that specific, is prolly pretty bad addicted to them. You ain't a smoker," says Davidson matter of factly.

"I tell you what I think." Hargrove leans closer to Grant over the table and glares at him, "I think this other person is actually the one responsible for everything. I think you're covering for them and you needed some elaborate bullshit story to make us think it was some ancient monster, when in reality it's just someone you want to continue causing harm to the people of this area. You'll get your time in prison alright. I just don't understand why you had to drag us into some campfire story to try and trick us into lessening your sentence. You will be held accountable. All I have to do is call the FBI and tell them I have you. I'm sure their questioning will be more...*extensive*. Good luck feeding them that bullshit."

"What if I took you to the tree? Would you believe me then?" he asks.

"The existence of the tree proves nothing other than the ground is fertile. I'm not hiking in the woods to validate your outlandish claims," says Hargrove, standing up.

"Please, I'll bet there are more bodies out there...or

maybe the Feyo is still there now… You'd have no choice but to believe it if you saw it for yourself!" he says.

Hargrove looks at her watch. "Okay then. If you can do it in handcuffs, we'll go play hide and seek with you in the woods. If we don't see anything, you're definitely being charged with those murders. The FBI will have you in a cell that's a lot less comfortable than ours, I promise. And if I was you, I would reconsider your decision of withholding the name of the person that helped you." She turns to walk out of the room. "McKay, Davidson, get him in the back of my SUV and grab some waters out of the break room. Hope you boys are ready to walk through the woods."

* * *

WE PREPARE HARGROVE'S SUV, a brand new Chevrolet. It was outfitted with all of the workings of an unmarked car. Outside of the large "Chief of Police" decal on the side, you wouldn't even know it was a cop car. We load him up in the very back, and all get in. Hargrove had instructed the few officers still at the station to be on standby, and to not speak a word of anything they had heard without her permission. She was adamant about keeping the entire Native American folklore story under wraps until we had him formally charged and awaiting trial. No need to have the town any more scared than it already is.

As we make our way to Sunridge Valley, I look in the mirror and see Grant silently crying in the back. I wonder if he's crying because he knows that we'll find nothing, and he's going to prison for the rest of his life, or if it's because he really thinks the Feyollocuani will be waiting for him out there.

I wonder if he really believes what he saw was real? Is it? Or is there just someone who is really good at playing on his obsession, and used him to do his dirty work? Either way I don't have a good feeling about looking around in the woods with this guy.

12:00 P.M.

WE MAKE it to the end of the long road that leads to the entrance of the valley. We pull behind a small white car with two young people in the back, very obviously scrambling to put their clothes back on. We wait a moment, then get out. Walking up to the window, Hargrove taps it with her fingernails and then makes a "get out of here" motion with her hands. They comply, and take off. We let Grant out of the back, and begin walking towards the woods.

"How far is that tree from here?" asks Hargrove.

"About two miles. After the first mile it opens up a little. There are old horse trails we can follow," says Grant.

"Alright, you lead the way then. Don't make me hike through the woods for nothing. If there's not something that corroborates your story, you're just shit out of luck," she says, throwing a judgmental look his way. He nods, and begins walking down an overgrown path off to the left side of the loop.

"Looks like it's mating season or somethin'," says Davidson, pointing to a pile of clothes at the front of the trail. I laugh and look back to the old barn, near where Molly was killed. I look extra hard at the area where I saw that...thing in the picture. Nothing is there, but I can't help but to feel uneasy thinking that if it *IS* real, it could be anywhere out here. Even if it was a person who has Grant fooled, they could be out here waiting on us. I'll keep my head on a swivel.

211

The first of the trail is thick with branches that have attempted to take it back over. We push our way through, and after about twenty minutes it opens up and becomes easier to navigate. We are now far enough into the woods that if he were to take off on us, we would have a tough time catching him. I speed up a little, and make sure I'm right on his heels. I look back to Davidson and Hargrove.

"Don't worry, I ain't passed out yet. No promises on the way back though. Y'all might have to carry me out," Davidson says, wiping sweat from his brow. I look into the woods behind them just in case this was all just a setup and Grant's partner is waiting for the right moment to jump out and overpower us. All I see is trees for now, so I guess we're okay. It's so quiet out here that we will definitely hear if someone tries to run up on us.

We approach a dense patch of trees, and Grant points to a small hand saw on the ground.

"That's the saw I used to get to it. It's in the middle of all of this. I don't know if I can get to it with these handcuffs on though," he says raising his hands up in front of us.

Hargrove glares at him, "I'll take them off, but just know that if you take off on me, I will not be chasing you." She pats her hand on her service weapon, "Understood?"

"Yes, of course," he says, walking to her with his arms outstretched. She removes the handcuffs and he rubs his wrists. He starts to push his way through the thick layer of trees and overgrowth, and we follow. It takes us a few minutes to be able to make it to the clearing. Once all of us are through, we stand in front of the tree Grant had described. As he stated before, there were two trees dancing around the original burned one. I feel uncomfortable just looking at it. It seems very out of place, yet very familiar...

Then, it all comes back to me. This is the tree I fell off of when I was younger. Peyton Goddard had dared me to try and get to the top of it, and I was just drunk enough to try. Maddy Thomas was there and I wanted to show off, in hopes that it would make her like me. I remember getting to the top, and in trying to celebrate, lost my footing and fell. I remember landing hard against the base of the tree, cutting my arm up badly. Lucky for me, Maddy's mom was a nurse and we went to her house to fix me up. I look at the base of the tree where I remember falling, but it looks like this is where Grant had started cutting.

"That's where its foot was sticking out and I was able to cut into there and get it out," says Grant bending down with me. A wave of heat passes over my body as I realize that it wasn't the tree that cut me when I fell, it was the foot of the Feyollocuani...*if it was real anyways*, this could all be a hoax. That could've been like...a dummy or something they put in there a long time ago to prank someone... Maybe it was like a plastic foot or something and that's why it cut me so badly... I keep my thoughts to myself, and look to the ropes that lay inside the trunk.

"So these were the ropes that it was tied with?" I ask, holding them up.

"Yep, they were pretty hard to cut too," Grant says.

"That's cause it's made with cedar and willow. Prolly got some kinda animal hide twisted up in there too. Indian rope is way tougher than that hardware store bullshit we have nowadays," says Davidson, picking up a piece of it and pulling it tight between his hands.

"Well, the rope is real and the tree is real, but it really doesn't prove anything. I thought you said there were probably bodies here. What else can you show us?" asks Hargrove, pulling her shirt away from her body and blowing down into it to cool down.

"I...I had hoped there would be. Have you guys found

anymore than the three?" asks Grant, with a worried expression on his face.

"No. Were we supposed to? Do you know of another person who has been killed?" Hargrove crosses her arms.

"No, but that's not good..." Grant looks around quickly.

"What's the issue?" she asks.

"That means that it's stronger. Once it gets its true strength back...theres nothing left... They basically just dissolve people and animals, and leave nothing behind. That's why I'm saying it's bad. If it's already that strong, there's really nothing we can do. It could be anywhere. We gotta get the fuck out of here," he says, putting his hands on his head and pacing in front of small open area beside the tree.

Hargrove rolls her eyes and groans, "Alright now you can quit with the bullshit, Grant. I'm tired of listening to it. No more games. Either tell us who you are covering for, or let's go back and get you processed so you can wait for trial."

Grant paces back and forth faster. His expression becomes more frantic, "Sorry, I swear I'm not bullshitting you guys. I don't know what I thought bringing you all out here. Maybe it left... Yea, maybe it went somewhere else and we're okay...maybe. Let's go please." Grant steps forward quickly and trips on a root, falling flat beside a thick bush.

"Ow fuck," he groans, rolling over to his back and putting his hands on his stomach. I walk over to him and reach my hand out to help him get back up. Just as he starts to extend his hand to mine, a black hand reaches around the back of the thick overgrowth and slaps his chest as another slides down under him. I quickly reach out to grab his wrist, but miss as he is drug backwards violently. He lets out an odd sucking sound, and his body sinks flat to the ground. His face completely dissolves in an instant and all that is left are his clothes. I fall back as I hear Davidson fire off four shots by my head.

"DON'T LET IT OUT OF YOUR SIGHT!" says Hargrove, now joining Davidson in firing blindly into the forest. I jump up and get my pistol out, running round the edge of the bush where Grant's clothes lay. Nothing is there but the trees. I look up, thinking maybe it climbed one and is about to jump down on me, but I see nothing.

"GET BACK TO THE FUCKIN ROAD Y'ALL LETS GO!" says Davidson, as he sprints back the way we came. Hargrove and I join him and run as fast as we can into the clearing. Looking back every few steps, I see nothing but the blur of trees and overgrowth as I run. We make it about a mile before I hear Davidson wheezing loudly.

"I don't ...I ... I don't think it's chasin' us now... hot damn," he says through labored breaths.

"I can't tell but we can't stop now, come on," says Hargrove, patting him on the back and jogging forward. I look back to the trail, and see nothing. *It could be anywhere...* I turn and begin running as fast as I can again, passing both of them. My legs feel like they are going to explode, but I'd rather feel this pain than...whatever the fuck I just saw happen to Grant.

We make it back to Hargrove's SUV, and Davidson and I jump in the back. She hops in and puts the gas pedal to the floor, spinning us around and out of the loop, heading away from the mouth of the valley. I turn and look back to the start of the trail, and can just barely make out a pair of grey eyes looking our way as we speed off.

"I need to speak to you immediately, it's urgent. Where can we meet?" asks Hargrove into her cellphone. After a moment, she hangs up, and looks to us.

"I called Mike Banner," she says, wiping a tear from her face, "He's going to meet us at the co-op. Neither of you speak a word of this to anyone, got it?"

"The hell would we even say? What even just happened? I ain't ever seen no shit like that in my whole life!" says Davidson.

"Yea. Just...I just I don't know. I knew *HE* believed that...*thing* was real but I—I don't know what to think right now," she says. "All I *DO* know is that we are in over our heads by a mile now. We had to have hit it with a few of those rounds, but it was just... GONE...Grant just...disappeared too. How the fuck am I supposed to explain this?" She turns the radio up and continues to drive.

* * *

I THINK of the way Grant looked when the Feyo had...done *whatever that was*. His face just sunk in and went away... It was so fast, yet it is playing back in my mind in slow motion. Like each atom of his body was broken down into nothing, like the way styrofoam burns... His eyes open and staring right at me... He was right the whole time and we thought he was just some crazy idiot that was trying to lie his way out of some murder charges. Then we led him right to it. *What even is that thing? Is it what he said or something else? Could it be a person with some type of weapon we don't understand? No...It couldn't be. I didn't even think stuff like that was possible. What the fuck does that mean that it can be real? What else is real that we don't know about?*

I put my head in my hands. I can't imagine what the people of Culver will think when we try and explain this... Hopefully Mike Banner will do that for us. There's no way we could release that information without an immediate backlash. No one would believe us anyways. We sit in silence for the remainder of the ride to the co-op.

Pulling in, we see a black SUV backed in the the corner of the lot. Hargrove backs in beside it. Mike gets out of the SUV, and into ours.

"How can I be of assistance?" he asks.

"You can assist us in telling us what the actual fuck is going on. Tell me you know what this fucking...*thing* is," Hargrove says, glaring at him.

He looks back to her, then to us with a confused expression, "What...thing?" he asks.

"Feyollocuani," I say.

His expression changes to one of intense concern. He looks to Hargrove. "You've seen it?"

"Seen it? It almost fucking killed us! It killed our suspect right in front of us! Did you know about this? Did you know there was a God damn...whatever it is running around here and didn't tell us?" Hargrove asks, gripping the steering wheel tightly and grinding her teeth.

"Yes. But you can't be too angry, you and I both know that no one in your department, including you would have believed me. This is pretty bad. It should have been gone by now."

"The fuck you mean gone by now?" asks Davidson.

Mike sighs, "Look. There's a lot about this that is privileged information but…since you guys have seen it first hand I'll let you know. Just know all of you will be signing Non-Disclosure Agreements after this, okay?"

We all nod our heads to signify we understand, and I scoot up in my seat.

"The FBI has been tracking these for two decades. As of right now, there are at least six that are active in North America, including this one," he says.

Hargrove gasps, "Are you serious? How? Where? Six? What are you doing about them? Will the—"

"Look, I know this is a lot to take in, and frankly it isn't something I'm truly at liberty to be speaking on at this time," Mike says. "But just know that once it gets to this level of strength, they typically leave the areas in which they were dormant. They tend to go deeper into the woods where they can feed without intervention. Once at full strength they only need to feed every few weeks, and large game tend to be their go to. I have never seen one stick around this long. That's why I told you the other day you had at most a few murders left."

"So, what's next then?" asks Hargrove, visibly frustrated, "We just kind of hope it goes away? What am I supposed to tell the media? What do I tell the people that are at risk of being…vaporized? Or whatever that was? They know we had a suspect and who he was. How the hell do I explain that he just got fucking dissolved in the woods?"

Mike reaches over and puts his hand on her shoulder, "Listen, as crazy as it sounds, it's going to be okay. This isn't the first time this has happened, and we will solve it. We can make this look like you are releasing your suspect to us. We can make a show of it, trust me. We'll wait a few weeks and put out a statement saying he killed himself in his cell or something along those lines. Happens every day. You can say his other accomplice escaped and we are pursuing them elsewhere. That would explain any more disappearances or loose ends really."

Hargrove takes a deep breath and closes her eyes for a moment. She exhales, "Okay. But what if it doesn't leave? What if it just keeps on doing that? Can we kill it? We shot at it no less than ten times earlier and I guess it didn't do anything to it. What about the accomplice? If they didn't flee they could be assisting that *thing* in killing more people…"

"Yea shooting it won't work. It can heal itself pretty quickly. The only luck we've ever had is to tie them up, decapitate them and encase the head in concrete. For some reason that's the only way we can get the bodies to stop regenerating and then, they will actually burn. Once the body is burned, the head is useless and we usually crush or burn them as well. We have tried to study their behavior, but haven't been able to learn too much. It's just that by the time we know about them, they are already too strong and the risk is too great to even attempt. That's why I wouldn't worry about the accomplice. No one can control them, and if I had to guess they likely ended up the same way your other suspect did. These things are truly untouchable at a certain point. The standard method is to just…let them go away on their own and monitor the area. But with companies bull-dozing thousands and thousands of acres of formally unoccupied forests, this problem has ramped up ten fold over the last few years," Mike says. "If anything else happens, let me know. For now, that's how we'll take this. I will have my team begin working on the media element of all of it. Tell your force that the transfer has happened already, and go ahead and gather all of your physical evidence as well as audio recordings, any witness statements or anything of any relevance. I'll send some people to your station to grab it. I'll give you a call tomorrow before we have press briefing. We'll do our best to make it as seamless as possible for you and your team. I apologize to all of your for not being more direct, I had hoped you would never see it. I'll make the call for the mock transfer to happen ASAP. We have enough people in the area to make it look legitimate. And just so we are clear, it is in your best interest to keep this information to yourself. Those NDA's will be in your inbox before the end of the day." He gets out of the SUV and into his, and pulls away.

Hargrove runs her hands through her hair and turns to us. "I need you guys to align yourselves with this immediately. Not a fucking WORD of this gets out. I will brief Chief Marks, as he deserves to know. I don't know if he will be able to believe it, but I will do my best. No one else can know. I feel personally responsible for this to some degree by taking him up on the offer of driving out to see it. I should have known that wouldn't go well. It's my fault he is dead."

"You could not have known this was going to happen. I mean… who would have guessed he wasn't lying. Who would have guessed any of it really? I have so many questions I want answered," I say.

"I have a feeling we'll never get any answers. I bet we will be trying to understand it for the rest of our lives. Let's just hope that we never see it again. I understand if either of you need to take some time off to try and…cope," she says, pulling out of the co-op.

"Ain't takin off till I know that thang is gone. Think we

should try and cut its head off like that guy said?" asks Davidson.

Hargrove tilts the mirror so she can see him, "No. Stay as far away from that area as possible. I'll have Magnolia shut that road down completely until further notice. As soon as we get back to the station I need you both to start collecting any and all evidence about this since the start and get it to me. I want all physical stuff boxed up and all files sent to me then deleted from your computer. If anyone asks, the FBI has formally taken over the investigation. If someone keeps pressing, direct them to me."

We nod in agreement. We ride in silence all the way back to the station, no doubt all thinking the same thing. It's one thing to see what we saw, but for Mike Banner to be so casual about it was…unsettling to say the least. *If he was so quick to tell us what he did, what else is there about them that he omitted? What other types of things like this exist all around us, with different Mike Banner type people in charge of keeping them secret? Was all of this actually a much bigger deal than he said? Will there be more deaths? Are we in more danger than he's letting on? Will it recognize us? Will it hunt us down?*

Hargrove picks up her phone and dials a number quickly. "Hey. I know I said not to, but I need you to come in for an hour or so. I need to brief you on a major development," she says. I hear a muffled response on the other end, and she hangs up.

"Wonder how he'll react?" I ask.

"Hopefully better than us. He's been through a lot, but not something like this," she says, turning into the station. We see three Black SUV's parked in the front of the station, all with large "FBI" decals on the side.

"Guess he was right about making a show of it. Makes sense, but how did they beat us here?" asks Hargrove, trying to find a spot. She whips around to the side and is almost hit head on by the green WCDX van, speeding through the lot. She veers left, just a few feet from the van and comes to a stop in an open space.

"Those idiots must have a drone watching the station or something. No way they'd know they were coming," she says.

"Mike Banner prolly called in an anonymous tip if I had guess," says Davidson, "Adds drama to the show."

She unlocks the door and steps out, "Maybe so, less questions from the public if they get to see the FBI drive away from the station on TV."

* * *

"Helloooooo Culver, Parker Cowan with WCDX News! Is it true that the FBI is taking over the investigation of the Vampire of Culver?" Parker shoves his microphone into the face of an FBI agent who is standing in front of one of the SUVs closest to the door. He doesn't respond, so Parker moves to the next agent, standing on the other side. "Parker Cowan with WCDX News! Is it true that the FBI is taking over the investigation of the Vampire of Culver?" he doesn't respond either. Frustrated, Parker turns and sees us. His eyes light up, and he walks our way.

He puts the microphone up to Hargrove. "Hellooooo Chief Hargrove, Parker Cowan with WCDX News! We had a loyal listener call in and tell us that the FBI is taking over the investigation of the Vampire of Culver, is that true?"

Hargrove straightens herself, and leans to the microphone to respond. "Yes. The FBI has made the determination that they will be taking over. They will release a press briefing sometime within the next day or so. I have been advised to let them answer any further questioning. I can assure you that they will work swiftly and effectively to put everyone responsible behind bars. They are also assuming custody of Grant Lungston at this time. I am grateful that they have offered their expertise and resources to ensure the safety of our town is secured."

Before Parker can ask any more questions, Hargrove walks around him and into the station. We are followed by six or seven FBI agents, and the doors are shut behind us. The agents follow us inside and instruct us to start preparing any physical evidence that they can remove. Everyone in the station works quickly and quietly, as we see the WCDX cameras outside trying to get better angles for Parker.

* * *

"Hellooo Culver, I'm a dipshit who doesn't realize everyone hates me," says one of the patrol officers. Everyone laughs for a moment while taping up the last few boxes. We hand them off to the agents who make a grand display of placing them into the SUV's. They had an agent in plain clothes put a bag over his head, and placed him in handcuffs. They walked him out, and shoved him into the back of one of the SUV's. *Damn they really thought of everything. This must not be the first time this has happened.* Parker Cowan's camera man made the mistake of getting a little too close, and received some harsh words from one of the agents before being shoved to the side. *I guess he didn't learn his lesson.* They pull off, WCDX van right behind them. I'm sure people will be going crazy seeing that parade of FBI vehicles go through the town.

Everyone goes back to what they were doing before we got here, none the wiser that we just handed off evidence of something much bigger than just a few murders. Davidson and I share a glance, and I can tell that it's upsetting him now that we just handed all of that over. I don't guess I really care though, it isn't like any of it was really relevant outside of

Grant's interrogation. No one would ever believe that he was telling the truth. I just worry that this whole thing will get to Davidson, as he's pretty strong in his faith. I'm not sure how someone like Pastor Tim would be able to explain something as unbelievable as that away. *I doubt there is a verse in the Bible about Feyollocuani.*

We see Chief Marks walk in, wearing a grey shirt and gym shorts. I've never seen him in anything other than a uniform so it almost looked like a stranger. He walks into his office, giving us a nod as he passed ours.

"I think he's gonna call us liars," says Davidson, now standing on the other side of my desk.

"I don't know, honestly. I think he will definitely need some time to try and understand it but I don't think he will think we're outright lying," I say.

"Guess we'll find out. Either way that's a bunch of shit to hear all at once. Hell I'm still confused," he says, lowering his voice as another officer walks by.

* * *

After around forty minutes, we see Hargrove emerge, and stick her head into our open office area. She stares at Davidson and I for a moment, then nods and walks away.

"Whole lotta words she said without sayin' anything, huh?" asks Davidson.

I smile and nod. A few moments later, Chief Marks comes in wearing an angry expression. He looks to us, and motions for us to follow him. We get into his office, and he shuts the door behind him. Davidson and I share a look of nervous anticipation as Chief sits in his chair and leans back.

"Just to be clear, none of this leaves this office, got it?" he asks, eyes darting back and forth between us.

"Got it," we say at the same time.

He leans down and pulls open the bottom drawer of his desk. He produces a glass bottle with a brownish liquid and three styrofoam cups.

"I used to drink from this bottle of bourbon every time I closed out a big case, until Sarah died. I kinda stayed away from drinkin' until my head was on a little better," he says pouring a little bit of the liquid into each of the cups. Davidson and I remain silent.

"I know we didn't really close this out, but I bet this is as close as we will ever get to knowing what the hell happened," he says, handing us each a cup. "I'm sure once the last FBI agent leaves this place we will never hear from any of them again. Here's to hoping that God forsaken thing gets the hell out of town before it does any more damage."

The three of us finish our cups, and Chief collects them. The three of us sit there in an awkward silence for a moment before he pulls two pieces of gum out of his pocket and slides them to Davidson and I.

"So…did y'all get a good look at it?" he asks.

"Not really," I say. "It happened so fast that all I really got to see was its hands and what it did to Grant."

"Man. Sorry I wasn't there. I feel bad roughing that man up, especially now that I know he was being honest. Who knows though, maybe he led y'all out there hoping it would kill the three of you and spare him," he says.

"I just really think he was trying to prove it to us. I think he knew he was in over his head and had no other way to try and get out of any accountability. I just worry about whoever was helping him. Now that they are probably seeing the news report that he's in FBI custody, there's no telling what their next move will be," I say, unwrapping the gum and beginning to chew it.

"Yea…If they're smart, they'll get the hell out of town and take that…thing with them. Who would've thought something like that would be real... Even our seasoned out of towner detective here couldn't have figured that one out huh?" he asks, looking to me with a smile. He sits up and puts his elbows on the table. "All I know is, I'm going back home. I'll pause my thoughts on it until tomorrow. I suggest you boys head out also. It's gonna be weird until we're certain that thing has left."

Davidson and I exit his office, and gather our things. We walk out of the side door and head to our cars.

"Damon," Davidson says, placing his hand on my shoulder, "Are you sure you're alright? That was some real crazy shit. It scared me half to death and I wasn't right up on it like you. Aren't you like...freaked out?"

"I appreciate the concern man, but I'm okay. I don't think my brain has really grasped it yet, though. Too much all at once really. I'll be okay," I smile and unlock my car.

"See you tomorrow then, buddy."

CHAPTER 26

Still down to hang out tonight? Need me to
bring you anything?

S *hit. I totally forgot about Evelyn coming over.*

> Yea sorry, it's been a rough one today. Bring
> some food and I'll pay for it. Alcohol is
> optional but I will definitely be making a drink
> the second I get home.

Maybe she'll get something good, I'm starving.

I put my phone down and walk into the gas station I had stopped at. I'm not sure how long I had sat there, but my brain isn't really operating correctly. It wasn't until Davidson had stopped me outside of the station that I truly thought about everything.

"Are you sure you're alright?"

Now that I'm thinking about it, I'm really not sure the last time I was…*alright*. Not that anything had been particularly bad before all of this but it wasn't particularly good either. I think I had grown too comfortable with suffering in my own mediocrity. I was wasting away without even realizing it. After today…after seeing Grant…*disappear*, it really twisted my mind up imagining that I was going to die out there too. I know I've had more nights than I can count where dying seemed like the best option, but something about today and not being in control of the outcome is really bugging me. I've never been one to freeze up, but that stuff isn't supposed to be real. That wasn't some crackhead we had to help a landlord evict, or a drug dealer we busted….that *thing* was…I don't even know. I've never been superstitious or anything but something about seeing that thing look back at me at the end of that trail has me feeling so uncomfortable and I can't stop it. I need to hurry home so I can ease my nerves and take my mind off of it.

8:00 P.M.

I LET EVELYN IN, and she hands me a large bag.

"I didn't know what you'd want so I just got us chips and salsa from that Mexican place," she says smiling.

"That'll be just fine."

I place the food in the kitchen and pour myself another drink. This is at least the third since I've been home, but who's counting anyways. Evelyn sits another bag down, and pulls out a bottle of tequila and a six pack of sodas.

"So where's the doggy? Maybe she'll let me love her this time," she says.

I realize that I haven't seen her in a few minutes so I call for her and she doesn't respond. I walk to the front and open the door, and see her sniffing at Evelyn's car.

"Girl, relax that flannel is long gone, come on!" I say

holding the door open. Daisy investigates for a few more seconds before trotting up to the doorway. She takes one long glance back at the car, before entering and deciding to investigate Evelyn's shoes. She seems content and begins wagging her tail.

"See, she likes me. All is well," says Evelyn rubbing Daisy's head.

"She isn't typically a fan of women," I say, opening up the bag of food.

Evelyn gets up and takes a big swig of the tequila straight from the bottle, "Well, maybe you've just had the wrong women around. She can probably tell who was going to hurt you and scared them off."

She was probably right, but I think it might have been the other way around. I can't say I've been the best partner to anyone since I was in school. Work typically dictates my mood and time, and doesn't allow me to really open up the way I need to for a relationship to work. Not with Evelyn, though. There is a comfort with her that I can't quite explain. It's like I've known her for years. When I'm around her I'm not really worried about what happened at work, just excited to hear what she has to say next. I wonder if she feels the same way.

"So I heard on the radio that you guys are turning over that case to the FBI, is that a good or a bad thing?" she asks, crunching loudly on a tortilla chip.

She must've read my mind. I take a quick drink and reply, "A little bit of both, I guess. I wish we could've closed it out, but as long as it's over I'm okay with it. It's been too crazy around here."

"Oh, you guys aren't always chasing vampires around?" she asks, tilting her head and smiling. *If she only knew what that smile did to me.*

"Only on halloween when they get too drunk," I say, finishing off my drink.

"Mind if I use your restroom?" she asks.

I point her down the hall and she steps away. Hopefully she isn't turned off by my basic decor in there. It isn't like I have many guests, and have never really cared to splurge on remodeling that old bathroom. As I pour myself another drink I drop a piece of ice into the floor. I bend down to grab it and am transported back to the woods for a moment, reaching down for Grant's wrist and he's dragged backwards and *dissolved... I wonder if he felt anything? The look of fear across his face seems to be tattooed into my brain. How did we not see that thing coming? How did we outrun it? Did it let us go on purpose just to fuck with us?* I snap myself out of the flashback and rub my eyes.

"You okay?"

I didn't realize Evelyn had seen that.

"Yea, I-I just zoned out for a second is all," I say, as I feel my cheeks get hot with embarrassment.

She smiles and walks over to me, putting her hands on my sides and giving me a quick kiss on the forehead. I put my hands around her waist and pull her in, kissing her softly on her lips. She returns the favor and we embrace for a moment. She bites her lip, and looks up to me.

"Back in the zone yet?" she asks, spinning out of my arms and back to the kitchen table. She winks at me as she selects the biggest chip in the bag and dips it into the salsa. If only that happened every time I had bad thoughts, I'd really be...*alright.*

"Oh, and what happened to your eye? Bad guy get too frisky or something?" Evelyn asks, crunching her chip loudly.

"I wish! At least I could hit a bad guy back. It was this countertop. The other night I got tripped up somehow and smashed my face on it," I say, patting the edge of the counter.

I had forgotten about my black eye entirely. I was hoping it would have been healed up before I was around Evelyn again. *Maybe she doesn't think I'm an idiot.*

Over the next hour we finish off the chips, and a few more drinks. It's like with each word she says, I become more attracted to her. The way she talks, laughs and even the way she always moves her hair behind her ear, just for it to fall back down is perfect. Maybe it's the alcohol, or maybe it just *IS*. If she feels even half of the way I do right now, this might turn into something special. She starts playing music on her phone, it's some indie artist that must be her favorite as she begins singing and dancing in the living room. *A little more upbeat than the classical music in the car.* I join her and she puts my hands around her hips, and starts spinning us around. Her hair flies into my face as I hear her sing the chorus of the song loudly. *She even sings beautifully.* I know this moment will be a core memory for me, no matter what happens. If she decides to move away and never speak to me again, I'll always have this memory to look back on.

The song ends and she goes to step around me back to the kitchen, but slips on the carpet. I catch her and guide her down to the floor. We laugh, and she kisses me.

"Thanks, sorry I just love that song. Classical music for the car rides and *this* for the...dancing," she says.

"It's okay! I'd fall in this living room a hundred times with you if you wanted me to," I say moving her hair out of her face and kissing her forehead.

I stand up and reach my hand out to help her out of the floor, and it comes back again. I see Grant's eyes as he feels the Feyo's hands press against his body, and that horrible sound he made. He dissolves again, leaving only his clothes sitting on the ground. *My legs burning from the thought of running and my ears ringing from Davidsons initial shots...How do bullets not hurt it? How does...anything make sense with this fucking thing...* I close my eyes and feel a hand on the side of my face.

"Damon? Are you okay? What happened?" Evelyn asks, and I realize I had just been frozen in place for a moment. She was kneeling in front of me with a concerned look on her face. I sit down in front of her.

"Yea... Yea I'm okay I just had a really rough day. I can't get it out of my head, honestly. I'm sorry if I ruined that moment," I say.

She gets up, and grabs my drink from the counter and brings it down to me, sitting down. She puts her hands on my knees, "You know, you can tell me anything. It isn't like I'm going to tell anyone."

"I know," I say, taking a quick drink before continuing, "but I honestly don't know how. It's a lot." I rack my brain thinking of a quick lie that could satisfy her concern without confessing what had really happened.

"You don't have to, but if you want to, I have all of the time in the world. Let's go outside and get you some air," she says, standing up.

We walk out to my porch and sit on the top step. She lights a cigarette and blows the smoke away from me, placing her other hand on my back and rubbing it. She leans her head to the side, smiling. Hard to argue with that look.

"Well, I will tell you but I don't want you to like feel bad for me or anything," I say.

"Consider it done," she says, changing her face from a smile to emotionless for a moment before giggling.

"Well," I say, trying to decide what I'll let out, "Unfortunately, I saw a man die today. Right as I was trying to help him up, just like I was going to help you up earlier. When I reached out for you it just kind of came back is all."

"Oh, I'm really sorry. I didn't mean to fall down, honestly." She frowns a little and rubs my back again.

"No, don't think that was your fault. You didn't kill him… or did you?" I joke, making my finger in the shape of a gun and pointing it at her.

"I'm innocent!" she says, taking a long drag from her cigarette. "But really I'm sorry you had to deal with that. How did he die if you don't mind me asking?"

I think for a moment and respond, "I don't really know. He just…died."

"That's rough. Did you know him?" she asks.

"No, he was a suspect in a case we are working on."

"Oh, wow. That's horrible. I hate that you had to see that. You guys must all be so exhausted with everything that has been going on," she says standing up, "So sorry for the timing, but I need to use your restroom again! Be right back, I promise!"

I breathe out, thankful she had to walk away before I accidentally told her everything. She's so easy to talk to that everything just kind of comes out like that. If I told her what I had actually seen, she might think I'm crazy and just leave and go back to her hotel. *Will that be the hardest part of all of this? No one would ever believe me so who the hell can I even talk to about it?* I don't want to begin something with this woman without being honest. I'm just not sure when an appropriate time to let someone know you saw someone dissolve before your eyes in some horrifying and unexplainable way would be…

I take another sip of my drink and look out into my yard. The wind is blowing and the air hitting my face feels great. I take another drink and try to lay back onto my porch to wait for her, but I accidentally lay on something. I sit back up and reach behind me to see what it was. It was Evelyn's ciga-rettes, *whoops.* I hope I didn't break any of them. I find her lighter and put it on top of them, and sit them beside me.

"Tequila goes right through me I'm sorry," she says,

walking over to me and sitting back down. She takes a drink of her tequila and places her hand on my back again.

"Oh, there they are!" she says, reaching down and grabbing the cigarettes, "Was looking all in my bag in there thinking I brought them back in. These things are too expensive to be losing!" She laughs as she pulls one out and lights it.

As she places the box back down, I pick it up. I shake them in front of her, "These things are bad for you anyw—" I stop. I realize now in the light of the porch, that Evelyn smokes Strada 308's. The same cigarettes they found in the driver's seat of Lewis Parley's truck. The same cigarettes that Davidson was certain weren't Grant's. My head starts spinning and I stand up quickly, almost losing my balance.

"What's wrong? Are you having another flashback from today? What do you need me to do?" she asks.

"Where did you buy these?" I ask, raising the cigarettes up to her.

"I buy them online…my mom used to smoke them when I was little…why? What's wrong?" she asks, projecting her genuine confusion.

I realize now that she would have no way of knowing that we found them. Grant didn't even know until we already had him in custody. That's why his reaction was off. *Davidson was right. They weren't his. They were Evelyn's.* My face goes numb as a million thoughts flood into my mind at once.

"Damon…please, tell me what's wrong," she says. I turn away from her. *Was she Grant's accomplice? Was she here to kill me? Was this whole thing a setup? Were all of these moments fake? How can I be so fucking stupid?*

"So when were you going to tell me you knew Grant Lungston?" I ask, still facing away.

"Wh-what are you talking about?" she asks, her voice cracking slightly.

"When were you going to tell me that you helped him hang up those bodies?" I ask, turning around to face her.

Her expression changes from confused, to one of sadness and a single tear rolls down her face. Before I can react, she pulls out a small revolver and points it at me.

"How about we go inside," she says through her teeth.

I sit quietly on my couch as Evelyn paces back and forth in front of me, her finger on the outside of the trigger well of the revolver. *Maybe I can overpower her quickly and take it from her...or maybe I can make it to my room where my pistol is...* I decide I'm too drunk and need to focus on how to talk my way out of this situation. Evelyn wipes a tear from her eye, and sits criss cross a few feet in front of me.

"I need you to know I didn't touch those bodies, Damon. Not a single one of them," she says.

My mind races. *How can I believe her? How was I so trusting? How could I not see that she was hiding something like this? What else did I miss?*

"Why would I believe you? How could you lie to me like this? Were you planning to kill me the whole time? All this joking about a fucking vampire or something when it was YOU all along! You and Grant playing around with a fuck-ing...monster? Who are you? I could've died today because of you!" I say, my anger overpowering my fear for the moment.

She briefly drops her head, and I take the opportunity to

lunge for her revolver. She jumps up quickly, dodging me, and I fall flat onto the floor. I roll over and she has the revolver pointed directly at my face, finger now on the trigger. I see the front of each round in the cylinder. *She isn't bluffing. I need to let this play out before I get killed in my own living room.* Tears pour down her face, and she wipes them away with her free hand.

"Look Damon, I promise I don't want to hurt you, but you HAVE to calm down. Just chill the fuck out and listen to me a moment…okay? Please? *PLEASE?* It's not what you think!"

I slowly nod, "Okay. Say what you have to say. I'm not going to be stupid. I don't want to die. Just put the gun down, I promise I'll let you talk. I'm sorry I lunged at you." I put my hands up, and slowly sit up. She takes a few steps and motions for me to get back on the couch. She grabs the bottle of tequila and sits it on the ground by my feet, then she gets a chair from the kitchen and sits in it a few feet in front of me.

"I'll tell you what. Let's both relax a little. Take a sip of that tequila and ask me what you need to. I'll take a sip, too. I'll answer you honestly, you deserve that. Then I'll ask a question and we'll take turns," she says while placing the revolver on the floor. I take a large gulp of the tequila from the bottle and hand it to her. *This seems like a cheap trick just to make me drunker and easier to evade. Oh well, not like I have much of a choice here…*

"So who are you then, and why are you really here?" I ask.

She takes her drink, and stares at me for a moment before putting her hair behind her ear.

"I am Evelyn Moore. That was not a lie. Me being here for my mother was not a lie either, at least all the way."

"What do you mean?" I ask.

"Nah babe, it's my turn," she says, another tear rolling down her face.

"Okay, what's your question then?"

"Was it Grant that you saw die today?" she asks, reaching for the tequila again.

"Yes. He was trying to prove to us that he wasn't lying. He confessed everything about how he had been searching for the Feyollocuani for years and found it here. We didn't believe him, and called his bluff. I mean who the fuck would? He paid for it with his life, but now we know he was telling the truth. It was what killed him right in front of me. He literally fucking...dissolved. It was so fast," I say. "Now, tell me the truth. Did you help him hang up those bodies?"

She breathes out and closes her eyes a moment, likely processing the news of Grant dying, "No. I didn't. I drove him to the church, and he did his thing. When we left from there we went out to the highway and rode around for a while as he tried to explain why he wanted to throw you guys off the trail of the Feyo. I also drove him to the school. I never touched either of them though, honest. He was convinced he had to display them like that to appease the Feyo in exchange for eternal life or something. He was really off the deep end with his understanding of the history of the Feyo. Nothing I could say would change his mind. The cop I didn't even know about until the day after I gave you a ride home. Grant actually tried to approach me as we left the tavern. He saw you and took off. He is who I was on the phone with at the restaurant that next day. He was beyond spooked and told me he was going to turn himself in. I told him not too, but he was dead set on it."

I think back to that night, when Evelyn seemed bothered for a moment. Had I been less drunk I may have actually been able to see Grant then... *Would it have changed anything if I did see him? He could've led me to the Feyo to cover his tracks and I wouldn't have been able to fight it.* I take a drink from the bottle and hand it back to her. She takes a drink, then smiles a little.

"Did he tell you about me? Was it your plan tonight to arrest me?" she asks.

"No, don't turn this around on me. My partner suspected those cigarettes weren't his. Forensics found them wedged in the driver's seat of Lewis Parley's truck. That was actually his tavern we met in. He was "Big Lew." I had no idea it was you until now. Why did you help him then if you didn't take part in displaying the bodies? You didn't want to be…immortal or like…a Feyollocuani? What was he to you, anyways?" I ask.

She laughs a little, shaking her head. "He had this delusion of grandeur about him. He thought he was so smart, and all the of the people in the tribes he met could see that. They knew he was too proud to listen to their warnings. I actually didn't even meet him until I was in Magnolia. In the grand scheme of things, he was a stranger to me. I too, was searching for the Feyollocuani for a long long time. This will probably answer more questions than one," she takes a long drink of the tequila and sloshes it around, looking at how little is left.

"Damon," she says, looking deeply into my eyes, "The reason I'm here, and the reason I helped Grant, is because my mother was killed by a Feyollocuani when I was fifteen. I loved my mother with all of my heart. Her and I used to take walks in the woods every single day to talk, and to get away from my dad… That was our thing. One day we decided to try a new trail she had found on a map that was supposed to lead to a waterfall. We got turned around somehow and ended up lost. We eventually found the waterfall late that evening, and it was beautiful. It had a walking path that went underneath it that had a large open area that was big enough to sleep in. We decided it would be safer to sleep underneath it for the night so we could make our way back through the woods in the daylight the next day." Evelyn stops for a moment to wipe the tears from her eyes again.

"The next morning when we woke up, we started walking back the way we came. About twenty minutes later, we saw what we thought was a man crouched on the edge of the trail. We approached him but when we got close, he heard us and turned around quickly. We were still about thirty feet from him when he just sprinted at us. Mom stood in front of me and he grabbed her...and she just dissolved. Just like Grant did in front of you... When he was that close and I could look into his eyes I realized it wasn't a man, but some-thing...*different.* I took off running as fast as I could, but when I looked back it wasn't even chasing me. Just standing there staring at me, totally expressionless. I kept running until I came out into a clearing and saw a family hiking. Once I told them what had happened, they called the police. Once they got there, they obviously didn't believe me. They told me I was just a scared kid and that someone likely just attacked her or she got lost, and that I had imagined the whole...dissolving thing. For years I had these vivid dreams about different hikers getting killed by it," she says finishing the rest of the tequila.

She continues, "My dad blamed me for it. Said I made her go to that waterfall and it was my fault someone killed her. She left me a large inheritance, that my dad legally had no right to, as it was specifically stated in her will that I would get it when I turned eighteen. My dad always said I would have to give him some on my birthday since all of that was my fault. Lucky for me he died three days before my birthday in a car crash. He was drinking and driving. Anyways, I kind of always kept what happened to my mom inside until I visited a tribe ceremony during college. I was researching the influence of western culture in Native American tribes of today, when I saw their ceremony of sacrifice for the Feyollocuani. I was so terrified by it that I had a panic attack. The medicine woman of the tribe took me in and gave me a tea that calmed my nerves. She then took me to their keeper of stories and I told her about my mother. She let me know about the history of the Feyo. It was kind of therapeutic to know that I wasn't crazy, and what took my mother was actually real."

"I'm sorry for your loss. That's horrible to have seen that at such a young age. I can't even imagine it. Seeing it today was enough for me, and I've seen a lot," I say, contemplating whether or not to try again for the revolver now that it is just sitting there.

"Thank you. And sorry for yours, too. Isn't it kind of ironic at least that both of our mothers died young and my dad died from drinking and driving? I thought of bringing it up when we were driving but I felt like it would seem like I was trying to "one-up" you. Anyways, the keeper of stories… I spent years speaking with her, and trying to find out everything I could. When I had finally built up a little confidence, I decided I wanted to see one. I begged her to tell me where one was, but she refused. She said it would bring bad luck on her and her tribe. She said my anger would cloud my judgment and I would get myself hurt. One day I was visiting my mother's grave and I decided I needed to kill the one that killed her. I put it in my head that if I could kill it, it would help me move on," she says.

"So, did you? Did you kill it?"

"No. I camped out in those woods for weeks. I even found the exact spot where she stood. I spent so long standing there, hoping it would come back and I could kill it right there. Unfortunately, I never saw it at all. I went back to the keeper of stories and told her about what I had done. She scolded me, and said that it had likely moved deeper into the woods, or had been killed. She told me that years ago there was a group of men who had decided they wanted to go kill the ones near native lands to ensure their safety. She thought that maybe they found it and killed it. So, I let it go for a while. I lived my life. I got smarter with the money my mother had left me and started a marketing firm that became successful enough that I could do whatever I wanted. About a month ago I decided I would go back to the keeper of stories and tell her about my progress. She told me that a man had recently been to see her, on the hunt for a Feyollocuani. Told me about how he was delusional, thinking he could find one and gain its power and eternal life. She said he acted dangerously and they had to ban him from returning. She told me his name, and that he had went south on his hunt. I did a little digging and I found him. Got his number through an old employer, and I just called him up." She stands up, grabbing the revolver and goes to the kitchen.

"What do you want to drink?" she asks.

"Just whiskey," I say.

She pours two glasses for us, and walks back into the living room. I think that now would be a perfect time to run around her and grab her gun from the kitchen counter where she left it. I decide against it, as I don't think she actually wants to hurt me. Plus, she's answering a lot of questions that I likely never would have gotten answers for otherwise. *I hate that getting to know the real her doesn't even matter since I will have to find a way to arrest her at some point anyways, since she helped Grant in some way. Or, maybe I don't have to... she said she didn't do anything outside of driving. She could be lying, though. She still hasn't said WHY she helped him yet.*

"So…he answered your call? Then what?" I ask.

She sips the whiskey and makes a face. "Yup. I asked if that's what he was really doing and he confirmed. I lied to him and said I was on a similar journey and would like to join him. He gave me an address and had me meet him there. It was that bigger man's house. When I finally got there, that man was already dead and in the truck. He told me about his encounter with the Feyo, and that he fully believed it had spared him as a thanks for what he had done. He said that he wanted to make sure the police were as confused as possible, so it had time to get stronger and fully repay him by giving him eternal life. He said once that happened, he would make sure that it happened to me as well. I knew he was crazy, and I didn't want to get in his way. For all I knew at the time, he was lying and had killed that man. I told him I didn't want to take part in anything to do with the bodies."

"But that isn't what you wanted, right? What did you want?" I ask.

"He was too stupid to understand that it wasn't even possible. I just wanted it dead. Something about knowing someone else was determined enough to find one reignited my hatred towards them. Knowing I was so close made all those feelings from my youth come back. I decided I would dedicate the rest of my life to finding and killing them all, and this was going to be how I started. I led Grant on as long as it took to get to the Feyo. He kept insisting I stay away until it was strong enough. In retrospect it seems like that was a good thing."

"So how do you plan to do that? Aren't they hard to kill?" I ask, taking a drink. I release the tension from my muscles, becoming more relaxed. No need in being on edge anymore, might as well enjoy this moment of transparency while it lasts.

"That's what they say. I had hoped to be able to find them still trapped and weak and cut their heads off. That wouldn't be too hard. But since dipshit Grant had to make this one strong…I don't know. It really complicates things," She says, taking another drink.

"So where do I play into this? How did you find me? Why? Were you trying to distract me?" I ask angrily.

"I didn't go looking for you. Meeting you at the tavern was by chance really. I had been going to that bar every few days since I got here. They have really good chicken salad and it was usually a good time. I heard the bartender talking to you, and overheard that you were a cop. Then the whole thing with the guy happened. I would be lying if I told you that distracting you wasn't on my mind at the time, but once we started talking, I had a great time. It became more of a distraction for *me*. I really enjoyed talking to you, and all of this has been real. Outside of the whole…lying about the reason I'm here and playing into the vampire thing," she says, smiling for a just a moment. "Damon, I swear to you it's all been real. I'm sorry I lied to you, I really am. I just knew you'd arrest me and I would be totally fucked if you guys never got to see it. You wouldn't believe either one of us. If that had happened, I might have died out there with Grant today…speaking of, why did the FBI say they took him into custody?" she asks.

"They know about the Feyo. They have been tracking them for a long time, actually. They have killed some even, but their plan for this one is to just…let it go deeper into the woods. Apparently they think it is safer to leave them alone when they get to this stage in strength," I say.

She looks back to me, astonished. She finishes her glass of whiskey then yawns. "Would have never guessed that to be honest. I bet they know where they all are. I wish I could find a way to get into their database and hunt them down with that info… Did they say anything about knowing someone was helping Grant?"

"Yea, but if they knew it was you, they definitely didn't tell us. They told us we should stick with the story of the accomplice fleeing the area. I would get rid of your phone if I was you though. If they do decide to pursue finding everyone he was in contact with, I'm sure they could find that easily," I say.

"Fuck. You're right. I'll do that first thing tomorrow, then I'll…" She trails off, then looks up to me. She begins to cry, and looks away for a moment.

"That means I'll need to get away from here. It means I'll need to get away from you," she says, walking back to the kitchen and grabbing her revolver. She comes back into the living room and stares at me. "You have to let me leave. *Please*. This is all I have. I have to kill them. You don't under-stand…I know you're just going to try and arrest me the second you can I just know it. I can see it in your eyes. But just know, NOTHING is stopping me from doing this for my mother. How many more mothers and fathers and kids must be out there, in danger at all times because of those fucking things? I promise you I'm not some bad person. I don't want to cause harm to anyone, *ESPECIALLY* you."

She was definitely right. As drunk and angry as I am, I have done nothing but think of different ways to overpower her to be able to take her in since I saw those cigarettes. As much as I like her, she's a criminal and that's what I do…I find the bad people and put them away. *She isn't really bad, though…I get her reasoning. Had the Feyo not killed anyone, what harm would she be doing to anyone but herself really? …In the grand scheme of things I guess I would be the bad one. I did nothing to avenge my mother, and even took part in doing the very thing that killed her several times. As fucked up as it seems, even while sitting here being threatened with a gun has been the closest I've felt to anyone in as long as I can remember.*

"I'm not going to arrest you Evelyn. I can't. You didn't hurt anyone. Grant was the real criminal here. I get why you want to do what you're doing, but why? It's too dangerous. What if it kills you? If not this one then the next? What if you make it stronger and it goes out and does what it's done here, in another town? Maybe I could help you find other ways to move on that don't require risking your life?"

She paces for a moment, then stares at me. "Promise?" she asks, raising her eyebrow. I nod my head, and she unloads the revolver and places it on the table. "I'm really sorry, Damon. I didn't want to hurt you, I promise. I wish that first night I could've somehow told you everything. I feel so bad for having to lie to you, but I didn't expect this to…go so well I guess. And being honest, I don't know what will happen. I just know that I have to kill them. I feel like I can't sleep until I know they're gone. This feels like my purpose in life. I need this. I've exhausted all other means of closure."

"I promise. It's okay. Just know if the FBI asks me about you, I don't know any of this," I say. I imagine Mike Banner showing me her picture, and asking me how I was so easily fooled. *I'm sure she could tell me the sky was falling and I'd believe her. Something about her makes me so trusting and comfortable. Even after knowing she lied, it's like that never even happene*d.

"Thanks. Maybe if they are just leaving it alone they won't even look into it. Maybe I could even still talk to you… I would really like that." She sits down beside me on the couch, and leans her head onto my shoulder.

CHAPTER 28

10:45 A.M.

I yawn, and try to move my left arm, but it's trapped. I open my eyes to see Evelyn still asleep against my shoulder. We must've just fallen asleep after the tense moment went away. I try to move my legs and realize Daisy is laying across both of our laps. *Where was she when everything was going down? Why wasn't she growling at her or trying to help?* She must really think she's a good person. I may not be able to trust Evelyn just yet, but I definitely can trust Daisy. That must be a good sign. My head is pounding, and I recall how much I drank and the fact that I had mixed tequila and whiskey. I need to get up and get some headache medicine before…

"Oh shit!" I say, rolling out from under Daisy and Evelyn.

"Huh?" she asks, waking up.

"Sorry! I'm late for work, we must've passed out!" I jump

up and run to get ready. I find my phone in the kitchen and see that I had several missed calls from Chief Marks.

> Sorry Chief, I missed all my alarms. Won't happen again.

> I understand. Was just worried.

I bet he's thinking I drank too much trying to cope with the situation. That or he thought I got killed by the Feyo... Not a chance he'd think I was actually hanging out with Grant's accomplice, being held at gun point and then sleeping casually with her on my couch. I brush my teeth and head back to the living room. Evelyn is flat on her side, cuddling with Daisy. I walk over and kiss her forehead, and go to my car.

I go through a drive thru and pick up a bag full of cheese-burgers and fries. It has always been a custom at the station that if you show up late, you have to bring everyone something. *I need to remember to give Davidson hell for not doing that on the day he was late. Well, I guess I could let him slide given the circumstances of that day...* I need something on my stomach anyways. Now that I think about it, I only had a few chips last night. That explains why I was able to pass out so quickly.

* * *

"Practicin' to be a delivery boy when they fire you for being a part timer?" Davidson asks, grabbing one of the bags from me and sitting it down on an unused desk. I laugh, and sit the other bag down.

"So what's been going on today?" I ask.

Davidson motions his arm and turns slowly in a circle, "You're lookin at it. Ain't done a damn thing really. Hargrove was here earlier to tell us when the FBI's doin that press briefing, then left with Chief."

"Do we need to go to it?" I ask, opening up a greasy burger and sitting it on my desk.

"Nah that's why they left. They wanted minimal presence. They said they were gonna go just to show their faces. It ought to be on soon. I'll pull it up on my computer." He rolls his chair over to his computer and goes to the WCDX website. Turning his screen so that we could both see, he laughs and points at the top of the screen. It is a banner that reads: "HELLLLLOOOOOOOOO CULVER" that scrolls back and forth, bouncing between two badly pixelated ads for a dentist.

"The lack of self awareness with that shithead is somethin' else," he says, scrolling down the page, "Ahh, looks like it already started."

We see Mike Banner standing at a podium in front of the WCDX building. He is speaking very monotone, echoing the same statements he had said in Hargrove's SUV yesterday.

"Guess he's just gonna give 'em this script and take off," he says, while scratching his head, "I think that'll work, especially with some of those airheads in that audience."

"I hope," I look around to make sure no one is listening, "Maybe that thing is gone. I'd like to have some normal days again. I didn't realize how much I missed those."

"How normal was your night last night?" he asks. "I was worried you'd quit after that. I really wouldn't blame ya, though. I considered it for a moment myself, if I'm being honest."

"Shiiiit, you know they're going to have to pry you out of here," I ball my burger wrapper up and throw it into the garbage. "I just drank too much and passed out before I set my alarms."

He shakes his head, and focuses back on the computer screen.

"As far as the other suspect goes, we have reason to believe that they fled the area once Grant was in custody. We will continue to monitor the situation, and ensure the safety of the area. That is all I have for now, and I will not be taking questions at this time," says Mike, and he quickly walks away from the podium. He is bombarded with questions from reporters, but exits without responding to any of them.

"Yep, the ol script and dip," says Davidson. He tosses his burger wrapper towards the trash, missing badly. "Shit," he says, getting up to throw it away.

* * *

"REASON TO BELIEVE *that they have fled the area*" plays back in my head. *Do they really think that? Or were they just saying that to appease the press? Do they know about Evelyn?* If they do, they either don't care, or have something planned that they wouldn't even think of sharing with us. I wonder if she's still asleep, or if she's up and gone. She said she still wanted to talk to me, but I wonder if that was just her trying to keep me from arresting her. She might not ever speak to me again after this. She could be long gone by now. I hope not. I hope she isn't out there in the woods trying to kill that thing alone. *How is she going to do it at all? She could have all the help in the world, and it probably wouldn't matter. What's one woman to a... thing that can kill you just by touching you? Grant said it took groups of warriors trying to trap it for it to even work. Maybe I should help her? No, that would just get us both killed...*

The whole night plays over and over in my head, and I think of when she said she camped out in the woods waiting for it. She's definitely way more courageous than me. I don't want to be in the same city as that thing, much less going straight to it. She is something else. Maybe she won't totally abandon me and we can hang out again, with less tears and guns.

* * *

CHIEF WALKS INTO THE STATION, carrying a large bag from the same Burger Stop that I got our food from earlier.

"Well shit," he says, seeing an officer eating one of the other burgers. "Oh well, I'm hungry as hell anyways. Watching that boring ass FBI guy talk had me day dreaming about some french fries. Oh, and Hargrove told me that Devin Stevens has checked himself into a psychiatric hospital. I really appreciate that you guys were able to handle that situation without any problems. Maybe he'll be better for it." He reaches into the bag and produces a handful of Burger Stops signature crinkle cut fries, holding them high in the air before disappearing to his office.

"Who do y'all think the dude that helped Grant is?" asks a young patrol officer, peeking into the bag of food.

"No idea," says Davidson, sneaking a few more fries, playfully slapping at the officers hand as she reached into the bag. "What you thinking, Damon?"

I shove a fry into my mouth to buy some thinking time. *I wish I could say, "Well, I think she's beautiful and funny! She slept on my couch last night after holding me at gunpoint. It was great!"* Unfortunately, I'll have to get good at lying until I figure out what my new normal will be.

"I think it's probably an FBI agent," I say, leaning back in my chair.

"Huh? How so?" she asks, finally able to outsmart Davidson's bag defense and grab her a burger.

"Think about it, we've never seen the person. The FBI didn't really seem too worried about finding them either. I think they know who it is and don't care. Maybe Grant was their target the whole time. Maybe he was traveling the country doing all this, and they had an agent go undercover to help catch him. Maybe even fed him that fairy tale to make him seem crazy so he could plead insanity at trial," I say.

She ponders my response for a moment, then nods her head, "Yea that actually does make sense. All those government agencies are crooked as hell anyways. No tellin' what the truth really is." She walks into the lobby, and Davidson and I glance to each other.

"No tellin' is right," he says.

* * *

OVER THE NEXT HOUR, Davidson and I take turns looking through reports, trying to dredge up something interesting to start working on now that our focus isn't dedicated to the murders. Outside of stolen property and domestic disputes, Culver is pretty safe. Well, before this anyways… When I was promoted to detective, I thought it would be like the old movies where there was some murderer on the run every few weeks who would accidentally leave breadcrumbs of evidence along the way. All a part of his master plan, only to monologue too long when confronted by some hot shot detective in the end and get captured or killed.

Unfortunately, the real life cases involve monologues from crackheads who try to justify stealing lawnmowers and copper. I wonder how long it will take the town to exaggerate the "Vampire of Culver" story, turning it into something like a modern day Dracula tale. How many generations will it take to forget something like this? I don't think anyone could even come close to guessing what has actually happened. *How long will the memory of Grant being killed play in my head? I hope it gets a little easier.* I think about Devin

Stevens, and how his life will carry on after losing Molly. I hope he gets the help he needs at that hospital.

My thoughts are interrupted by a text message from an unknown number:

Hi! It's Evelyn. This is my new number! Sorry it took so long, hope I didn't worry you!

I smile. At least now I know she didn't totally abandon me.

I thought you'd have been on a flight to another country by now, but I'm glad you transferred my number.

Nah, maybe later. Too much work here for now. Speaking of, can I see you tonight? I'd like to run something by you.

I think for a moment. *What could she want to run by me? I hope she doesn't want me to cover for her doing something stupid. Then again what does it matter really? She's going to do what she wants no matter what. I honestly admire that about her. I need something to motivate me like that so I'm not just back to writing suicide notes alone in my room again.*

Of course, just promise that there are no hostage situations this time okay?

Promise! See you later! XoXo.

I put my phone down as Chief Marks walks into the office area. He points to Davidson and I and turns his head towards his office, indicating that we should follow. We make our way to his office and shut the door behind us.

"We have an issue," he says calmly.

My heart rate increases, expecting him to say that he knows about Evelyn and her involvement or something.

He continues, "I just got off the phone with Hargrove. She's sayin' that the Fosters called and reported that someone has stolen one of their cattle. Said no fence was broken or anything, so it couldn't have gotten out."

"Fuck. It hasn't left then. Hopefully it will soon though," I say.

"I'm worried it will move out of the woods and into the town. Maybe it has like a taste for the area or somethin' now," he says, clicking a pen and rocking in his chair. "Hargrove says she's going to call Mike Banner and see if there's anything we can do to make it get out of here quicker. In the meantime…first thing in the morning y'all need to make an appearance at the Foster's farm. Don't go off in the woods or anything, just show up. Two Magnolia officers will be there too."

"Got it," Davidson says.

We exit the office and start to clean up for the day. We don't speak on it, but I know Davidson and I are sharing the same thoughts. *What if Chief was right, and instead of going away like they said, the Feyollocuani comes out into the town? What if we can't stop it? What happens? Does the FBI come in and try and trap it then? What would even happen if a whole town saw something like that... People would go into a real panic. I hope it just goes away.*

CHAPTER 29

7:00 P.M.

"Sorry, I had to stop by a few stores," says Evelyn, setting a large bag on the floor near the table.

"That's alright. So what's up? What do you need to run by me?" I ask, grabbing my glass of water from the kitchen.

"Is that straight vodka?" she asks, sniffing the glass.

"No, my liver needs a day off," I say, lying. I really just didn't want to be too drunk in case things go south, like last night. I don't think she would do anything like that again, but I also didn't think she was assisting a deranged man who wanted to become immortal, yet here we are.

"Understandable," she says, pulling out a large scroll and rolling it out on the table. It is the same map Davidson and I had found the original "Coalition Treaty" markings on. She had drawn all over it, with arrows and circles and little notes.

"So," she says, crossing her arms. "I think I have a plan."

"So you're really going to go out there and try and kill it? Alone?" I ask, matching her cross armed stance.

"Yup. You can help if you'd like, but don't feel obligated. I just wanted to see if you thought this plan was stupid, or not."

She leans over the map and points at the center of the triangle where the tree was. "It's probably still hanging around here, or at least close. So step one is to get all the way there without it getting me. I think what I want to do, is come this back way." She moves her finger over a few inches to where there is a small creek that twisted through the valley.

"How will you get there? And where did you get this map?" I ask.

"I'll just have to go five or six miles past that Lewis guys house and hike over the hill and down into where the creek is, then follow it. I think the noise of the water could mask the sound. And I got this from the little building behind the courthouse. Something to do with Union County tourism. A bunch of nice old ladies in there," she says.

I lean down to the map, and point at where the creek is closest to the triangle, "But as far as your plan goes, what about this distance? Whether it hears you coming up the creek or not isn't really important, is it? If you have to walk around three hundred yards into a clearing it would see you, right?" I ask.

She smiles, squinting her eyes, "I thought you were a detective." She moves my finger to the bend of the creek. I look closely and realize there is a cave opening drawn there with the small writing "Black Bear Cave" above it.

"So...you think it's in the cave? Why?" I ask.

"Because it makes the most sense, silly," she says, taking a drink of my water. "They hunt in the day time, but they go to sleep at night just like us. That's how many tribes were able to trap them."

"So what, you want to close the cave off and trap it there to let it die?" I ask.

"Nope, follow me," she says, heading towards the door. I follow her out to her car, and she opens the trunk to reveal a large net.

"Uhh… is that just a net? You plan to catch it with a net?" I ask.

"Not just any net, this is a commercial fishing net. Strong enough for big ass fish and strong enough for Feyollocuani," she says smugly, crossing her arms.

"Are you sure? Aren't they like…super strong?" I ask.

"Stronger than us of course, but not impossibly strong like a shark or a dolphin…both of which get caught in these nets every day."

"Well sharks and dolphins can't dissolve humans," I say, raising my eyebrow.

She smiles and shuts the trunk and walks back in. She sits down on the couch and yawns. Daisy slowly walks up and sniffs her feet before laying across them.

"Oh yea, I meant to ask," I say, sitting down beside her, "What was with that flannel? Whose was it? Daisy never freaks out like that."

"Grant's," she says dryly.

"Makes sense then, Daisy is a good judge of character." I lean down and pet her head.

Evelyn smiles and leans forward. "So…what do you think? Do you think it will work?"

"I don't know. I think it's too dangerous. I think you're underestimating how strong it could be. If it does work, what's the plan then? Carry it through the woods?"

"It really isn't much stronger than we are. They are surprisingly human like…and *WHEN* I catch it…" She gets up, stepping over daisy, and goes to the bag near the table. She pulls out a short cable with handles on the ends. "This!" she says, putting the cable across her neck, sticking her tongue out and closing her eyes."

"What is that?" I ask.

"It's a cable saw. It's used for cutting through small branches and other stuff. And by stuff I mean the neck of the Feyo." She smiles and reaches into the bag again, pulling out a large burlap sack. "Then I'll put the head in this, and we will mix up some concrete in a bucket in my trunk. Then we will take it to a bridge and throw it off. Without the head, the body can never regenerate and will wither away."

"I'm just scared that you'll go out there and get killed, and I'll never see you again. I don't like the thought of that," I say.

"Well then lover boy, come with me. Protect me." She puts her wrist up to her forehead, striking the classic "damsel in distress" pose.

I stand up, walking over and putting my arms around her. I kiss her on the cheek, and look into her eyes. "I wish I was brave like you, but I don't know how I could help. What if we just let the FBI figure it out? They already know it's still in the area. What if you just stayed here with me for a while, and then we took a road trip to find one that's a little more… dormant. That way you're safe, and you still get to avenge your mother."

She kisses me quickly, and smiles. "Not an option, detective. This is happening. Let me kill it. If I kill this one, killing the rest of them will be easy. I'm going to go tomorrow night, with or without you."

I take a deep breath and imagine her out there in the woods, alone. I lower my eyes at her, "Okay. I'll help you, but I have one condition."

"What's that?" she asks.

"If it kills me, you have to take care of Daisy."

"Deal," she says, kissing me again, "But I'm going back to the hotel get some sleep. I need to be as awake as possible out there. I recommend you do the same. After this is over, who knows, maybe I can come get some rest *with* you... You still haven't shown me your room." She bites her lip for a moment, then pets Daisy. She quickly gathers her things and we walk to her car. "Damon, I would understand if you didn't want to help me. This is my own fight. Don't feel like you have to. I won't be upset, I promise."

"I know. Be careful. See you tomorrow." I shut her door for her, and watch her leave for Magnolia.

I understand that I don't have to help her, but I just can't imagine her attempting to do all of that on her own. She's courageous and smart, but I don't think it would be enough. It may be her "fight", but letting her try it alone is a death wish. It can be my fight too. It isn't like I have anything else going on. Worst case scenario it kills me, and it isn't like that affects anyone but Daisy. For several years now, I've been considering doing that myself, but every time I imagine Daisy having to see me that way. She wouldn't understand and would think I abandoned her, and I really just couldn't do that to her. *I have to help Evelyn kill this thing.*

I walk back inside, petting Daisy and touching her nose.

"Wish you could help us. I know you'd tear that thing up without flinching. I love you."

She wags her tail, likely unaware that tomorrow I'll be putting my life at risk. If we aren't successful it's possible that we're also putting all of Union county at risk, or worse. I finish off my glass of water, and begin to get ready for bed. *I imagine what it would be like to have Evelyn in that bed with me... Will definitely be something worth looking forward to if everything works out. Well, that and...living.* I take a long look at the half empty bottle of whiskey in the freezer, and decide against it. I need to be as focused as possible for tomorrow.

. . .

2:15 A.M.

I WAKE UP, covered in sweat and about to urinate on myself. I guess all that water decided now was the time it needed to come out. I stand up and stretch, and look at my phone.

> Good night! XoXo.

She sent that around nine, so that means I got to sleep at a decent time. I keep the lights off to try and save my sleepiness so I can salvage the last few hours before I need to get up. I feel my way across the hall to my bathroom. I relieve myself for what feels like an hour, and start to feel my way back to my room. While crossing the hall, I get the feeling someone is watching me. My hair stands up, and I squint my eyes down the hallway. I don't see anything and begin to walk into my room when I hear a floorboard creak in the living room. I make my way slowly and quietly to my closet and grab the sawn off shotgun I keep in the corner. I crouch low by my doorway and listen.

I hear another floorboard creak, this time sounding like it's coming from my kitchen. I slowly peek around the doorway, pressing my left shoulder firmly against it as I creep into the hallway. In the darkness I still can't see anything. I sigh. I guess I'm just on edge from thinking about going into the woods looking for the Feyo. I stand up and flip on the hallway light to confirm that nothing is there. The hallway is empty... but just out of the corner of my eye, I notice a singular grey eye staring at me near the entrance of the kitchen. I point the shotgun directly at it and pull the trigger.

The hallway erupts with wooden splinters and dust as my ears begin to ring. I rack the shotgun and move forward, hoping to see the Feyo laying there with its head in pieces.

Nothing is there. I spin and around wildly, ears still ringing. The kitchen is empty, except for the debris I created by blowing the corner of the wall off. *I'm surprised this shotgun even fired, I haven't cleaned it in years.* I make my way to the living room. Nothing here either. I turn to go back into the kitchen and out of nowhere, a black hand swings wildly at me. It misses my face by a few inches, and I fall backwards. I hit the ground and pull the trigger, this time hitting the Feyo directly in the chest as it leaps towards me. It flies into the wall and falls down, laying in a heap on the floor. I sit up and quickly rack the shotgun again and point it at its head. I pull the trigger but nothing happens. I rack it again, and nothing. I must've only loaded two shells and now I'm fucked. The Feyo then starts to get up and I turn to run. I feel a pressure on my side, then a sudden wave of heat passes over me, as everything goes black.

* * *

I'M jolted awake by Daisy stepping onto my ribs. She must have jumped up on the bed and landed on me. I look around wildly and it's pitch black in my room. I push her aside and roll to my phone. Two-fifteen a.m. *Holy shit.* That dream was too real this time. I could see it. I could *FEEL* it. I need to go to the bathroom, but first I need to make sure this was a dream and that thing isn't inside my house. I jump up and go to the closet, grabbing the shotgun. I reach to the top of the closet into a box of shells, and ensure that it's fully loaded this time.

I burst through the doorway of the bedroom, flipping on the hallway light and looking directly at the corner entrance to the kitchen. It's still intact. I clear the kitchen, then the living area and turn quickly back to the hall. Nothing. Daisy joins me in the hallway, head turned sideways and tail thumping against the wall. I go to the restroom before laying back down. *I thought these dreams would be over by now.* I grab my phone and text Evelyn.

> I know it's late, but what were you saying about the dreams you had after your mom was killed? Sorry if this is too personal for a text. Goodnight.

I place my phone back down and think. Maybe Evelyn was having similar dreams. I need to tell her about these. Maybe she knows a way to make them stop. It's almost too much to deal with sometimes.

CHAPTER 30

8:00 A.M.

I check my phone, and still don't see a response from Evelyn. I'm sure she is trying to sleep in. I made sure to be up and at the station a little earlier, so as soon as Davidson gets in, we can head to the Foster's farm. I start a pot of coffee and a patrol officer walks up.

"You see where they got Raymond Stokes on a DUI last night?" he asks.

"Oh no!"

"Yea apparently they found him in one of his boss's company trucks up against a utility pole. Truck still in drive. No real damage besides the transmission if I had to guess. He had a damn fifth of vodka in his hand too. They got him in Magnolia right now since it was one of their officers that found him."

"Damn. I thought he was doing better," I say.

The officer grabs a cup, and begins to put sugar in the

bottom. "Yea, but it looks like he can't out run that problem of his. Doesn't help that he had to see that man in the church like that. Hard to get that out of your head." He pours the fresh coffee into his cup and walks away.

He is right about that. Any time my mind is unoccupied it loves to show me all of the horrible things I've seen over the last few weeks. Hopefully after tonight I can fill my head with better moments to outweigh those thoughts. Things like Evelyn... I wonder if she would want to take a vacation to the beach or somewhere relaxing. Somewhere far from this city and all of its problems. Even if she doesn't, I might. I need some distance from all of this, as soon as possible.

I sit at my desk and wait for my coffee to cool, organizing and throwing away old things that I no longer need. Davidson shows up, carrying a box of donuts.

"Well well well, a cop with some donuts. Might as well have worn a pig mask," I say, reaching for the box.

He laughs, and goes to make himself a cup of coffee. "Yeah they love to make jokes when I stop there. They said they're likely closing up shop soon and moving out of Union County, so I thought I would grab some while I still can."

"Why?"

"Their dad owns the place, and he said it just doesn't feel safe anymore. Said he might sell and open up somewhere closer to the ocean for a new start," he says, selecting a donut from the box.

9:30 A.M.

WE ARRIVE at the Foster farm, and are greeted by two

Magnolia officers. The two brothers are standing at the gate to let us in.

"How are you?" I ask to Cain as he shakes my hand.

"Be a lot better if I knew where my cow was," he says.

We all walk down the driveway to the edge of their main yard.

"Dad ain't feelin' well, so we'll take y'all down there to the spot where she was. Not sure what y'all can do but maybe y'all can see somethin' we don't," says Abel.

We begin to walk into their open field along their fence.

"So when did you realize it was missing?" I ask.

"It was around lunch time yesterday. We had been up all morning working on a pole barn on the other field across the way. We had a bite to eat then came over here to make sure the water troughs were full, and all the cows were up by the barn. They are normally down in the corner of the fence 'till night time by the shade tree. We did a head count and realized we were one down. Checked the whole fence and she was nowhere to be found," says Cain.

"No cameras or anything?" I ask.

"Funny you ask. We just started putting cameras up everywhere, after…you know. Didn't think to have one all the way down here, though."

We continue walking the fence, looking for anything that might indicate someone actually stole the cow. Davidson and I both make sure to appear very observant and make it look like that was actually what we are doing here. We both know that the Fosters won't be seeing their cow ever again. I just hope that it's the last one after tonight. We make it down to the corner of the fence, where there is a large post, and the fence is metal instead of wood like the rest.

"Why is the fence different here?" asks Davidson, "Someone break in right here before?"

"Naw. There's a creek bout a ten minute walk that way,

and the cows used to love to break this damn post down and go lay in it. You ought to see how hard it is to get those fat heifers out of there. We had to beef this spot up a little. Worked so far," Abel says.

"I'll be damn," says Davidson.

A creek. The same creek that I'll be in later tonight. I wish we could just come this way, would save us a lot of hiking. Evelyn's theory that it's in a cave near here would make sense then. All it has to do is walk a few minutes then get it a free meal, and go back to sleep. I bet it has no intention of leaving any time soon with this setup. *But what happens when it runs out of cows? Will the Fosters be next?*

"We'll keep an eye out. We know what y'alls brand looks like. Can't hide a cow too easy but you never know. Hope something comes up and y'all can get it back. Thanks for showing us," says Davidson.

"Me too. That's a three thousand dollar beef cow. Every butcher in Union county is on alert to give me a call if it shows up there. Thank y'all for comin' out. Even if it doesn't bring her back," says Cain.

Oh it won't, I think to myself as we walk back up to the house. I'm regretting the donuts now as I feel the sweat rolling down the back of my legs. When we finally make it back to the car, Davidson blasts the air conditioning and puts his face right up to the vent.

"Glad I don't have to work in a damn field all day. I'd be as dead as that cow they're missing,'" he says.

"Oh yea me too. I just hope that it's the last one they lose," I say.

He shakes his head as we pull away from the farm.

* * *

ARRIVING BACK AT THE STATION, we spend the rest of the day going through the motions. Outside of a few call ins about speeding, the station seems to be back to its old self. Exactly what I wanted. At least that's what I thought, until right now. Looking around at how everyone seems to be really busy, but is actually pantomiming work until the end of the shift is depressing. *Is this what I want the rest of my career to be? Sitting around and waiting on something to happen?* This is probably what got me to the place I was in to begin with. I have to do something different to make sure I don't end up like Raymond Stokes, passed out with a bottle somewhere.

My phone vibrates.

> Sorry, I took some sleep meds to make sure I
> had plenty of sleep. We'll talk about the
> dreams when I see you tonight. If you're still
> wanting to go with, we can meet at your
> house.

I'm glad to see that she is awake, but I had hoped she had a change of heart, and wanted to take me up on just moving on to an easier target. I guess not. I confirm that I'm still going to help her, and get my things together to leave.

"See you tomorrow!" says Davidson as I walk out of the side door.

I hope so, I think to myself. If I make it in tomorrow that means we were either successful in killing the Feyo, or it's long gone. Either one is a win for me.

8:00 P.M.

I HEAR Evelyn's car pull up, and I walk to open the door. She walks in carrying a black bag. She sets it on the table and gives me a quick kiss.

"Missed ya!"

"You too! What's in the bag?"

She walks to it, and pulls out a bottle of whiskey. "I figured doing this a little buzzed might be easier... What did you want to know about my dreams?"

"You had just mentioned that after your mother was killed, you had dreams of other people dying. If you don't want to talk about it, I understand."

She opens the bottle and takes a quick drink, "Oh, yea. After she was killed I would have these really vivid dreams where I would be back out there in those woods, and I would see the Feyo kill someone, then I would wake up. It was really scary. Why?"

"Well, I've been having dreams too. I had one last night. I've actually had one before pretty much every bad thing that has happened here. I...I was wondering if it was related somehow."

She pulls out a chair, pointing to the one beside it, "Sit. Tell me about them, please." She slides the whiskey in front of the chair, and I sit down.

I tell her about each dream in vivid detail to the best of my memory. Explaining how each one was vaguely foretelling the next event. She sits, cross legged, listening intently. When I explain the one from the night before, she places her hand under her chin, and begins biting her fingernails.

"What's wrong? What does it mean?" I ask.

She takes another drink, and slides the bottle back to me. "It means you had to come in contact with that Feyo in some way, and since you said you didn't see it until the other day, it had to be something from before. But that doesn't make sense, since it was dormant. You saying that it was somehow talking to you is odd, also."

"Actually I did come in contact with it," I say, holding my arm up to show her the scar. "I didn't realize until I was there at the tree with Grant. Its foot was actually sticking out of part of the tree I fell on when I was younger. We were all too drunk to notice. So what does it mean? What does it touching me have anything to do with the dreams? Is it trying to like…communicate with me? Wasn't that what it was saying by telling me it would see me soon and stuff?"

"No. The tribes didn't really understand it. Also, the Feyo don't speak so it isn't like they could help them learn anything, really. But any time someone was near a Feyo and it touched them, or killed someone close to them, they would have those dreams. They think that the Feyo projects their experience or intentions to all of the others in a way, and because it has made contact with you, you get bits and pieces of what's happening. Like it has imprinted itself on you in a way. I have never heard about it actually talking though, and now that I think about it, I never really heard anyone speak in any of my dreams. I may have to ask the keeper of stories about it. Maybe it spoke to Grant somehow too and that may be where he made the jump to thinking he could become one. Maybe it was tricking him. BUT, that means there are two different ways to interpret your dreams." She reaches over and grabs the whiskey again, this time taking a large gulp.

"What is it?"

"The good news is that they go away. The keeper of stories told me that the reason my dreams stopped is because the Feyo that killed my mother was likely killed, or is now in a dormant state. The better news, is that the chance that we will see it tonight just went to one-hundred percent, and my plan will surely work."

"Not if we don't go. We could do it another night, when we are a little more prepared. Maybe we could get some like big cage or something to put by the cave and—"

She puts her finger over my lips. "Shh. It's happening tonight, babe. I've come too far. I have to get this over with."

I sigh. "Okay. But, does this mean that the people with me when it killed Grant will have dreams as well?"

"Very likely. Like I said, it isn't fully understood. So let's go kill that fucking thing, so they never have to have them again."

I take a drink of the whiskey, and as it burns my throat, I imagine poor Davidson having to deal with a dream like I did. I wonder why he didn't tell me? Then again, I didn't tell him either. I bet he didn't want me to worry. That's probably why he brought donuts.

Evelyn stands up and grabs the bottle. "Let's do this. Hope you're ready to do some hiking."

I stand up and walk to the kitchen. "I'll meet you out there, I'll just be a second." She exits, and I hear her car crank. I grab two very large bowls. I fill one with water, and the other with dog food. Daisy runs into the kitchen and looks at me with her head tilted. I set both of them on the floor, then fill up the sink with water. I lean down and kiss her forehead. "Daisy, if I don't come home I promise it wasn't because I wanted to stay away. You are the best girl in the whole world and I love you with all my heart." I ruffle the fur on her back, and go to my room to grab my pistol, thinking back to the time I wrote those words down. *I have to come back to her, she doesn't deserve to be left alone.*

I swallow hard and walk out, Daisy looks at me one more time, tail wagging. Almost like she knows it will all be okay. *I hope she's right.* I leave the door unlocked, because I know if this doesn't go well that Chief Marks will come looking here first if I don't show up to work tomorrow. As I sit in the passenger seat of the car, Evelyn puts her hand on mine.

"You really don't have to help me if you don't want to," she says.

I look to her, feeling tears come up in my eyes, "I'm coming, just don't make Daisy wonder why I didn't make it back okay?"

"Oh, we're coming back. I feel it."

WE PULL OUT, and head for the valley.

CHAPTER 31

We find a spot to pull over around six miles past the house of Lewis Parley. *I wonder if they will find a way to sell that house? How would they explain what happened there to the new buyers?* Evelyn backs the car into a small clearing and puts it in park.

She looks to me, "Last chance to change your mind. You sure you want to do this?"

"Are you asking me, or was that directed at yourself?" I ask, rubbing her arm.

"No. I'm ready."

"If you're ready, then I am," I say.

We get out of the car and open the trunk. She pulls out a can of mosquito spray and we spray each other down. I fake a cough and pretend to fall over. She laughs and pulls out two backpacks from the trunk.

"This one has the net, the cable and the bag. The other is just extra flashlights, waters and some snacks for while we wait. And this…" She pulls the bottle of whiskey out and takes a drink. She passes it to me, and after I take a sip, I place it into the second backpack. I grab the heavier one with the net inside, and we cross the road to begin walking into the woods.

"If we just keep walking directly southwest we will run into the creek in a few hours, then we just have to follow it to the bend," says Evelyn, pulling out a compass from her pocket and tapping it with her finger.

We begin our walk into the woods, checking every few minutes to ensure that we are going in the right direction. Several spots we have to detour because of how thick the woods are. We don't want to risk using the cable saw for anything but the Feyo, so walking around was the only option. After a few hours of walking, Evelyn stops on a fallen tree to take a break.

"Didn't expect there to be this much shit in the way," she says wiping her brow and grabbing a water from the backpack.

"Yea this sucks," I say, sitting down beside her. I drink from my water, and hear a limb crack. Evelyn and I both turn our flashlights off and hold our breath. She squeezes my leg as we hear a branch crackle over our head. She grabs her flashlight and points it up in the direction of the noise and clicks it on. The light bounces off of the eyes of a large owl, who isn't happy about it. It flies off, snapping small branches as it goes.

"God damn. I thought that was it for us," says Evelyn, getting up and putting the backpack on, "Let's get this over with. Creek should be close."

We begin walking again and around thirty minutes later we arrive at the bank of the creek. It's fast moving and narrow, creating a calming murmur of sound as the water flows over stones and fallen branches. Seems just loud enough to mask our footsteps as we approach the Feyo. I just hope it's really sleeping and we aren't about to be caught in a bad spot. Not much I could really do with a pistol and a flashlight.

We get to where the creek begins to bend and Evelyn puts her hand across my chest, and her finger over her mouth, then points into the darkness on the other side of the creek. In the moonlight I can barely make out the opening of a small cave about a hundred yards away. The cave is dead center of the bend, and it looks like the net will definitely be big enough to cover the entire entrance.

"We should go ahead and cross," she says as she begins to step into the water. Luckily the creek is very shallow where we are, only coming up to our shins as we slowly walk across. We move at a snails pace along the water until we get to the cave. I shine my flashlight around, being careful not to point it at the opening. I can't see any animals or anything around that would spook us as we attempt this.

I mouth the words "So what now?" to Evelyn as she slowly takes her backpack off and places it on the ground. She points to two small trees that sit atop the cave. She mimes a wrapping motion around them. I set the backpack down, and begin to pull the net out. She grabs some rope, and before I can process it, she holds on to one end and throws the rolled up portion directly in front of the cave. It lands a few feet on the other side and I put my hand over my mouth. *What the fuck are you doing? You're about to wake it up!* I think, looking wildly at her.

She smiles, placing her hand against the side of my head and whispering into my ear, "We will put the net over the mouth of the cave, tying it off to those trees loosely. Then we will stand on the bottom of each side. I threw the rope so that when the net is up, we can tie it around the opening. When it comes running out, we will pull the rope, closing the net."

I nod my head. It makes sense, but she needs to be more careful. This will only work if it goes exactly right. If not, we're both dead and no one will ever figure out what the hell happened. *We have to get this right.* We unroll the net, placing the opening towards the cave. Together, we slowly walk it over to align it. As we walk in front of the cave, we both stare into it. It's pitch black inside even though the sun will be rising soon, and luckily there isn't a pissed off Feyo standing there wondering what the hell we are doing. We slowly begin to pull the net up to the top of the cave, lifting and walking along opposite sides. We hear a fluttering noise and freeze.

Three bats fly out of the cave, narrowly slipping through the small opening we had yet to cover. We stand there holding our breath hoping that the bats didn't awake the Feyo. After a few moments we continue to lift the net. We wrap the ends together using a zip tie behind the trees. Evelyn walks down and grabs the bundle of rope. I step down across from her, and she tosses it over the net to me. I tie a slip knot so that when it pulls the net, it tightens the rope. I'm thankful for the few weeks of Boy Scouts I took when I was younger. Evelyn walks around to me. She steps on the net at the corner of the cave and mouths "Just like this."

She walks to me and holds me tight. She gives me a kiss, then looks at me for a moment. She leans to my ear and whispers, "It's going to go right. I just know it is. Thank you so much for helping me." She kisses me again, then pulls the cable saw from the backpack and shoves it into a cargo pocket on her pants. She puts the backpack back on, and blows me a kiss as she walks to the other side. Once she's standing on the corner, I match her on my side, and hold on to the rope. She picks up a large rock and throws it as hard as she can across the creek. It cracks loudly as it bounces off of a tree. No noise comes from the cave, so she does it again, this time the rock breaks a small branch off of a tree and it falls loudly to the ground.

Before I can register what is happening, I feel my feet being pulled out from under me as the Feyo erupts from the cave and into the net. I hold onto the rope as tight as I can, but it is ripped from my hands as the Feyo slams into the water. I jump up and run for it, but it goes under. It begins violently sloshing back and forth trying to exit the net, causing it to get tangled in a fallen tree at the waters edge. Evelyn runs across the creek to try and capture it.

"Grab the rope before it gets out!" I say loudly, running to join her.

"It's stuck!" She tugs hard on the rope as the Feyo spins wildly within the net, covering us both with water.

I reach under the water and free the rope from the branch it was stuck on, and help her pull as hard as I can. It won't budge. I turn away, and put the rope over my shoulder and drive my feet into the bank. I start to feel the tension loosening, hands burning from gripping the rope so hard. All of a sudden we hear a *THWAP* as the rope snaps, sending Evelyn and I to the ground hard. I turn to see the net, rolling backwards into the creek. Evelyn and I jump up just as we see the Feyo free itself from the net, and stand in the water. For a moment everything seems to stand still, as it stares intently at me. *Fuck.*

"RUN!" Evelyn yells, as she turns and sprints. I join her and we take off away from the creek. I turn to look back and the Feyo is running effortlessly behind us, not making a sound. I cut to the left, and slam into a tree that was leaned against another, and fall flat on my back. I roll to get up and see the Feyo launching towards me, arms extended. I jump up, just as a bottle of whiskey explodes in its face, knocking it backwards. One of its outstretched hands misses my face by inches, and I feel Evelyn tugging at my arm.

We sprint away and the muscles in my legs feel as if they're going to rip from my bones as we make our way towards a clearing. My feet slipping in my wet socks as I try and create distance between myself and the Feyo. I look back, and no longer see it chasing us, but I keep running anyways. We make it to the edge of the clearing and reach the corner of the Foster's fence. We jump it, and begin running towards their barn, just as we hear a hard *THUD* against the fence behind us.

We turn around as the Feyo makes it over the corner, and begins running towards us. We scramble past a tree along the fence, and Evelyn twists her ankle on an exposed root and collapses in front of me. I reach down to pick her up as I'm running but in my exhausted state, we tumble forward together. We come to a rest by the fence. We turn around to see the Feyo in mid air, grey eyes lit up by the rising sun. I brace myself and throw my arm around Evelyn, just as the Feyo is ripped backwards violently by a lasso wrapped around its neck. It lands flat on its back with a *THUMP*, creating a cloud of dust. I hear the gallop of horses as a second lasso sails through the air while it tries to flee. The lasso lands perfectly around its midsection, trapping its arms. Cain Foster pulls hard on the rope and brings it back down to the ground.

"Throw me another rope!" he yells to Abel.

Abel tosses one to him, dismounting from his horse and running to the Feyo. In a matter of seconds they have it tied up with its legs and hands together behind its back.

"Better start talkin' motherfucker!" says Abel, kicking it in the side. I help Evelyn up, and we jog to the Foster brothers.

"You won't have any luck with that, they can't speak," says Evelyn, pulling the cable saw out of her cargo pocket.

"Huh? They?" asks Cain.

Evelyn puts the cable underneath the Feyo's neck, and stomps on the back of its head. Its face now buried in the dirt, she begins ripping the saw back and forth.

"Lady, what the fuck are you doing?" asks Cain, reaching to try and stop her. I reach out and stop him, shaking my head. We watch as Evelyn saws through the neck of the of the Feyo, each movement creating a gut wrenching noise. She makes it all the way through, and kicks the head a few feet towards the fence. Abel vomits.

"Fuck you!" she says, throwing the saw down. She reaches into her other cargo pocket and pulls out the crumpled burlap sack.

"I can't wait until every last one of these fucking things are dead," she says, picking up the head of the Feyo and putting it into the sack. She slams it on the ground a few times and looks up to us. "Sorry, uh… that's just been a long time coming. Let's get out of here."

Cain interrupts, "Y'all planning on telling me what the hell is going on?" We start to reply when we see an old man walking towards us. His steps seem very labored, and he's putting a lot of trust in his walking cane.

"Dad! Why are you out here? You need to be resting!" says Abel.

Mr. Foster waves his hand at Abel. "Oh whatever, I'm fine. I heard all this damn hollerin' and I had to—" He stops, looking down at the lifeless body of the Feyo, then to Evelyn holding the sack. He scratches his head, then looks to Cain, "Better get the side by side with the bed on it down here. I always knew they were real. Now I know what took my damn cow. Evil bastard."

Confused, Cain follows his fathers orders and hops back on his horse and heads up to the barn. Mr. Foster hobbles closer to the Feyo, and jabs it with his walking cane a few times.

"So what the hell is it then?" asks Abel, the color now gone from his face.

"Feyollocuani, and praise the Lord it's dead. Evil like that needs to be down there with the Devil. Today seems like as good a day as any to start that brush fire. We'll toss it in there."

"Feya…what? I don't understand. We can't burn someone's body out here Dad that's wrong," says Abel.

"We can and we will. That ain't no damn person, anyway. And don't worry 'bout understandin' it. Just worry 'bout pickin' it up and putting it in the side by side." Mr. Foster puts his hand on my shoulder. "And no offense, but I seen you with them other cops and I ain't trying have any more law men sniffing around. Can we just keep this between us?"

"None taken, and absolutely. The fewer people that know about it the better. Union County will be safer now, and we don't need to worry about having to explain all of this," I say, looking at the sack in Evelyn's hand.

He nods, then takes a few steps back as Cain pulls up in the side by side. Abel and I grab the body of the Feyo and toss it in the back.

"Now hop in, we gotta get this fire started," says Mr. Foster, pulling himself into the passenger seat.

Evelyn and I get in the back seat, and Abel hops onto his horse. As we head to the brush pile, she leans her head on my shoulder. Looking down at the burlap sack, I wonder if the Feyo is still…alive in there. *Will trapping it in concrete just be a prison for it, or is it dead?* I transfer my focus back to Evelyn as we pull up to a large pile of dry tree limbs and sticks. We hop out and Cain and I toss the Feyo's body into the pile. Abel walks up with a jug of gasoline, pouring it in various spots around the pile.

"Y'all step back a little!" he says as he takes a lighter from his pocket and ignites the gasoline trail he had made. The wood immediately bursts into flames, and sweat begins running down my face. I yawn, not realizing how tired I was. I don't know how I'm going to make it to work in a few hours. I don't even really care to go. Maybe I'll call in and rest with Evelyn. We watch as the flames finally reach the Feyo's body. It turns the smoke solid black as it burns away. I notice a tear roll down Evelyn's face, and put my arm around her.

"Cain, give these people a ride back to wherever they came from. I'm sure they're ready to get home," says Mr. Foster as he walks up to us. He shakes mine and Evelyn's hand. "The smell of this fire has me wantin' a biscuit." He hobbles away, and Cain pulls a set of keys out of his pocket.

"We'll take my truck. Where y'all headed?" he asks. We tell him, and he raises his eyebrow, "Well damn no wonder y'all look like shit then. That's damn near ten miles from here."

We laugh and follow him to a truck, about a hundred and fifty yards from the fire. On the way, I go ahead and send Chief Marks a text, telling him that I won't be in to work. *I wish I had the courage to just quit. After all this, I don't really feel like being a detective is my thing. I should be doing something more...fulfilling.* Now that the Feyo is dead, it isn't like anything will really be worth showing up for. I'm sure the crackheads would be just fine without me asking them questions.

ARRIVING AT THE CAR, Cain turns to me and asks, "So...that was what killed that man in the lodge right? That means we ain't finding the cow either, huh?"

"Yes sir. I'm sorry you guys had to be a part of all of that. Unfortunately, that does mean that the cow is gone as well," I say.

"Damn. Well at least it's dead now."

"Yup, thanks to you! Very grateful that you two were there. We'd be dead if you weren't," says Evelyn, getting out of the truck.

"Not a problem. We were out looking for whoever—or I guess *WHAT* ever was stealing cows. Guess we both got what we needed. Was it uh…was it really a vampire?" He asks.

"Not quite," I say.

"Dad is gonna have to explain to me what the hell it was then, since he acted like he knew all about it," he says.

"I'm sure he will, man. Thanks again," I say as I exit the truck. He pulls away, and we walk to the back of Evelyn's car. She pulls out a bucket and a bag of quick mix concrete. We cut open the bag and pour most of it into the bucket. She steps around to the back seat and pulls out two gallon jugs of water.

"Can you grab a stick or something to mix this with?" she asks, pouring the water into the bucket. I find one about ten inches long, and help her mix up the concrete. Once it is mixed, she opens the burlap sack and dumps the Feyo's head out into the concrete. It plops in, eyes facing towards us, still grey and emotionless. Looking into its eyes again sends a chill down my spine. I know it can't hurt me anymore but I just feel like it's still…*watching*. I take the stick and shove it deeper into the bucket.

"Now we've gotta let this dry. Let's go to your house and rest," she says.

"Sounds good to me."

I place the lid on the bucket, and put it into her trunk. We pull out into the road, and I look into the woods where we started our hike yesterday and smile. I could've never pulled something like that off alone. I wonder what else I could accomplish now that I have someone around to push me like that. *Well, IF she stays around.* I wonder what her plans are now. She reaches for the radio and turns the volume up, then rubs my thigh.

"Told ya we'd do it," she says.

* * *

We make it back to my house, both so exhausted that walking up my steps feels like climbing a mountain. I go to sit down on the couch, but Evelyn interrupts me.

"No, don't sit just yet. We have to shower first. I have to wash that... I have to wash that off of me," she says, turning to walk down the hallway.

"I understand. There are towels and stuff in the closet. I don't have any feminine smelling items you'd probably use, but I'm sure it will work for now, though. You can go first if you'd like."

"Oh? You mean you wouldn't want to join me?" she asks, turning back to face me.

I swallow hard. I hadn't even considered that as a possibility. *In this moment I can't think of anything in the world I'd rather do...* "I mean... If you... if you're okay with that, I would love to."

She walks over to me, stepping out of her shoes and gracefully tossing them near the door. She stands in front of me for a moment before crossing her arms and pulling her shirt up and over her head in one motion. She glides onto my lap and places her right hand on my shoulder, using her other hand to remove her bra. I watch it fall to the floor, then look back into her eyes. She smiles and leans down to kiss me, her fingers making their way through my hair. She backs away and straightens her back for a moment, just enough for me to catch a glimpse of her breasts. I pull her back to me and roll her onto her back on the couch. I remove the rest of her clothes, making sure to kiss her from her neck to her thighs in the process.

She pulls my shirt over my head and throws it against the wall. From beneath me, she removes my belt. She wraps it around the back of my neck, pulling me in for another kiss. I take a moment to admire her beauty, running my hand all the way up her body and stopping near the side of her face.

"As much as I'd love for you to fuck me right now, let's get this filth off of us first," she says, pulling herself up, "and besides, I already said you needed to show me the bedroom. I think it's a little more fitting for the occasion."

She jumps up and holds her hand out for me to grab. She leads me to the bathroom and we begin fulfilling her request of washing the *"filth"* off of our bodies. I'm not sure if the sweat and mental anguish we obtained from our time with the Feyo could be categorized as "filth", though. More like *"rot"* or a *"sludge"* that will be stuck to us forever... *However, in this moment all I can think of is the way the water from the shower is running down Evelyn's smooth body. The way she looks with nothing on is much more amazing than I could've ever imagined... Like something you'd see in a magazine... Definitely not the type of body that has ever been pressed against mine before now.*

CHAPTER 32

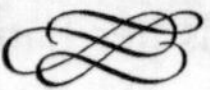

1:45 P.M.

I awake to Daisy's tail slapping my hand. I roll over, and realize Evelyn isn't in the bed. I sit up, and my entire body aches. Hiking through the woods really kicked my ass. Running away from the Feyo kicked my ass. Hell, everything that has happened since finding Lewis Parley in that church has kicked my ass... I stand up and stretch for a moment before walking into the hallway. Evelyn is at the table in the dining room, eating cereal and looking at a laptop.

"Good morning, sleepy head!" she says. "Would've made you some breakfast, but you hardly have anything in here."

"That's okay, how'd you sleep?" I ask.

"That was probably the best sleep I've had in years," she says. Especially since uh..." She winks at me, and begins typing on her laptop.

Her wink reminds me of this morning after our shower.

The same wink she gave me after pulling me into my bed and continuing what we started on the couch. Entering her for the first time was something I will likely never forget. That and the way her body looked as we made love is now permanently burned into my brain, and I can't wait to see it again. *I'd love to right now, actually. Right here in this kitchen...*

"Catching up on work?" I ask, manually overriding my train of thought.

"Sort've."

"What's that mean?" I ask, sitting down beside her.

"Well," she says, turning the laptop towards me, "Looks like the closest Feyo is in New Orleans..."

The screen displayed an online forum where someone had attached a picture of a map.

"What am I even looking at?" I ask.

"It's a map of a few known Feyo in the United States. This is a forum I started following a few months ago. Some of the info is probably bullshit but some is at least kind of accurate. Whoever this person is, has mapped out several of them. See, look," she says, pointing to our location on the map. It had Union county highlighted with "Dormant" written on it. It wasn't exactly right, but close enough to have likely led her here if Grant hadn't assisted.

"How did they get this information?" I ask.

"No idea. They might be working with that team from the FBI or something, it's hard to know. This forum is pretty much anonymous, and there aren't like character profiles or anything. Either way, if they knew this one was here, surely they're right about this one," she says, pointing to New Orleans, Louisiana.

"So you're serious about wanting to continue? You want to go everywhere and kill these things?"

"As serious as a heart attack," she says, grasping her chest and pretending to fall over.

"When would you want to go there?"

"As soon as possible. The sooner they're all dead, the better. I want to be able to move on. I decided after they're all gone, I want to sell my business and just retire. I'd like to travel, and be comfortable knowing that the Feyo are all gone," she says, shutting the laptop.

"I understand but—"

"But what?" she asks. "I have to do this. This is what I was meant to do. I understand if you don't want to be a part of that, don't feel like you have to be roped into all of this."

I think for a moment. I knew this time would come the second she told me she wanted to kill them all. I guess I just kept it out of my head because I wasn't prepared to face it. This beautiful woman, who fulfills everything I could ever imagine wanting in a partner, is about to leave me behind. If she leaves here, there is no way I would ever see her again. I'd just go back to being the same shell of a person, going through the motions again. *Will this be what finally pushes me to get out of here?*

"I-I really wish I could Evelyn, but I can't just quit my job and I don't have enough vacation for all of that."

"Why not?" she asks, squinting her eyes at me.

"I have to have money, and it isn't like I could work while driving all over the country."

"Money isn't a problem here. If you come with me, you'll never have to worry about that. I mean if you just wanted to work when all this is done, there are police stations every-where," she says.

"You're right. What about Daisy, though? I would have to take her with us. I don't really trust anyone to watch her."

"Even better!", she says, standing to pet her. "So…what's it going to be?"

I close my eyes and think. *On one hand, I can go with this woman I barely know, traveling the country trying to kill those...*

things. On the other hand, I could stay here and rot away like everyone else. I think back to the night all of this started, and the note I had written. Is that what I want to go back to? I think I'll finally take my mothers advice and get the hell out of Culver.

"I think I'll join you."

She holds me in a long embrace, then kisses me several times very quickly.

"Good. Was thinking I would have to hold you hostage again."

3:30 P.M.

"ALRIGHT. On the count of three...One. Two. Threeeee!" Evelyn says as we push the heavy bucket off the side of a bridge. It crashes into the water, sinking immediately.

"Do you think it's dead? Or is it just...stuck in there forever?" I ask.

"It's definitely still alive right now, but after a few days it will die. At least that's what the keeper of stories said. Kind of like how humans can stay alive for a few seconds when they are decapitated, just...weirder and longer," she says.

I shudder at the thought of the Feyo just laying there in darkness. I wish I could understand what they really are. Maybe Evelyn will let me meet the keeper of stories and I can figure out where they came from. This situation has brought a new curious energy to me. The weirdest thing I ever witnessed before all of this was just people being strange. Three weeks ago I wouldn't have even thought of something like the Feyo as a possibility, now here I am tossing its head into a river. Weird how life can change so fast.

"Now, to quit your job," she says as we get back in her car.

"Not looking froward to it," I say.

The truth is that I don't even know what to say to Chief. He's put so much time into me, and leaving him down a detective seems really disrespectful. Thinking back to all of the moments he'd seen something in me and let me keep my job, even when I knew I didn't deserve it. I start to have second thoughts.

"I just wish there was a way I could do this that would be the right thing for everyone. My boss is a great guy and he doesn't deserve to be abandoned like that. He's basically family," I say.

"Well…how happy were you before this? Like, with the way things were?" she asks as she pulls back on to the road, "Why don't you just take tonight to think on it? I have a lot of packing and stuff to do anyways. Sorry I gave you an ultimatum earlier, that was rude of me. Just know that if you spend your life only making other people happy, you never will get to experience what's best for YOU."

I shift in my seat, "I still want to, and I get what you're saying. I just need to find out the best way to go about it. I need to get some things together too. I definitely don't want to go back to what I was doing. Just being completely honest, this has been the happiest I've been in a long time. Even though you held a gun to my head…"

She smiles and grabs my hand, "I promise that won't ever happen again. I'm sorry. The feeling is mutual, though. I've been keeping myself so busy with everything I never really stopped to feel anything. Spending this time with you has helped remind me that I need to do that more often. I can't lose myself in all of this and not actually experience life and have fun. No matter what ends up coming of all of this, I uh…I need you to know that you've really been important to me. I really mean it."

I pull her hand up to my face and kiss it. "Thank you. I feel the same way." The rest of the ride back to my house, I think deeply about how I'll tell Chief that I'm done. I wish I could just write a letter to him or something, but he deserves more than that. I think I'll probably go in early and get it over with, like ripping off a bandaid. That way if he's mad or wants to have a long talk about it, I'll still have time to pack a little. I really don't think I'll take more than a few things. I don't have much anyways. As long as I have Daisy and some clothes, I'll be alright.

8:00 P.M.

"Kinda sad isn't it?" I say to Daisy as we look at the two small bags I have sitting on my bed. I decided I'd take one suitcase of every day clothes and one with the few nicer things I have in case we get a chance to eat somewhere special. I filled the rest of the bag with the few pistols I have and the shotgun. I hope I never need them, but knowing that I'll be leaving this house unattended for a while I don't want anything to get stolen. I know it would probably help to eventually sell this place to have some spending money but there's no chance in hell I ever will. It's pretty much the only thing I have left of my mom. That's the only reason I've even kept it this long. Something about it still being here makes me feel like she's still here in a way.

I look to my glass of whiskey on the nightstand, now room temperature from sitting there for so long. I think I'll just pour it out. Tomorrow will be a long day, and something about Evelyn asking me if I was happy before really made me think about how much I've been drinking. I told myself I would stop after this case was over, and now it's over. Maybe I'll see how many days I can go without it. I really don't feel the need when I'm around Evelyn anyways, so I'm sure she'll help.

I grab the picture of my mother off of the wall, and look at it for a moment. It is a picture she had me take when I was fourteen, of her on the steps of the porch reading a book. It's really blurry, since I didn't really know how to use cameras then. I hope one day I can have a child that loves me as much as I loved her. I place it back, and get ready for bed.

CHAPTER 33

8:00 A.M.

$\mathcal{I}$ pace back and forth in front of my desk. I arrived at work a little too early I think. I just wanted to be here early just in case Chief Marks or Davidson was here. I have already taken all the things I wanted to keep to my car, so that way I can get out of here quickly once I get this over with. I've already had two cups of coffee and I think that if I have another, my heart will beat out of my chest. I'm really not ready for this.

"Howdy part timer!" Davidson says, walking into the office holding another dozen donuts.

"Well uhh… uhh, I'm like, well uh…" I struggle for words, as I really wasn't expecting to have to confront him first.

"Damn son, spit it out!" he sits the donuts down and grabs a glazed one, biting it nearly in half.

"Man I…I'm done with this… I'm quitting today." Saying it out loud made my skin hot.

"Huh? You get an offer from somewhere else? What? Why?" Crumbs fall from his face and he sits the donut down, mouth still open.

"Yea man…but no there aren't any offers, it's really hard to explain…" I realize now that I haven't even told anyone about Evelyn for fear of them finding out the connection. *I should've put more thought into this. They are going to think you're fucking crazy.*

"I'll be damn… you hit the lottery didn't you?" His grin growing as he picks his donut back up and finishes it.

"Shit man, I wish. I just met someone, and she brings an opportunity that requires me to quit and move. I hope you guys aren't mad," I say.

"Mad? Shit, I envy you buddy. Congratulations is in order. You? With a woman? I'd have never guessed it," he says, slapping my shoulder, "Live your life while you can. You got my number if you ever wanna talk it out. Till then, I guess I gotta get to working twice as hard to fill your shoes. I always knew you'd outgrow this. You're a smart cat, always have been. It was bound to happen one day."

"I appreciate it man, honestly. You've been a great man to work with. I couldn't have asked for a better partner, or friend."

Chief Marks walks by the doorway and into his office. My hands go numb thinking about how the next few minutes will go.

"Good luck with that, buddy. I'll leave you to it. I gotta go take a statement from the gas station owner down the street. Someone tried to rob it wearing a beer box as a mask yesterday around lunch and somehow made off with six hundred dollars." He walks over and gives me a long hug, then places his hands on my shoulders. "Like I said, you have my number. I'll always pick up if you call, buddy. *ALWAYS.* It's been good, brother. Stay safe for me." He grabs another donut and walks to the side door. I catch a glimpse of him wiping a tear from his eye as he steps out. I feel a wave of sadness hit me. Eight years of being with him five to six days a week, ending with a hug and a pat on the shoulder. I'll definitely be taking him up on that phone call.

I make my way to Chief Marks office and stare at the door a moment. I take a deep breath, and knock a few times.

"C'mon in," he says.

He's eating a biscuit while looking at his phone, and in this moment I imagine him as a father figure that I never had. I feel like I'm a teenager that is about to tell my father that I've wrecked into his car or something. The only conversation I've had with my dad in the last fifteen years is when he was trying to figure out where we lived, and I lied to him and told him we lived in Australia. I knew he knew that I was lying because of the area code, but I had hoped that it pissed him off. He never called again.

"Whatcha needin'?" asks Chief.

"I'm quitting today… uh now," I say, brain outrunning my mouth.

He sits his biscuit down and drinks from his mug of coffee. He sighs and sits silently for moment. "Why? Is it because of that…*thing*?"

"No, it isn't that. Someone has just…uh… I don't even really know how to explain it Chief… I—"

"Who is she?" he asks, grinning.

"Uh…her name is Evelyn and—"

"Listen son, no need to explain it to me. More times than I can count, I've said I was going to quit. Hell, I took my badge off and even set it on this very desk at least five times in the last three years. Sarah even encouraged it before she was taken from me, but I always powered through the feelin'. There's nothing I regret more than not quitting. I should've cashed out my retirement and bought a damn camper to travel the country while I still had a little time with her… I'll never get that time back, and I think about it damn near every day. If this person means even half of anything to you, I support whatever you have going on. Go out there and live, have fun, love her with everything in you, son. You'll be better for it. If you ever want to come back, that desk will have your name on it. You've been a damn good detective, and if it means you're happy, I'm happy."

I feel my eyes swelling with tears as the relief of his statement settles in. Before I can respond, he comes around his desk and holds me in a long hug.

"Now get your ass out of here before I start cryin' too," he says, shaking my hand vigorously. I place my badge and service weapon on his desk.

"Thank you for giving me the space to succeed. Call me if you need anything," I say as I exit his office.

Walking to my car feels surreal. Coming here every day for so long, I never imagined that there would be a "last time" I walked out, especially this soon. I stare at the old boot propping the door open and feel tears forming in my eyes. I think of when my mother told me that "The hardest things to do, are usually the best for you. Real growth comes from pain."

THE NEXT FEW hours I feel numb as I make my way home and gather my things. None of it feels real, and the feeling I had in the office hasn't left. Evelyn should be here any minute. I pace the living room while Daisy watches me confused. I've peed no less than ten times in the last two hours and I feel like I should go again.

I hear a honk in the front yard and peek out of the blinds. It's a black Mercedes sprinter van that is parked sideways behind my car. Evelyn pokes her head out of the window and waves back and forth. I grab my bags and walk out, as Daisy follows.

"I figured we needed something a little more appropriate, what do you think?" Evelyn asks as she exits the van.

"I think it's badass honestly, what happened to your car?"

"Traded it in on this. I don't have a need for it now that there's a whole man and a dog involved in the operation. Judging by your bags I'd say you decided to tag along?" she asks, petting Daisy.

"Yes ma'am. Quitting went a little better than I expected and I decided I'm ready for a change, so here I am. Regular civilian Damon McKay, at your service. Scooby doo was booked up, so Daisy will have to do."

She walks over and kisses me, grabbing one of the bags, "Anything else you need?"

"Just let me run grab Daisy's food and I'm ready to go."

I walk back inside, grabbing her food and two bowls. I stop by the breaker box and cut the power to the house. Walking back through, I recall all of the nights I spent here, alone. The late nights, drinking and passing out on the couch, the takeout and the anguish of feeling lost. I don't have that feeling anymore. I think about my mom, lecturing me about girls at that same dining room table before prom, being sure to give me a comically large bag of condoms from the health department before I left. *I wonder what she'd think about Evelyn...* I lock the door, and walk to the van.

"Ready?" Evelyn asks.

"As I'll ever be." I look back to the front porch as we pull away, and imagine my mother at the bottom of the steps, waving at us. I smile, thinking of what she would have to say about what I was doing.

I'm finally following your advice, Mom... I'm getting the hell out of Culver.

EPILOGUE

"See how good he is? See just how *GREAT GOD IS?* Oh Lord in heaven, thank you! Thank you for moving that evil into the right hands and out of our town! AMEN!" says Pastor Tim.

Several responses of "Amen!" Bounce off of the walls of the church, directly into the ears of Preston Walsh. He hasn't been listening for the last thirty minutes, instead rolling around in his memory of the last few weeks. Back to the time where something pulled him to this very church, trying to tell him that something very bad had happened. *What did it mean? What really happened that night?* He had heard rumors and knew one of the people responsible was arrested, but as far as details go… *What could be so evil that it sucked him in?* He had come to terms with knowing it wasn't him that did anything wrong, but he couldn't shake the feeling of it meaning something much deeper than he could understand.

Maybe it was a sign from a higher power trying to convince him to find faith again. Maybe it was some supernatural premonition that he would never understand. Maybe it was nothing and he was just losing his mind… His mind racing with possibilities, he decides that it has to at least be good that he's here at all. Nothing wrong with giving the church a chance. He sits up straight, focusing all of his attention on Pastor Tim.

* * *

Doc Thompson leans back in his chair, releasing a long sigh. The computer screens in front of him displaying images of Lewis Parley, Molly Baxter and Walker Hamilton. The FBI had taken all of the documents and data related their case with the promise on following up with him if any major development occurred. *Yea, right...* Doc knew that even though they would likely assign the sharpest forensic scientists and pathologists in the country to these images, he would never hear from them again. What they didn't know, was that he always saved backups for every picture and note he has taken since his first day here in Culver.

As he clicks back and forth on the images, he wonders if the FBI was even right at all in their assumption that the man they took into custody was who committed the crimes. As far as he knew, there weren't any fingerprints or DNA samples available to compare to. He had heard the guy just turned himself in and that was it. It seemed as if there was minimal follow up on the other person at all. Those detectives hadn't even returned his call the last time he tried to reach them. In his mind he knows something is fishy with the way the FBI handled it. No one has conjured up even a rumor as to how that man or his accomplice did those things to the bodies. He rubs his temple at the thought of never being able to understand what really happened.

He pours himself another glass of wine, making sure to preform a silent "toast" to each of the victims before finishing it off. He clicks the small "x" in the corner of all the images and powers his computer down. Grabbing his bag, he takes one more long look at the blank computer screen. Part of him hopes he never sees anything like that ever again. Deep down he knows he will spend the rest of his life trying to get answers to the only thing that ever left him scratching his head in his entire career. He switches the lights off, and heads home.

* * *

EARL DAVIDSON SITS on the edge of his bed, staring at the wall. He thinks briefly about the dream he had a few nights ago, and rubs his hands over his eyes. He couldn't quite remember it entirely, but he knows it is the culprit for his lack of sleep. He wonders if he will have nightmares like that again. He wonders how many times he will think about how close Damon McKay came to dying right in front of him, grateful he didn't have to see another friend get taken. He thinks of how many times he had nightmares after ending his deployments in the Army. Those dreams only started to fade away in the last decade or so. He hopes the nightmare wasn't an indication of the return of trips to see a therapist. He was better equipped now to deal with those things, but those nightmares never included monsters from Native American history, though.

He lays back down, hoping that the recent news of Damon leaving the force wouldn't inspire other officers to leave as well. Damon is a good man and he's happy to see him with a spark of joy in his eye for once, but it hurts to know he will have a much more boring time at work. He prays for Damon to have good luck in his new venture, then attempts again to go to sleep.

* * *

JACOB GREENE PLACES a bank bag into the safe in the back room of the tavern. He places a stack of stapled receipts on top before closing the safe and walking back to the main area of bar. The sound of the neon lights greet him and he looks out to where just an hour ago, twenty patrons had filled the space. If he closed his eyes, he could almost see them again. He's made it a habit over the years to learn almost every frequent customers name, secrets and anything else they were willing to share. He had always wanted to be a therapist, but found that this setting worked much better than a cold and lifeless office.

He thinks for a moment about that police officer and the woman that he left with not too many moons ago. He hasn't seen them since. He hopes that maybe they fell in love and decided they would much rather share drinks at a more secluded location. He hopes to at least see the police officer again so he can hear all the details about Big Lew's killer. He hates that he never got to retire the way he wanted. Jacob walks to the front door and turns back to the bar once more. Before he closes the door, he stares at the back wall at the new sign that reads:

"In Loving Memory of Lewis Parley"

* * *

A BEER BOTTLE smashes against a concrete tomb, the shards of broken glass absorbed by the overgrowth at its base.

"Damn bro that has to be like bad luck or something," says a teenager, who is urinating on a piece of rotted wood nearby.

"Everything is bad luck around here. Who gives a fuck? Bet you can't make a bottle in that hole!" Says a young woman who is seated on another tomb above the boy who threw the bottle.

"Okay, Jules, challenge accepted! You have to show me your tits if it goes in, though!"

The other teens laughter bounces off the surrounding piles of eroding concrete that make up the forgotten cemetery. They spend every weekend in the summer sneaking out here to share whatever alcohol they've collected throughout the week. Jules was the oldest, just turning twenty last winter. She is usually able to grab enough to get a good buzz, but she enjoys the solitude far more than the alcohol. Anything to be away from her apartment in the French Quarter.

"Deal," she says, tossing the boy an empty bottle.

He takes aim and launches the beer bottle nearly forty feet towards a large, unmarked tomb that has a basketball sized hole in the upper right corner. The bottle smashes right at the top of the hole, sending most of the shards of glass upwards into the sky.

"Fuck! That was so close! That's got to count for something, right?" asks the boy, "Come on that's worth at least one tit right?"

"No sir! Better luck next time, dumbass," says Jules, hopping down and gathering her things. The group walks towards the edge of the rows of tombs and exits the cemetery.

The shards of the beer bottle that weren't thrown beyond the eroded tomb, still slowly trickle into the opening of the hole. Falling like snowflakes to land amongst the sediment and loose debris that has made its way into the tomb over the years since it has been forgotten. A single shard slides into a small hole in a piece of cloth that protrudes from the rubble, likely created by a small insect that was burrowing to find escape from the predators nearby. The shard comes to rest in the corner of an open, grey eye.